"We shouldn't do this. We both know it. It's too dangerous."

He nodded, but she wasn't fooled. It was clear that while he agreed that a physical relationship between them was dangerous, he was past caring about the consequences. His next words only confirmed this impression and signaled her fate.

"There's something here, Izzy. Maybe has been for a long time." He stared at her, perfectly still except for his restless hands, which roamed to her waist again, and then up her torso until his thumbs just brushed over the sides of her breasts. "We need to figure out what that is."

She'd been afraid he'd say that.

He kissed her, taking another irrevocable step down the road that separated friend from lover. There was no question of her kissing him back, not when she felt the vibrating urgency in his body, the warmth of his lips, and tasted the peppermint in his mouth. Not when she wanted him as much as she did.

Books by Ann Christopher

Kimani Romance

Just About Sex
Sweeter Than Revenge
Tender Secrets
Road to Seduction

ANN CHRISTOPHER

is a full-time chauffeur for her two overscheduled children. She is also a wife, former lawyer and decent cook. In between trips to various sporting practices and games, Target and the grocery store, she likes to write the occasional romance novel featuring a devastatingly handsome alpha male. She lives in Cincinnati and spends her time with her family, which includes two spoiled rescue cats, Sadie and Savannah.

If you'd like to recommend a great book, share a recipe for homemade cake of any kind or have a tip for getting your children to do what you say the *first* time you say it, Ann would love to hear from you through her Web site, www.AnnChristopher.com.

ROAD to
Seduction

Ann
Christopher

To my husband, as always

 KIMANI PRESS™

ISBN-13: 978-0-373-86103-3
ISBN-10:   0-373-86103-6

Recycling programs
for this product may
not exist in your area.

ROAD TO SEDUCTION

Dear Reader,

Poor Eric Warner.

You remember Eric, right? The millionaire cousin of Andrew Warner from *Tender Secrets?* Well, guess what? Eric's about to get his world rocked by...wait for it...his best friend from college, Isabella Stevens.

Isabella has changed—at least Eric *thinks* she has—and the sweet little girl next door is now the sexiest woman Eric's ever seen.

Who'd have thought?

Eric doesn't like all these changes—he's perfectly happy as a player, *thank you very much*—but what can he do? Ignore his growing passion for Izzy? Hide it? Get over it?

Of course not.

So now, with his heart in her hands and his mind made up, Eric will use this weekend road trip to win Isabella. To charm her...seduce her...love her.

After all, what a Warner man wants, a Warner man gets.

Happy reading!

Ann

P.S. Don't forget to look for Senator Jonathan Warner's story, which is coming in September 2009. I like to think of it as Barack Obama meets an African-American Murphy Brown. Cheers!

Thanks to:

My Web mistress and animal expert, Frauke Spanuth, who answered my questions about sick dogs; and to my great author friend Caroline Linden, who helped me plot this book and thought of the title. Now if I could only get her to write the next one for me....

Chapter 1

Whoa, thought Eric Warner. Who was *that?*

Whoever she was, he wanted her. Bad.

He froze, his hand poised to ring the bell of his friend Isabella Stevens's apartment in an old baby-blue gingerbread Victorian, and tried to decide what to do about the sexy woman walking up the sidewalk toward him.

Now was not the time for a hook-up with some random passing woman. He knew that. He'd just arrived here, in Cincinnati, to pick up Isabella, spend the night and take her to the Florida wedding of some of their college classmates in the morning. That was the only thing on his agenda for the weekend.

But…damn. Look at her.

She was carrying a couple of plastic bags of groceries and walking a small dog on a leash. Short and lush, with healthy brown thighs and shapely calves rippling her fluttery flowered skirt, she wore one of those strappy tank tops that hugged every ample curve. Dark glasses covered a pretty face and sheets of sleek black hair skimmed her shoulders.

Bottom line: she was a knockout. World-class.

She worked it, too. There was a little extra strut in her step that was probably caused by whatever she was listening to on her iPod, and, seeing the sway of her hips, he thanked God for portable music. Her lips moved and she sang under her breath, in her own world and oblivious to Eric and his X-rated fascination with her mouth. Watching that supple body flow, he felt the curl of an electrifying knot deep in his belly.

Maybe she was a neighbor of Izzy's... Maybe Izzy could introduce them... No, he couldn't wait that long... He should go ahead and introduce himself now... No guts, no glory...

Putting his overnight bag down, he moved to the edge of the porch, ready to charm, bribe or beg, whatever he had to do to get inside this delicious woman's panties at the earliest possible moment.

And that was when she saw him.

Her face broke into a wide, incredible, thrilled grin and something within the obviously malfunctioning gears of his brain lurched into place. Right before his disbelieving eyes the woman shape-shifted or morphed or *something* and became... No, it couldn't be... Yes—yes it was...*Isabella*.

What the—?

Izzy. His *best friend*. The free spirit who'd been like a sister to him since the day he met her in college seventeen years ago. The woman he'd never *ever* lusted after.

Izzy, for God's sake.

With a sickening twist in his gut, all his erotic fantasies burned red-hot and incinerated in a pretty good impression of a satellite reentering the Earth's atmosphere, but the mistake wasn't entirely his fault. She'd lost weight. That was it. And her hair was different. Longer and straighter or something. And he hadn't seen her in almost a year. He wasn't a complete lunatic.

"Eric!" Izzy ripped the buds from her ears and ran the last several steps up the walk to him. "You're *early*."

"Ah..."

That one lame syllable was all he could manage because this

whole scene was way too freaky. His mouth flapped open and closed like a door on a well-oiled hinge, but words continued to fail him. *Think, man, THINK*. He tried again, but this second attempt at coherent speech produced only a strange gurgle from somewhere in his throat.

Luckily Izzy didn't seem to notice. With a squeal of excitement, she dropped her bags and launched herself at him in a blur of thrilled dimples and white teeth.

It was the wrong time to touch her, but that didn't stop Eric from opening his eager arms, catching her and pulling her as close as humanly possible without snapping her ribs like toothpicks. Her chin hooked over his shoulder, and suddenly she was everything wonderful and familiar—the friend he knew and loved, same as always.

And yet that alarming new sexual awareness was still there, too. He shoved it aside, hard, and tried to ignore it.

God, she felt good.

A shudder rippled through him, and he wallowed in the *rightness*—so strong it bordered on perfection—of holding Isabella. It was only now, at this moment of touching her again, that he realized how much he'd missed her since he last saw her. His work travel had tripled, but that was no excuse. Almost a year was way too long to go without seeing her, and he swore to himself he wouldn't let so much time pass between visits in the future.

Her wonderful light smell—she always reminded him of water, sunshine and air—washed over him, and the craziest thought ran through his mind:

It's good to be home.

He clung, sinking his restless fingers deep into her gleaming hair and reveling in the feel of her lush breasts against his chest. Never in seventeen years had he noticed Izzy's breasts, but— whoa, boy—there was no ignoring them now.

His conscience, which was slow but still functional, finally intruded.

This was wrong. Touching Izzy while thinking sexy thoughts

about her was wrong, wrong, WRONG, and he was going to stop. *Right now*.

Well, not *right* now, obviously, but soon... Pretty soon. Eventually.

But he didn't stop. Against all standards of decency and common sense, he tightened his hold on that supple body and wanted more. Wanted *her* with a ferocity that bordered on physical pain.

At last she pulled back. Eric, feeling bereft, peeled himself away and slowly slid his hands down the warm silk of her bare arms. Afraid to say anything at this strange new moment and give away his insanity, which he devoutly hoped was only temporary, he watched as she rummaged in her purse for her keys.

A hard knot lodged in his throat and he tried to swallow it down.

He would not lust after, long for Isabella and ruin the single most important friendship he'd ever had.

Distraction came in the form of the Yorkie, who yapped and bounced around Eric's legs, apparently of the opinion that he could leap into his arms if he jumped high enough.

Eric's dry mouth finally worked. "Hey, Zeus. Look at you, buddy."

The fur around his little black face had been trimmed since he saw him last, and he looked like a soulful-eyed teddy bear with brown muzzle and eyebrows. Flustered and grateful to have something to do with his hands other than grope his best friend, Eric stooped to catch the dog, who was wearing a tiny Cincinnati Reds tee with the number 00 on it, hooked him under his arm like a football, and rubbed his soft little head. Zeus squirmed and smiled his tongue-dangling smile at him.

Eric scratched behind Zeus's ears and grinned at Izzy. "He's a monster. Have you been feeding him raw steak?"

Isabella beamed with motherly pride. "He's six pounds now. You didn't think he'd stay a puppy forever, did you?"

"I should've kept him for myself." Eric lowered Zeus to the porch, where the dog danced on his tiny brown paws, his entire body wriggling with excitement.

"Don't even try it." Izzy continued to root through her enormous purse. "You gave him to me. Best birthday present I ever got."

"You think?"

"I *know*. So did they kick you out of the office?"

The reminder of the place made Eric snort as he picked up his bag. His elegant office was beginning to take on the rough outline of a prison every time he thought about it. "Nah. It was time to call it a day."

"What's up with the *suit?*" Smiling, she gave him a pointed once over. "Who drives for an hour and a half in the car wearing a *suit?*"

Staring down at his starched-but-rumpled white shirt, Eric felt a little sheepish now that she pointed out the obvious. Since he didn't want to tell her he'd been so anxious to see her he hadn't even *thought* of taking the time to change before he left Columbus, he decided to ignore the question altogether.

"What's up with you?" he asked instead. "You can't return phone calls anymore? What's with the silent treatment?"

This was a sore spot with him, one he intended to address immediately. Her phone calls and text messages had tapered off to next to nothing in the last month or so, and the few messages she did send had gotten a little cryptic. The upshot was that he was now officially worried.

His protective gene, which was dormant when it came to other women, kicked into hyperdrive with Izzy. Always had.

What was bothering her? School was out for the summer, so he knew it couldn't be one of her little kindergartners giving her a hard time learning his or her ABCs. Money, on the other hand, was always a potential issue. She didn't make much and wasn't exactly Alan Greenspan when it came to managing it. Or it could be—he swallowed hard—*boyfriend* trouble.

This last idea, for some reason, made him feel like smashing something to smithereens, running over it a time or two with a steamroller, and then incinerating it with a flamethrower.

"*Well?*" he demanded.

"Sorry," she muttered. "It's been a busy month."

Busy? This was her explanation for not keeping in touch with him? Was she for real? She'd have to do a hell of a lot better than that if she wanted to get back in his good graces.

"How's that?" he snapped.

His tone must have been rougher than he intended, because her head jerked up and she gave him an exaggerated pout. "Uh-oh. Someone's being a grouchy puss today."

"Don't start."

He flashed her a dark look because his equilibrium still hadn't quite returned to normal, and he was in no mood for teasing. But she scrunched her face up into a purse-lipped glower, and he had to laugh.

"I don't look like that," he told her.

"Yes, you do. Is this about the Hong Kong deal? Did it close?"

"Yeah."

"That's *wonderful*. Congratulations. Another triumph for the CEO of WarnerBrands, eh?"

Eric grunted, feeling unaccountably surly. "Yeah, well, I've been trained for this since birth, haven't I?"

Izzy's genuine delight for his accomplishments big and small had always been one of the best things about her. But now it sort of pissed him off.

Opening a Hong Kong branch of his family's multi-billion dollar clothing company, as she well knew, involved his spending large amounts of time in China during the next few months. Was she *that* anxious for him to be thousands of miles away? They barely saw each other now, and they only lived ninety miles apart. How would things be with him spending half his time overseas? Had she thought of *that?*

Yanking her jangling keys out of her purse at last, she eyed him with concern. "Let's get you upstairs. You're wound tighter than a top."

"I'm alright."

This was a lie, but he wasn't about to confess that his real problem was that he suddenly wanted to do things with her that were still illegal in some states.

The second her back was turned to open the door, he swiped his suddenly sweaty brow, and followed her inside and up the narrow staircase leading to her apartment.

At the threshold, he paused.

Wait, said a little voice deep inside his head. *Wait.*

Eric hesitated while his thoughts coalesced into something vague but disturbing. With sudden clarity he knew that if he went into that apartment now, with Isabella, something…irrevocable would happen. He couldn't think *what,* only that it *would* happen, and whatever *it* was would be huge.

The simultaneous certainty and uncertainty froze him in his tracks, but after a second or two of this foolishness, he gave himself a hard mental smack. What the hell was wrong with him today? *Get a grip, Warner.*

Shaking his head, he stepped into Izzy's huge, high-ceilinged living room in time to see her walk to the kitchen and put the groceries on the enormous center island.

"Beer?" she asked over her shoulder.

"Thanks."

Yeah, he wanted a beer all right. He wanted a beer, and then he wanted a full psych eval so he could figure out who'd messed with the settings on his brain. What'd gotten into him? Checking out an attractive woman was one thing—hell, everyone did *that*—but his fierce new physical reaction to Isabella, well, that was just sick. *Sick.*

"Thanks for driving to Jacksonville with me," she told him. "I couldn't afford plane tickets *and* the hotel."

"I'd've been happy to—" he began.

"I know you would have, Daddy Warbucks, but I didn't want you to."

"I've known mules less stubborn than you." he muttered. "Why couldn't we have just taken the Lear? I get to use the Lear, you know. Comes with the job."

Izzy snorted. "What's the carbon footprint on flying that baby to Florida and back just for the two of us?"

Eric rolled his eyes and kept quiet. It was hard to get a

decadent lifestyle going with Isabella hanging around all the time, acting as his social conscience.

Taking the glass she poured for him, he wandered into the living-room half of the enormous space, sank onto the comfy, overstuffed tan sofa, adjusted a couple of pillows behind his back and heaved a long, contented sigh.

Thank God he was finally here.

Isabella had the best apartment in the world, all lightness and air, and a perfect reflection of her eclectic personality. Tall ceilings, huge windows on three sides that always seemed to catch the sun, and lots of cozy chairs with pretty little pillows and throws tossed over the arms. But there were also several carved animal statues, a handful of Oriental figurines and an African mask or two.

A giant red pot of tall pussy willows sat on the hearth, with more pots and candles on the mantle. Bookshelves overflowing with a little bit of everything, including romance novels, Stephen King books and more mysteries that he could ever count sandwiched the fireplace. Wait, was there a new section? He squinted at the titles. There *was*—a whole shelf lined with books like *Speaking Your Dog's Secret Language* and *Be the Leader of Your Pack!* Eric chuckled.

Sipping the rich, vaguely sweet lager she always kept around for him, he relaxed another thirty percent and wondered idly if a man could come from the sheer pleasure of drinking an icy beer at the end of a long day. But then she sat right next to him, tucked her legs under her, took her sunglasses off and gave Eric a good look at her smiling face up close.

That was when the trouble *really* began.

Chapter 2

She'd always been attractive, of course—nothing new there. A thousand years ago, at Princeton's freshman orientation, he'd met her, registered her attractiveness and put her firmly in the adorable category, thereby removing her from the list of "women he wanted to have sex with" and putting her into the category of "women he could be friends with."

Over the years, his friendship with Izzy had become too central to his existence—too *vital*—to ever risk screwing it up by making it sexual, not that he'd ever entertained sexy thoughts about her.

Until now.

Izzy had always stayed fun and cute, and life as he'd known it had sailed along problem-free. Today, however, there was a problem—a *big* problem—and she was causing it. She wasn't showing him much cute. About zero percent, actually, compared to about a thousand percent sexy, and he didn't like it.

Everything about her was suddenly tempting—the worst kind of forbidden fruit. Those black corkscrew curls were now super-straight and shiny and he wanted to dive into them. And her skin sure looked irresistible. Normally sort of a coffee-heavy-on-the-cream color, it now had a healthy red tinge to it. She looked as though she'd been getting lots of sun—especially across her sweet chipmunk cheeks that didn't look so chipmunk-y at the moment. The deep dimples on either side of her mouth were still there, but now her cheeks looked—like the rest of her—smooth and sleek.

Vaguely aware of her watching him with that same bemused look on her face, he let his unwilling gaze fall to her mouth and immediately regretted it. A tight, painful knot of longing grew in his belly, torturing him. Such lips she had—moist and lush, as tempting as a bowl of plump, ripe Bing cherries dribbling with juice. A wave of heat crept up his neck, shot past his ears, across his face, and headed north until his scalp tingled.

He wanted…to kiss those lips. That and more. Helluva lot more.

Caught again, he flicked his gaze up to her eyes, and there were two huge, almond-shaped, long-lashed, sparkling brown problems. What was going on here? Had someone switched Isabellas on him? No one had eyes like this… No one could be this beautiful. Surely he'd never seen this amazing face before.

Or was it that he'd never really *looked* at it?

"Oh, hey. Wait a minute." Izzy clunked her glass down on the side table and fixed him with a look. "Where's Jasmine? I thought you were bringing her to the wedding."

"I didn't feel like it."

Izzy snorted. *"Didn't feel like it?* I thought things were going so well."

Eric shrugged and sipped his beer. He hadn't thought about Jasmine in several hours, and didn't particularly want to start now. "Not really."

"What. Since when?"

He started to get exasperated because Jasmine wasn't worth this much interest. He couldn't understand Izzy's continued curiosity, nor did he particularly want to discuss his former sex buddy with her.

"What's with the questions?" he wondered.

They frowned at each other, and Izzy's jaw tightened into the throbbing, obstinate angle that told him he better answer her question, and he damn well better do it *now*.

"Look." He sighed and tried to look rueful lest Izzy think he was a heartless bastard. "It wasn't going anywhere. It's over. That's that."

Those sharp, shrewd eyes narrowed with the laser precision that always made him squirm like a guilty ten-year-old with a bat, a missing baseball and a smashed window.

"She was getting serious, wasn't she?"

Denying it, much as he wanted to, seemed pointless. "Well…yeah."

Isabella waited, but he had nothing further to say on the topic. He didn't need to recount every excruciating detail of last night's ugly parting scene with Jasmine: his confirmation that, yes, he really was going to the wedding in Florida, and, yes, he really wasn't going to take Jasmine.

And then, the thick layer of butter cream icing on top of the misery cake: he really *would* be driving all that way alone with Isabella. The shit had really hit the fan then, with Jasmine hurling accusations of cheating, selfishness and lack of commitment.

He'd expected a certain amount of pouting about the wedding. Maybe it *was* selfish of him, but he wanted to spend some time catching up with Isabella and seeing his friends in Florida. Jasmine was not—and never would be—a big part of his life, so why bring her along and introduce her as though she was? It wasn't like he'd die of loneliness during a few days without her.

So, yeah, Jasmine's moping was fine, and he'd expected and deserved it. But when she'd launched into a tirade about the evil Isabella and how his relationship with Isabella came between *their* chances of long-term happiness—as if they had one!—he'd had enough. There was no way he'd give up, or even scale back, his relationship with Isabella. After seventeen years? Get real.

His temper good and lost, he'd let Jasmine have it with both barrels, and that'd put the period at the end of their relationship. The last he'd seen of her had been her door slamming in his face. Funny, though. Six fun months with her and he couldn't work up too much upset—even over the loss of the sex, if nothing else.

His only regret was that, despite all his best efforts to keep things casual, Jasmine had gotten the impression that they had some sort of a future together. He'd inadvertently hurt her and for that, and *only* that, he was sorry.

"So... Another one bites the dust, eh?" Izzy asked, a new, unfamiliar edge of bitterness in her voice. Her lips twisted and, way back near her ear, her jaw began to throb. *"Men."*

Eric stared, watching her mutter something dark and unintelligible before she took a long sip of beer. He wondered what *men* had done to her that was so awful she needed to say the word with such revulsion. Like she was picturing dung-covered flesh-eating slugs or something.

"Uh," he began, choosing his words with caution. "Did something, ah, happen?"

Snorting, she stared down into her now half-full glass, her shoulders squared and rigid. "You could say that—"

The cordless on his side table rang. Silently cursing the interruption, Eric picked up the phone and handed it to her.

"Hello?" she said.

A man's voice—low, deep and smooth—came over the line.

Izzy listened and glowered and everything about her changed in an instant. The second she heard whoever it was, a light went out in her eyes.

Seeing this, Eric's muscles stiffened with a primitive anger and the need to protect. To maim, if need be, because that didn't sound like her father or brothers on the phone. It was the silky tone of someone who wanted to seduce, and Eric ought to know because he'd used that exact same tone often enough. Seething in silence, he waited for Izzy's reaction.

"Yeah, well, it's not really a good time," she snapped. "Eric's here and we're going to eat soon. So why don't you call back in...oh, say, *never*."

Eric gaped, feeling his eyes grow wide as dinner platters. What the hell was going on? Izzy could be hot-tempered here and there, sure, but he'd never seen her like *this*. What had this punk done to her?

More talking from the man; it sounded like wheedling now. Eric strained his ears trying to eavesdrop but couldn't understand a word.

"Fine," Isabella told the caller. "You have one minute, Joe." She hung up and stood up, looking both agitated and incandescent with anger.

Eric fumed and watched her from behind the red film of his sudden fury, not at all certain what his role was here. He knew what role he *wanted* to play, though: avenger. Whoever had done this to Isabella—hurt her and made her so angry—deserved to die a lingering death that involved a dark dungeon with sound-proof stone walls, and Eric was just the man to deliver that sort of justice. When he caught himself wondering where he could find a set of brass knuckles, it occurred to him that he needed to dial back his irrational anger a little. But he didn't think he could.

He'd temporarily forgotten she was dating someone, and re-membering now was a surprise. Yeah. That was it. He was just really surprised, not *jealous*. Never in his life had he been *jealous* and he wasn't *jealous* now.

Even though Isabella had—fury shuddered through him again and he tried unsuccessfully to tamp it down to some manageable level—slept with that SOB, he wasn't *jealous*.

Joe, she'd said his name was. An architect, right? No. A cor-porate type. How serious was it? For the life of him, Eric couldn't remember. Izzy'd talked about Joe here and there, but he'd never paid much attention.

He was paying extra attention now, though.

"Who was that?" Eric demanded.

Izzy glanced around and looked surprised to see Eric still

there. She fidgeted, crossing her arms over her chest. Then she undid her arms and ran one hand through her hair.

"Joe," she finally said. "He's coming up."

"Why?" Eric stood and tried to rein in his flaring temper. "What's he want?"

Izzy went to the front door. "The cheating bastard wants me to marry him," she said over her shoulder, each syllable vibrating with righteous anger. "Like I'm that stupid."

Leaving this bombshell to detonate inside Eric's brain, she disappeared down the steps. Eric stared after her, aghast, while the startling word reverberated like a gong, making him feel both like vomiting and smashing something.

Marry… Marry… Marry…

The distant sound of the outer door opening and that male voice, louder now, worked Eric's strained nerves. He paced back and forth in front of the windows, listening to their footsteps on the stairs as they came closer, and then Izzy reappeared with Joe right on her heels. Eric goggled, as though he'd just seen a Martian parallel park his spaceship, and so did Joe.

No freaking way, Eric thought. *No. Freaking. Way.*

If I had a long lost twin.

They were ringers. Dead ringers for one another.

No kidding—he and Joe the Jerk could've doubled for each other in a movie. Same height. Same skull trim and dark skin. Same mustache and goatee. Same shirtsleeves, with white dress shirt, dark suit pants and red tie loosened at the throat. The only difference, as far as Eric could tell, was the shoes, but a quick glance at Joe's feet told Eric that they had the same taste in footwear, too; Eric's own pair of $300 black Cole Haan oxfords was currently sitting in his closet at home.

Izzy made the introductions. "Joe Barker, this is Eric Warner."

Eric scowled at this invader of his peaceful sanctuary…this…this…*man* who'd slept with Isabella—*his* Isabella—and then broken her heart. The sorry punk didn't deserve to live and breathe the same air as Isabella for one more second, but Eric could take care of that. With punishment in his heart, he took a couple of steps closer and Joe did the same, looking every bit as pissed off as Eric felt.

Face-to-face, they stared each other down. Neither blinked or spoke.

Finally Joe held out his hand, a sign of weakness as far as Eric was concerned. They shook, both using the power-shake iron-grip that was universal manspeak for *I've got bigger balls than you and I'm going to take you off at the knees first chance I get.*

By some mutual but unspoken signal, they let go at the same time, and Eric dropped his hand, planted his feet wide, and prepared for war.

Chapter 3

Isabella fumed, watched the men and wondered how best to get rid of Joe, the man she'd thought she'd known but hadn't known at all. She still hadn't recovered from the other day and doubted she ever would. Their evening had started out so nicely. But now her head spun about how quickly their lovely relationship had unraveled.

Lovely relationship. Hah. It had all been a lie.

After a year of dating, they'd discussed marriage for the first time last month. She'd told him a little bit more about her past and shared parts of her life she'd never even told Eric. And what had Joe done? Had he supported her? Encouraged her? Told her he loved her no matter what and always would?

Hell, no. He'd cheated on her with his secretary, promptly confessed, pledged renewed and undying love for Isabella and asked her to marry him.

As if.

She watched uneasily as the men puffed their chests like two silverbacks about to battle for supremacy. The negative energy surrounding them reminded her of a black hole into which all the furniture might well be sucked.

With Eric's weird mood today—why *did* he keep staring at her like she'd grown antennae?—on top of his firecracker temper, she really needed to get Joe out of here before someone's blood got spilled. She shouldn't have let Joe in in the first place.

It'd be an even fight if it did come to fisticuffs, she thought. Eric and Joe were roughly the same height—*really* tall—with the same broad shoulders, narrow waist, and muscular butt and legs, although at the moment Eric's chest seemed to be the most inflated.

Their builds notwithstanding, though, they were nothing alike. Joe looked pretty good—she'd never kicked him out of bed, after all—but Eric blew every other man out of the water. Always had, always would, and it wasn't just his classic good looks and killer body, either. Lots of men had smooth dark skin, intense brown eyes and a lush mouth that made a woman wonder what miracles he could perform with his lips and tongue.

No, with Eric it was the indefinable *it,* and he had it in spades. That restless energy, that leashed power, that wide, slow, mischievous smile that was a *pow* right between her eyes every time she saw it, even after all these years.

Not for the first time, she congratulated herself on her triumph of self-control, of mind over hormone, that she'd achieved years ago. How else could a woman possibly be friends with a man like Eric Warner without experiencing an atomic meltdown of sexual frustration?

Not that he'd ever tested her self-control by, say, expressing the slightest attraction to her. His obvious and complete lack of sexual interest—when he so clearly loved women and had loved more than his share—had stung, but only years ago, at the beginning of their relationship. Now she was older and smart enough to know that Eric could really do—and *had done*—women some serious damage, if a woman was foolish enough to let him.

Actually, Eric looked like he was about to do some serious damage to Joe right now. He stood even straighter, squared his shoulders, and raised his chin. "So what do you do?"

"CFO." Joe's jaw tightened. "Phillips Financial. You?"

"CEO. WarnerBrands International."

Isabella watched them watch each other with grudging respect; two corporate titans meeting for the first time always felt like comrades, didn't they? Well…maybe not. Still, they seemed stalemated, and she was beginning to think the crisis had passed, but then Eric had to open his big fat mouth again.

"What's up? Izzy's not too happy to have you popping by, *Joe.*"

"Now, wait a minute," she interjected, annoyed. "I don't need a spokesperson—"

"*Bella* and I," Joe said, ignoring her and stalking closer to Eric until he was right up in his face, "have a few things to talk about."

"Not if she doesn't want to talk," Eric said.

After one last scowl at Eric, Joe looked at her. "Can I talk to you?"

"Sure," she said sourly. "And then you can *leave*. Excuse us, Eric."

Eric went utterly still. "Come again?"

Looking over her shoulder, she shot him a narrow-eyed warning look which he returned. Worse, he showed no signs of leaving the room and giving them some privacy. What the hell had gotten into him today? It was going to be a long, painful trip to Jacksonville and back if he carried on like this.

Get out, she mouthed.

Time stopped for ten long seconds while they glared at each other. Finally Eric snorted, wheeled around, and stalked off down the hall, but his brooding presence remained, looming over Isabella like a gray sky threatening sleet.

"I don't like him," Joe muttered.

"That's your problem."

Joe hesitated, apparently trying to decide where to start. Sighing, he ran a hand over his head, and his features softened. When he spoke it was with what looked like genuine regret, but with Joe, who could tell?

"You have to forgive me, Izzy. I can't live without you."

"Joe—"

"I'm sorry. It'll never happen again. I *swear*."

"I don't believe you. You're a liar."

Joe took a sharp, stuttering breath and hung his head in a pretty good imitation of shame. When he looked up again there were tears in his eyes that did nothing to change her mind.

"Please." He tried to take her hand but she snatched it free. "Let me try to make it up to you. Don't go to Johannesburg. Don't run away."

That last sentence had the sting of truth in it. Isabella blinked and tried to work up a plausible denial. "I'm not running away. I'm taking my life in another direction." She'd accepted a two-year teaching position at the new leadership academy for girls in South Africa. She hadn't even told Eric yet. "And you gave up any say about my career plans the second you jumped in bed with your secretary."

Anger crept across Joe's face, edging out any softness in his expression. "This is all about *him,* isn't it?" He jerked his head toward the hall down which Eric had disappeared. "He finally decided he wants you? Is that it?"

"No." *Where on earth had that come from?* "Eric and I are friends. That's all. He has nothing to do with this. What happened with us is *your* fault."

"Bullshit," he spat. "I've seen the way he looks at you. I've heard the way you talk about him. Do you think I'm stupid?"

"Joe—"

Vibrating with fury, he glared down at her. "Are you stopping somewhere to spend the night at some hotel? Are you telling me nothing's gonna happen *then?* You think I'm stupid enough to believe *that* whole setup'll be platonic?"

Beyond outraged, she decided it was past time for him to leave. She crossed her arms over her chest. "Eric is my *friend.*" Somehow she kept her voice low and calm despite the furious rush of blood in her ears. "He's been my *friend* for years, and he'll always be my *friend.*"

"Even after *I'm* gone from your life, you mean."

"You are gone from my life."

Joe flinched and she felt a moment's vindictive pleasure at hurting him a little when he'd hurt her so much. He dropped his head and made an incredulous, laughing sound, as though he couldn't quite get over her foolishness. When he looked up again, his eyes glittered, hard and bitter.

"You're naïve," he told her.

"No, I'm not—"

"If you think that any straight man can look at *that* face—" his flashing gaze raked over her "—and *that* body without trying to get you in bed, then you don't know a *thing* about men."

"You're wrong," she said, stung to the core of her soul because she was no seductress and there *was* one straight man that'd never wanted her and never would, a man who was immune to whatever charms she possessed and had been for seventeen years. "Eric doesn't want me."

Joe flinched as though she'd sprayed him with mace, and, too late, she realized her mistake. "I didn't mean—"

But Joe just laughed that same harsh, bitter laugh. "So everything would be different if he *did* want you, huh?"

"*No*. And it's none of your business anyway."

He stared her down and she blinked back the hot, unaccountable tears that stung her eyes. The painful silence lengthened until she wished she were anywhere else in the universe but here. She didn't want this scene, didn't want to talk anymore with this man and, most of all, didn't want to explain again that she'd never turned Eric's head, not even once.

"It's time for you to leave," she said flatly.

After giving her a long, searching look, he blinked and nodded. When he spoke again his voice was full of gravel. "I love you," he told her. "I'll always love you. This was the biggest mistake of my life."

You got that right, she thought, turning her head away.

"Take care of yourself, Bella."

With that, Joe turned to go. And as the door closed behind him she couldn't muster up any feelings of sorrow, loss or forgiveness for the man who'd been such a big part of her life. All she could think was: *good riddance*.

An hour later, Eric slammed around the kitchen, making dinner and working himself into such a state of agitation that his clothes, skin and muscles felt tight enough to suffocate. It was as though he'd been shrink-wrapped inside layers of plastic that prevented him from thinking clearly or even taking a deep breath.

This misery was his own damn fault, really, for hanging in the doorway and listening to every faint syllable of what he sincerely hoped was the last conversation *ever* between Isabella and her ex-jerk. Eric had had no business eavesdropping and he knew it. When had an eavesdropper ever overheard anything good? Why hadn't he known better?

Spying and eavesdropping were deeply shameful activities, and the guilt gnawed at his gut like a beaver with a fresh log and a dam to build. He should be hung by the thumbs for such a terrible transgression, and if Izzy kicked him out for violating her privacy, it'd be no less than he deserved. So, yeah, he was the scum of the earth, but he had much bigger problems to deal with than his regrettable lack of moral fiber.

Restless and frustrated, he went to the fridge, forgot what he'd meant to get, and, cursing, returned to the sink where he stared blankly at the shrimp in their colander. He reminded himself of the manatees in their tank at the Cincinnati Zoo—always swimming, never going anywhere.

Idiot. What the hell was his problem?

Glancing down the counter, he watched Izzy resolutely chop veggies for the salad and wondered if she was okay. After that jackass left a little while ago, Izzy had pretended she wasn't crying and Eric pretended he didn't see her red nose and eyes. Now he supposed they were both pretending they were having a perfectly normal evening together, the same as any other.

Hah.

Turning on the water, he began to clean the shrimp and tried to think. So he'd listened when he shouldn't have. The question now was: what, if anything, was he going to do about what he'd heard? His mind came up blank except for a few random thoughts swirling like feathers on the wind. Each time he tried to grab one and examine it, he wound up batting it further away:

Isabella was his friend.

Isabella was leaving the country.

He didn't want her to go.

Jasmine thought there was something between him and Isabella.

Joe thought there was something between him and Isabella.

Jasmine and Joe were wrong, of course. Nothing had ever happened between him and Izzy. No lingering goodbye kiss, no drunken night together after some raucous campus party, never even a longing glance. Their relationship had been as platonic as a date between Elton John and Ellen DeGeneres.

Until now…

No.

Muttering, he found a heavy pan, set it on the stove, and turned on the gas. There was no *until now* because nothing had changed or would change. If he repeated this mantra enough times, he'd surely believe it eventually.

Nothing had changed… Nothing had changed… Nothing had—

Except…something big *had* changed, hadn't it? Something *other* than his fierce new awareness of Isabella as a woman. Forget the Africa thing; Johannesburg was a plane ride away for someone like him who had a private jet at his disposal. No, the real issue was someone wanting to marry Izzy.

Marriage was forever. Maybe Izzy loved that idiot. Maybe she'd sleep on it, wake up in the morning, forgive Joe and tell him *yes*.

Then she'd be a soon-to-be married woman, wouldn't she? *Married.*

The thought sickened him, and feeling sick scared him.

God, it was hot in here. Turning down the burner, he poured olive oil and butter into the pan, wiped his brow, and tried to think. Why was the thought of Isabella getting married so unbearable? Hadn't he always known that in the distant, indistinct future, someone would snatch her up? Didn't he *want* her to marry someone, have a family and live happily ever after? Why was the thought of her building a life with a man like Joe so disturbing?

He and Joe were almost twins, physically and professionally. Isabella could marry a man exactly like Eric.

Isabella had chosen a man exactly like Eric.

The last thought stuck in his mind, insisting that he acknowledge it even as he sautéed the shrimp. *Isabella had chosen a man exactly like him.* Slowly, bit by bit, feeling as though he was battling a great mental deficit, he tried to connect the dots.

Dot one: Joe was Isabella's type.

Dot two: Joe and Eric were alike.

Dot three: if Joe and Eric were alike, and Joe was Isabella's type, then, by extrapolation…Eric was also Isabella's type.

Dot four… Dot four…

He struggled but couldn't get to dot four no matter how hard he tried.

Looking around, he checked Izzy's progress. Having finished with the salad, she'd mixed up a batch of brownies and was getting ready to put them in the oven.

"Don't forget to spray the pan," he told her.

"What?" Izzy froze, the mixing bowl poised over the rectangular baking pan. As though waking from a trance, she glanced down and looked mildly surprised to find a bowl and spatula in her hands.

"Oh. Sorry." She put the bowl down and reached for the cooking spray.

Eric turned back to the shrimp and stirred. His turmoil grew as other, more provocative thoughts came, crowding his brain to overflowing:

He was suddenly unattached. Isabella was suddenly unattached.

Why did those two things seem monumentally significant? They'd both been unattached at the same time before—hadn't they? Yeah, he was sure they had. Well…maybe not.

Izzy had had a few long-term boyfriends, including some jerk named Al in college, and then she'd had long periods when he didn't think she'd dated anyone, but he—well, to be honest, he generally had a flavor of the month, with next month's flavor on the horizon. But right now he couldn't think of another flavor he wanted to sample. Was that all there was? He *really* hoped not.

Taking the shrimp off the heat, he turned off the burner and shot Izzy a covert glance. With the brownies safely transferred to the oven, she was now enthusiastically licking the batter-covered spatula and had a smudge of chocolate on the tip of her nose. Something tightened in Eric's chest as he watched her.

God, he didn't want her to go. Not to Africa, not to be Joe's wife.

He wrestled with the Pandora's Box he didn't want to open but couldn't leave alone. No possible good could come of what he wanted to say next, but he couldn't *not* say it.

"You're pretty messed up about that Joe thing, aren't you?"

Izzy hesitated and then moved to the sink to rinse the brownie bowl. "I'll be okay."

This threw him for a loop. Could you be okay after someone you cared about cheated on you? Having never been in love—or anything close to it—he didn't know how these things worked, although his cousin Andrew (two years ago they'd discovered that Andrew wasn't technically his cousin, but Eric still thought of him as such) and his wife, Viveca, had seemed to fall in love pretty quickly, if not instantaneously, and he sure didn't think Andrew would be okay if Viveca cheated on him.

"You're better off without him. You know that, right?"

"I know," she murmured, scrubbing the bowl clean with a soapy brush.

"And what's this Africa business?"

She whipped around to glare at him with narrowed eyes, splashing bubbly water all down the front of her clothes. "You *listened?*"

Eric thought of doing the whole, *well, I might have accidentally heard a word or two while I was minding my own business in the bedroom* thing, but why bother?

"Yeah."

"Unbelievable." Defiant and outraged, she flapped a hand toward one corner of the living room, where a stack of flattened cardboard boxes sat, presumably waiting to be packed with her belongings. "I want to teach at the girls' school in Johannes—"

"You already did that in college, Izzy—"

The funniest little look shot across her face and disappeared so quickly he felt sure he'd imagined it. "That was just one semester, for an internship."

"—and people don't just up and move to South Africa."

"*I* do."

"*Why?*"

"This is what I'm doing with my life."

"*Why?*"

"Because those children are special and I can help them. I can make a difference in their lives."

"But you're a teacher here. You belong *here*."

"I'm needed *there*. Kids here want a new DVD or the next computer game. Kids there want to *learn*. To have a chance. And many of them have lost their parents to AIDS. I can do the most good *there*."

Eric floundered, at a complete loss. For the first time in their relationship, he couldn't understand Isabella. Her calm tone and determined expression told him he was getting nowhere, and his frustration level rose into the red zone. Maybe it was time to try a different tactic.

"And what about your personal life? What about getting married one day? Are you putting that on hold forever?"

She shrugged. "My life is leading me down a different path."

"A different path?"

A hissing sound distracted him and he discovered that the pasta was boiling over. *Wonderful.* He snatched the pot off the stove and burned his hand in the process. Cursing, he nudged Izzy out of her spot in front of the sink and poured off the water. The resulting cloud of steam only made him hotter.

He glared at her, this woman who was systematically ruining

what was supposed to be several relaxing days of fun. "What're you—a *nun* now?"

"I don't think I'm ever getting married," she told him.

Eric froze. *That* he understood. This statement sounded so unlike Isabella that a chill came over him. Looking at her over his shoulder, he swallowed hard and wondered why the hell Izzy's position on marriage mattered so much to him.

It wasn't like he was in the market for a wife. Why would he ever get married? So he could turn into a whipped, stoop-shouldered man like his father and his wife could turn into a Stepford Wife like his mother? *No thank you.* Not any time in the foreseeable future, if ever.

And yet…Izzy's determination to remain single still bothered him, and that was the weirdest thing. He couldn't just drop the subject, no matter how much he wanted to.

"Never say never, Iz."

She didn't answer.

In a day full of disturbing events, this small silence was the most troubling. He studied her.

Maybe it was the rigidity in her shoulders, or the flatness in those eyes that normally sparkled like the Hope Diamond. Maybe it was the utter lack of hope on her face, when she was a person who made Pollyanna look almost like a gloomy pessimist. Whatever it was, he didn't like it.

Still…it gave him the answer he needed:

Nothing. He would do nothing about his sudden attraction to Isabella. He would keep it to himself, and he would get over it. He would never—*never*—do anything to hurt her or their friendship, nor would he rock her boat right now when she was so vulnerable after Joe's infidelity.

Izzy had enough on her plate without her best friend trying to get in her panties, and she didn't take breakups well anyway. Back in college, when that idiot Al dumped her, she'd taken off for that semester in Africa in a clear knee-jerk reaction.

Hell, for all Eric knew, history was repeating itself here: Joe broke her heart, so she was leaving the country. Running and hiding in Africa, just like she'd done before. Maybe that was the only coping mechanism she had. Whether that was the case or not, the last thing she needed now was Eric sniffing after her.

No matter how hard it was, and he suspected it was going to be *very* hard, he would keep his feelings under wraps. Doing anything else would be unfair and…dishonorable.

His silent vow made, Eric felt much better because he'd chosen the right path. And much worse because he wanted her in his arms with an aching desperation. He felt empty and wrecked.

He didn't think he could shake it off any more than he could pitch for the Yankees. But…he would try his damnedest.

"Let's eat," he said. Case closed.

After dinner and cleanup, Eric talked her into watching *The Empire Strikes Back* again—it's the best movie in the entire series, no question, he always said—and then they said their good-nights and Eric disappeared down the hall into the guest bedroom.

Inside her own bedroom, Isabella lit her fresh-linen-scented aromatherapy candle, took a shower, threw on her matching pink cotton tank and boxers, and collapsed onto the bed with the remote. As usual, the pillow-arranging ritual—a girl could never have too many fluffy pillows—took several minutes, but finally she relaxed onto the down-covered heaven that was her comfy duvet.

Zeus, his eyelids droopy from a long day full of play, trotted into the room from parts unknown with his enormous blue plaid dog sleeping pillow—the thing was easily twice his size—gripped in his teeth. He dragged it to his corner between the nightstand and the wall, yapped once and ran out of the room again. Isabella smiled after him. A minute later he was back, this time carrying his favorite transitional object, a fuzzy pink floppy-eared bunny called Fluffles. Isabella watched while he arranged Fluffles on the pillow and then collapsed in his usual position, with his head resting on Fluffles's butt.

Isabella had just sighed with contentment, flipped to the Food Network to watch Paula Deen and was in the process of slathering her legs with her Bath & Body Works cream—Dancing Waters, of course—when Eric tapped lightly on the door.

"Come in," she called without thinking, her hands gliding up her bent right leg.

Eric walked in and opened his mouth to speak, but the words died on his lips when he saw what she was doing. To her complete astonishment, he studied her with a burning lust he didn't bother trying to hide.

Chapter 4

A warning bell rang in her mind—it was late, she was wearing skimpy jammies, they were in her bedroom, he was a man, she was a woman, they'd been drinking wine—but then time ground to a halt and it was too late for any remedial measures, like sliding her legs under the duvet.

She looked right into his eyes and delicious goose bumps erupted over every inch of her skin. Her heart stopped and then began the kind of furious gallop that made people reach for the phone to call 9-1-1. Stunned and frozen, she waited, not breathing, to see what Eric would do. The stark hunger in his face and intense interest in those dark eyes were not expressions she'd ever seen before, but, God help her, she liked seeing them now.

This was not Eric her friend. She knew that right away. This Eric was a complete stranger, someone she'd never before laid eyes on, a being as foreign to her as an alien just arrived on his spaceship. This was Eric the man, and he looked like he was excruciatingly aware of her as a woman, for the first time in their relationship.

He started at the bottom and didn't miss one millimeter of her body. His slow gaze traveled up past her feet and calves, paused on her thighs and then continued up to her breasts, where it stopped and lingered.

As though a switch had been flipped, her breasts swelled to aching, until it felt as though all the blood in her body had been diverted to her nipples. They were pointed and prominent now, she knew.

Eric knew it, too. His gleaming gaze zeroed in, as though he understood how her tank top abraded the sensitive buds every time her chest heaved for air, as though he wanted to suck her, hard, into his mouth as much as she wanted him to—needed him to.

Breathless with anticipation, she couldn't think or move, and, worse, was forced to indulge in seconds of unadulterated staring because Eric was still the best-looking man she'd ever seen, bar none.

He'd changed his clothes for bed and now wore black shorts and had a towel slung around his neck. Not exactly Armani, but with a body like *that* it hardly mattered. He moved and the simple gesture of rubbing the top of his head caused a rippling chain reaction of muscles all over his torso. Those wide, sculpted shoulders and arms pulsed with sinew and he was so *beautiful*—so incredibly stunning—that she wouldn't mind being struck blind at this very moment as long as she had this memory of him to sustain her through the darkness.

His lower body was as incredible. Butt, thighs, calves… muscles, muscles, muscles. Gleaming skin, too. Vast stretches of smooth brown skin, as though someone had taken a can of walnut spray paint to one of Michelangelo's statues and then breathed life into it.

It wasn't just the way Eric looked or looked at her that had her hot and bothered and tied her belly up in delicious knots. His masculine energy took up all the space in the bedroom, leaving none for the air she desperately needed to breathe.

Feeling feverish suddenly, shivery, she wished she'd turned

on the ceiling fan earlier. Yeah. Like *that* would help. Paralyzed, she waited for him to speak.

And waited…and waited…and waited.

Finally he gathered his thoughts. "I, ah—"

His voice was hoarse, so he cleared his throat and ran his tongue along his lower lip. That hot gaze flickered to her legs again and then abruptly snapped to her face, as though he'd realized he'd been ogling her. He flushed until his color was as bright as his glittering eyes.

"I forgot my toothpaste."

Toothpaste. Right.

This confession killed the sexual tension and left an awkwardness so excruciating she felt her cheeks flame.

"Oh," she said. "Sure."

Keeping her eyes lowered to the rug, she hopped down from the bed, hurried into her dark bathroom, and rummaged in the cabinet for the extra tube she always kept on hand. Nervous and clumsy, she knocked her plastic cup into the sink, where it clattered like a thousand metal trash cans. It took her two tries to grab it and three to replace it on the counter.

When she walked back into her room, she saw, to her uneasy surprise, that Eric was now standing right by the bed holding Zeus and absently scratching the rapturous creature behind his ears. Though Eric had been in her room millions of times before, he looked all around as though he'd never seen any of it and had to memorize every detail.

She watched while his gaze touched the gray walls he'd helped her paint when she moved in four years ago, the white trim…the nightstands with pictures her family and friends…the candle…the blue and white paisley duvet on the bed, the pillows…the TV…the bed again. The bed… The bed… *The bed*.

Isabella couldn't stand it—not the awkwardness, the tension or the unexpected and unwelcome heat in her body—anymore.

"Here," she said.

Focusing on some vague point over his shoulder, she thrust the tube at him and hoped he'd go back to his own bedroom where he belonged. When he didn't take it right away, she made the mistake of looking directly at his face and immediately regretted it.

Eric the friend was back, and she knew him well enough to see that he was bewildered. Troubled. Those dark eyes and lowered brows told her he couldn't figure out what'd just happened between them any more than she could, and his confusion touched her. Made her want to comfort him.

But she couldn't do anything like that now. Anything involving Eric's continued presence in her cozy room this late at night was way too dangerous, and she knew it.

He was too close. So close that his delicious, familiar scent— clean, fresh man, with sporty deodorant and a little spice thrown in, something from the Orient, she thought—blocked the candle's fragrance. So close that she could see the tight pores on his face, the beginnings of stubble on his chin and the sparks of blue, green and yellow in those piercing eyes she'd always thought were purely brown.

"Thanks," he said faintly.

His mission accomplished, he should have taken the stupid toothpaste and left. He didn't. Instead, he stared at her as though he'd been hypnotized to forget all about the original purpose of his trip to her room and to linger as though he couldn't bear to leave her.

Her frustration grew. *"Here,"* she said again, thrusting the toothpaste toward his chest, determined to get rid of him as soon as possible and by forcible expulsion if necessary.

He finally blinked. In slow motion, he grasped the top of the tube, brushing her hand in the process and holding—but not taking—the toothpaste.

For that one electrifying moment, as his hot skin touched hers and he stared into her eyes, her entire body sang with the beauty of Kathleen Battle at the Met. Sexual energy surged between them and it was both strange and right. That one touch of Eric's hand was erotic, breathtaking and unlike anything else she'd ever experienced.

It was also way too much for her.

"Anything else?" Dropping her hand and her gaze, she backed away, hurried toward the bed, and busied herself with the useless task of fluffing pillows. "I'm a little tired, so—"

"I'm good," he said, but *still* didn't move. After a pause, he said, "I can't believe Frank and Terri are getting married. Can you?"

She tried to grin, tried to pretend that feeling dizzying lust for him was normal, tried to put the desire behind them. But the new fever in her blood still burned hot and her hands still itched to glide over his skin.

It took her a long moment to answer. "I can't believe Frank and Terri ever managed to graduate. Remember that all-nighter we pulled to help him finish some lit paper junior year? That wasn't pretty."

He made an uncomfortable sound that was part laugh, part snort, and then lapsed into staring again. A good four or five beats passed before he opened his mouth, and another three or four before his voice activated.

"Well…I guess I'll just—"

"Yeah." She spoke quickly and focused her gaze on the pillows…the bed…the dog…anything but him. "Good night."

"Izzy?"

There was a plea in his voice, but she didn't want to hear it. She *wouldn't* hear it. If she heard it, she would look at him, and if she looked at him, she would go to him, and if she went to him they would make love. She knew it. There would be no stopping it. If they made love—*oh, man, she wanted to make love*—they would no longer be friends and, no matter what else ever happened between them, she always needed to keep Eric just as a friend.

"Good night."

She kept her voice soft but firm, and it worked. He moved away and then the quiet click of the closing door told her he'd gone at last. Weak with relief, she collapsed on the bed, listened to the hot rush of blood in her ears, and waited for sleep to come.

It never did.

* * *

"Don't touch that," Eric said the next morning when they set out for her parents' home in Greenville on the first leg of their trip.

Isabella snatched her hand away from the dashboard—cockpit, Eric called it—and shot him the angriest sidelong look she could manage.

They sat in Eric's pride and joy, a Mercedes SUV ML something-or-other. The gleaming black car had leather seats, a sunroof, a computer, satellite radio and enough bells and whistles for a respectable small aircraft. She was not allowed to touch any of them, not even, apparently, the knobs that controlled the air conditioning on *her* side of the vehicle. She supposed she should count herself lucky he'd let her sit in the stinking car at all without some sort of inspection to make sure her butt was worthy of the honor.

She'd had just about enough of Eric Warner.

He'd emerged from the guest bedroom this morning in a pissy mood, and it had gotten pissier as the hours wore on. He hadn't liked the coffee she'd bought, hadn't wanted Zeus to come along and possibly get hair in his precious car, and she hadn't moved fast enough when it was time to leave. No doubt she was also breathing too loudly, blinking too often and looking out the wrong window.

"I'm hot," she snarled.

He rolled his eyes behind his dark sunglasses. Without a word, he reached out and flipped a couple of switches and vents until a blast of arctic air hit her face, threatening the tip of her nose with frostbite.

"That's too cold."

"Dammit, Isabella." Keeping one eye on the road, he did some more adjusting of knobs and whatnot.

"Don't swear at me. I'm tired of your potty mouth." She'd been getting a steady stream of *dammit, Isabellas* today, and she was sick to death of it. It wasn't like she'd done anything wrong or was high maintenance or anything.

Well, sure, she'd made a couple of requests, but so what? Was it a big deal to ask once or twice for the driver to pull over so the passenger could use the bathroom? Was it really a hardship for him to switch from one of his ten thousand preprogrammed jazz stations and let her listen to a little Celtic guitar for a while? Was it *her* fault she'd forgotten her purse at her apartment and they'd lost half-an-hour while they drove back to get it? *Of course not.*

Maybe a walk down memory lane would help his mood. "Remember that time we drove to Florida for spring break? What was that—junior year? In a brown Honda Civic? That car was so old."

"Yeah, I remember. You forgot your makeup case and we lost an hour going back for it."

Isabella sighed. So much for distracting him with memories. "You're going to need to stop soon." She watched the green hills of Kentucky streak by her window and squinted against the sun's glare. "Bathroom break."

Another colorful curse. "We just stopped half an hour ago, Izzy. For God's sake."

"That was to eat. Now I need to go to the bathroom."

"Well, why didn't you go then?"

"Didn't need to," she told him. "And if I have to stop a thousand more times between here and Florida, you'll just have to stop, won't you?"

He seemed speechless with rage, which she found oddly gratifying after his snippy treatment this morning. All sorts of cords and veins in his neck throbbed with tension, and she could have happily watched them all day. But then she realized she was being childish, and, really, they couldn't drive all the way to Jacksonville like this. With her luck, he'd kick her out before they even got to Greenville.

It was hard to believe that all this misery resulted from their interlude last night. In the cold light of day, the episode seemed so…surreal. It hadn't really happened, had it?

The quivering, low in her belly, answered her.

Well, maybe it *had* really happened, but it was one strange, never-to-be-repeated moment out of time that she was perfectly willing to chalk up to too much wine at dinner.

They needed to talk, she decided, smoothing the hem of her skirt and staring down at her scarlet-painted toes in their fancy jeweled flip-flops. A good talk cured most problems, so that's what they'd do: talk, have a good laugh and move on with the rest of their lives. In ten minutes his black mood would be gone and everything would be back to normal.

"Look." Feeling fidgety and needing something to do with her hands, she grabbed another cinnamon candy from her cup holder, unwrapped it and slid it into her mouth. "I think if we just talk about what happened last night—"

"Can you pick that up, please?"

"What?"

"The wrapper." He loosened one tight-knuckled hand from the steering wheel and pointed to the red wrapper, which, sure enough, had dropped to the floor. "I don't want a lot of trash in the car."

"If you boss me around one more time, I'm going to jam this wrapper up your right nostril."

"Don't even try it."

She snatched the wrapper from the floor and shoved it into his stupid little Mercedes trash can instead. "So we had an awkward moment last night. Big deal. We just need to talk it through, and then—"

"Everything doesn't need to be *talked through,* Izzy." He seemed to have difficulty speaking through his rigid jaw. "I know you're big on that touchy-feely emotional nonsense, but I'm not. Everything does not need to be debriefed and dissected. Okay?"

Well, okay. She didn't need to be a nuclear physicist to know she was skating on thin ice and needed to back off. When Eric got like this, the best thing to do was give him a little space, let him sulk in peace and then wait until he was ready to talk.

Only how on earth was she supposed to give him space like this? They were stuck with each other until Monday. *Monday.* Three days from now.

Enough was enough. Mr. Passive-Aggressive was just going to have to deal with her right now.

"It's normal for us to feel a little attraction to each other, Eric, and—"

"I'm getting off," he barked.

With no further warning, he turned the wheel. The car, which was in the fast lane, skidded and hurtled across the other three lanes of the highway, dodging traffic at seventy-five miles an hour and headed for the off-ramp to a rest stop nestled at the foot of a tree-lined hill.

"WILL YOU BE CAREFUL, YOU MANIAC?"

Startled, Isabella stomped the invisible brake on the floor of her side of the car, grabbed the door handle for stability, and glanced around to make sure Zeus and Fluffles were okay in the backseat of this luxury deathmobile. Poor Zeus had slid across the leather and looked a little green under his fur, but his yellow bandana was still in place around his neck and his doggy harness had prevented any real harm. Catching her eye, he yapped and wagged his tail at her in a clear *I'm okay, Mommy* signal.

The car screeched to a halt in a space in front of the rest stop. Eric snatched the keys from the ignition, unlatched his seat belt and threw his door open. He leapt out, slammed the door and stalked away—*Buh-bye, jerk!*—but then he wheeled around and came right back.

Furious she braced herself for the onslaught.

Eric ripped the door open again and leaned down to shout at her. "Use the bathroom. Walk the damn dog. Get a snack. Get a drink. No, wait. *Don't* get a drink. Do *everything* you need to do because we are *not* stopping this car again until we reach the state of Tennessee."

Isabella flashed him a sweet smile and a rude hand gesture.

Eric's face went purple. Vibrating with rage, he slammed the door again, hard enough for the SUV to rock on its wheels and stomped off towards the vending machines. She could almost see steam coming out of his ears.

* * *

Isabella leaned against the enormous oak at the top of the ridge and enjoyed the light breeze on her face while Zeus, at the end of his long leash, bounced through the grass like a gazelle. It was probably wrong to envy a dog, but she did. Ah, to be young and free, with no worries in the world other than when you'd get your next slice of bacon. That was the life.

She, on the other hand, felt as edgy as a rat trapped in a tank with a python, and all thanks to her so-called best friend. *Jerk.*

Raising her hands high overhead, she leaned left, then right and tried to work out some of the tension in her shoulders and waist, but no dice. What good was stretching, anyway, when what she really needed was a tall margarita, heavy on the tequila?

She was just about to call Zeus so they could head back to the car and subject themselves to more of Eric's—she'd started to think of him as Captain Ahab—maniacal behavior, when his furious voice came up the hill behind her.

"Is-a-bell-a!" he roared.

She sighed and turned, wondering what grievous misdeeds he thought she'd done in the ten minutes since he'd seen her. Maybe she'd dropped another candy wrapper on the pristine floor of his car or, worse yet, gotten out of the car without fully retracting her seat belt.

"Yes, Eric?" She kept her voice sweet, knowing it would drive his blood pressure off the charts.

"I've been looking all over for you! I had some woman check the restroom for you! Where the hell have you been?"

"Right here."

"Here?" He summited the hill and stood under the tree, right in her face. *"Here?"*

"Problem?"

"Yeah, you could say that." Those same cords in his throat, the ones that had merely been vibrating earlier, now thrummed like harp strings, and she watched with detached fascination. "You might not want to hike half a mile away from an interstate rest stop without telling anyone where you're going—"

"I am *not* half a mile away," she began in an automatic denial, but then faltered when she glanced over Eric's shoulder and realized that the parking lot and building were, in fact, pretty far away and well beyond yelling distance.

"—because this is a good setup for a woman to get abducted, although I imagine anyone who abducted *you* would regret it before he got to the on-ramp."

"Oh, knock it off," she said. "I'm as abduct-able as the next woman."

"Is that an *I'm sorry I worried you, Eric?*" Cocking his head to the side, he held a hand to his ear as though he wanted to make sure he heard her forthcoming apology.

Now she felt bad, but this whole situation was *not* her fault. She'd only wandered so far because she was trying to work off a little of the stress *he'd* caused. If only he would stop being so stubborn and discuss the incident like the adult he pretended to be, they could have a perfectly lovely trip to Florida and back.

"No, I'm *not* sorry." Jamming her fists on her hips, she stuck out her chin and stood her ground. "If you would just snap out of your black mood and *talk* to me, we could—"

"Talk?" he said. "You want to *talk?*"

Some combination of the wild, glittering light in his eyes and the dangerous quality in his low voice cut through her bluster and struck fear in her heart. This was that strange Eric again, the one she didn't know and couldn't predict. The one she was wildly attracted to and needed to avoid.

She tried to shake her head *no,* but it was too late for backtracking and she could tell he was beyond listening anyway. In a burst of fluid movement, he stepped to her, slid his hands up under the bottom of her blouse and around her waist, backed her up to the tree and pressed his hips to hers.

"Let's talk, Iz."

Chapter 5

"Oh, my God." She couldn't think or talk while *Eric*—her best friend turned complete stranger—stroked the small of her back with hot, gentle hands and stoked that fever in her blood. "W-what're you doing?"

"I'm talking." His lips one inch from hers, he circled his hips and let her feel the incredible, terrifying evidence of how much he wanted her.

Panting and trembling now—this was *Eric!*—she dropped the leash and tried to push him away, with zero success. She wound up involuntarily clinging to thick, satiny arms as strong and immoveable as the tree against her back.

Her body, which was now far beyond her control, refused to acknowledge what her brain already knew: she was not supposed to know him this way. She was not supposed to know how big he was or how wonderful his hard length felt pressed against her aching sex or how passionate he could be.

This was never supposed to happen between them.

"You need to let me go," she whimpered.

"You started this, Izzy." He spoke in a husky bedroom voice he had no business using on her. "So let's talk."

"No."

"You want to know what's wrong with me?" He nuzzled her ear, burning her with hot, minty breath that sent bolts of electrifying sensation directly to her breasts and sex. "Here it is—I've got a serious jones for my best friend—"

"Stop it, Eric—"

"—and I'm a little freaked out by it."

"Don't."

"I've pretty much been hard since I saw you walking down the street yesterday." His gleaming gaze, dark with passion and need, focused on her face, which he cupped and stroked in a rough grip. "I want you, Isabella."

"No—"

"I want your mouth."

He flicked his tongue across her lips, tormenting her with the kind of kiss that inflamed but didn't satisfy.

"Eric."

"I want your breasts."

His hot hands slid higher under her shirt, skimming over the satin cups of her bra and hefting her breasts to test their weight. This was torture enough, but then he ran his thumbs over her nipples and she almost passed out. Ecstasy called to her, drowning out her self-protective instinct's feeble attempts to shout a warning.

"I want your thighs," he continued. "I want them wrapped around my hips."

No. Not that.

But his hands had already started their slow descent down her sides and hips to her skirt. Inching underneath in a belabored process designed to drive her insane, he spread those long fingers wide and kneaded as though her solid thighs were not a problem to be exercised away but a treasure to be worshipped.

"I want you. Want you. *Want you.*" Eric slid his hands out from under her skirt and up to her nape, tugged gently until her head fell back and buried his lips in the side of her neck. "Aren't you glad we talked?"

Dazed with pleasure, she clung to the smooth column of his neck. "You need to let me go so I can think."

"I'm *not* letting you go. Stop asking."

She could barely speak, but she gave it what she thought was a valiant effort, all things considered. "Y-you're blowing this all out of proportion. You had a little too much wine last night at dinner, and then you saw me in my p-pajamas and now you think it's a *thing,* but really it's just a passing attraction and you'll get over it."

"Yeah." He raised his head, and in his glittering eyes she saw excitement and relief, as though he were thrilled that she understood him so well. "*Yeah.* That's what *I* thought, too. Just a…a temporary insanity type thing that would go away in the cold light of day."

"Exactly."

Relieved to realize they were on the same page after all, she pulled back as much as she could and wondered how soon he'd let her go. Only he didn't let her go. His hands came out of her hair and slid around to cup her face, and her hopes fell even as her breasts throbbed again for his touch. When he stroked her cheeks with his thumbs, gently this time, she groaned, closed her eyes and let her head fall back against the tree, knowing she was lost.

"Here's the thing, though, Iz." He lowered his voice. "Open your eyes. Look at me."

Somehow she lifted her heavy lids and subjected herself to the fierce intensity in his expression. Even worse were his determination and raw passion, which he did nothing to hide. How could this be happening? *How?*

He smiled a lazy, wry, regretful smile—a devastating smile— and smoothed her cheeks again. "Here's the thing—you feel really good and this *thing* is strong. Really strong. It's not going to go away."

She shook her head in a gesture he didn't bother to acknowledge.

"Do you want to know what I've been wondering, Iz?"

Yes. "No."

His hands slid to her butt and he pulled her closer, wedging his hard length against the spot that ached and wept for him. "I've been wondering what it would be like to be inside you."

The seething image filled her mind and made her writhe against him even as she issued a meaningless denial. "No."

"Yeah. *Yeah.*" He pressed a gentle, lingering kiss to one corner of her mouth. "And I've been wondering how you'll look and sound when I make you come."

I've been wondering the same thing about you.

It was difficult to hold back those words as, bit by bit, the struggle left her, but somehow she managed. It was one thing to fight his touch—that was hard enough—but there was no way to resist his tender words. Listening to his husky voice say such unbearably sexy things to her was like rolling around on satin sheets or sliding into a hot bath. There was simply no way to resist the sensations or to keep her body from going pliant, and she wasn't even sure she wanted to. When he kissed the other corner of her mouth, she ran her hands up to his nape to anchor him close.

"And when I was in your room last night—Isabella? Are you listening to me?—when I was in your room last night, I kept thinking that *that's* where I belong. Watching that TV with you. Watching you put lotion on those legs. In that bed with you. Making love with you."

Her brain felt so sluggish now, her thoughts vague and loose. Was she dreaming? Was that it? Because this couldn't be happening. Not to her, not with Eric. And did he *mean* to do this? To jeopardize their entire seventeen-year friendship for the pleasure of having sex with each other—even if it did turn out to be the best sex of their lives? Did he think anything could be the same after today?

"We shouldn't do this. We both know it. It's too dangerous."

He nodded, but she wasn't fooled. She knew that while he agreed that a physical relationship between them was dangerous, he was past caring about the consequences.

"There's something here, Izzy. Maybe has been for a long time." He stared at her, perfectly still except for his restless hands, which roamed to her waist again, and then up her torso until his thumbs just brushed the sides of her breasts. "We need to figure out what it is."

She'd been afraid he'd say that.

Crooning deep in his throat, he kissed her, taking another irrevocable step down the road that separated friend from lover. There was no question of her kissing him back, not when she felt the vibrating urgency in his body, the warmth of his lips and tasted the peppermint in his mouth. Not when she wanted him as much as she did.

She automatically opened for him and sank deep, surging forward and up, searching and tasting him as he did to her. Groaning, he unleashed his hands and suddenly they were everywhere—in her hair, roaming over her back, kneading her butt, stroking her thighs—driving her higher, making her wilder than she'd ever thought she could be.

Her cries filled the air, embarrassing her, but she couldn't keep quiet. Not when he affected her this way. Eric. This was Eric. Eric… Eric… *Eric.*

For years she'd thought she'd known him, but now it was clear she'd known *nothing*. Not about his lips or his hands or his tenderness or his passion. This whole time he'd been a stranger to her, but now she wanted to learn *everything*. She needed all his secrets, had to open all the doors that had never before been options for her, had to discover everything about him.

"I want you," he whispered between deep, frantic kisses, over and over again. "Isabella? I want you… Want you."

"I want you, too."

Her confession loosed something in him and he shuddered, unable to suppress his body's reaction to her. A hint of a smile softened his swollen lips, and then he dove in again, kissing her with a ferocity that matched her own.

There was no telling how long they might have stood there,

or what else they might have done or said, if the distant sound of a dog barking hadn't pierced the absolute, primitive lust that engulfed her.

Slowly, by degrees, she remembered that she had a dog…she'd been walking the dog…the leash wasn't in her hand…

With a horrified gasp, she broke the kiss and looked wildly around. Eric clung, his fingers tightening in a reflexive refusal to let her go.

"Oh, no," she said. *"Oh, no."*

"What is it, Sunshine?"

"Zeus is gone."

It took several long seconds for her words to penetrate his sensual daze. She'd just opened her mouth to repeat herself when Eric blinked, cursed and wheeled around to look for the dog.

She looked, too, but there was no sign of Zeus, not in any direction, not for as far as her eyes could see. And on the other side of the rest stop, Isabella saw the highway, six concrete lanes of certain death for any living thing that trotted across its path.

"Oh, God," she said weakly.

Following her gaze, Eric took her hand. "We'll find him, baby."

Trying to hold back her panic, she nodded. All she had to do was look into Eric's face and see the resolve there, and she knew that if it was humanly possible for her dog to be found, Eric would find him. Tugging her hand, Eric took off at a run and they raced down the hill together.

Zeus, they quickly discovered, had made himself at home with a mountain of garbage bags outside the back door of the rest stop near the dumpster and had eaten…everything. They found the furry little idiot being sicker than, well, a dog. He lay there, groaning, amidst McDonald's wrappers, a pizza box and God only knew what other trash Eric didn't even want to think about. Isabella went into worried mother mode, scooped up the Yorkie—Eric wasn't about to touch him—and insisted that they get medical assistance.

Which was how they found themselves sitting side by side in red plastic scoop chairs in an examining room at an emergency veterinary clinic twenty minutes outside Knoxville, waiting for Zeus's prognosis.

Eric glared at the colorful poster of dog species by country against the far wall and wondered what the hell had happened to his life in the last eighteen hours to make it so unrecognizable. Driving to this stupid wedding instead of flying first-class or, better yet, taking the Lear. In a vet's office waiting for a dog that wasn't even his to have his little stomach pumped on account of gluttony.

Lusting after Isabella.

Man, was he lusting. If the crotch of his shorts got any tighter he'd no doubt have a potential career as a soprano for the local opera.

Leaning his head back, he closed his eyes and tried—*tried*—to put what had happened under that tree in perspective, but perspective was in short supply today. All he knew was that he burned for Izzy. *Burned.* With a fever that left a perpetual sheen of perspiration across his forehead and would no doubt melt the cheap plastic chair he was sitting in before the next ten minutes had passed.

Isabella. Who'd have thought that sweet, little, girl-next-door Izzy was so…so… *Everything.* So passionate. So responsive. So indescribably sexy. So *right* in his arms.

Opening his eyes, he shot her a sidelong glance and discovered her looking as shell-shocked as he felt. Her shapely legs were crossed, her lush, luscious mouth was slightly parted and her unfocused gaze had settled on the steel examining table. She wasn't doing anything especially tempting—holding Fluffles in a white-knuckled death grip didn't qualify—and wasn't exactly a nude Halle Berry beckoning to him from a satin-sheet-covered bed, but he wanted her just as much.

No, more. He wanted Izzy more than he'd ever wanted a woman. More than he'd known he *could* want a woman. The want settled into a hard knot low in his belly, tightened around his groin and squeezed his lungs until he could barely breathe with it.

Panic was right there, too, agitating him until he couldn't sit still and had to jump up, stalk over to the window and stare out at the supremely uninteresting view of some major intersection with a Burger King on one corner and a BP gas station on the other.

His rampaging thoughts refused to settle down. How could Isabella have done this to them? The list of her transgressions was long and serious. Changing the landscape between them by becoming so sexy that he couldn't ignore it. Awakening him to her sexuality and tempting him in unearthly ways. Scrambling his brains to the point where he couldn't think a coherent thought. What the hell was he supposed to do about all this?

And when—*when?*—would his throbbing erection go away?

His frustrated turmoil pissed him off because he hated not knowing what to do. Naturally he took it out on her. "I don't see why we couldn't have just given the dog a TUMS."

As usual, Izzy remained unfazed by his grumbling and gave him a withering look that was, he supposed, better than the bewildered look she'd worn a second ago. "TUMS are for humans. Zeus is a *dog* in case you hadn't noticed. He has a sensitive stomach. He can't just eat a *TUMS.*"

"Why not? He ate everything else."

This observation earned him a tongue click, which further irritated him. "Brilliant idea, Iz," he muttered. "Bringing a dog with a sensitive stomach on a road trip. How're you going to get the smell of dog sick off my leather seats?"

Those dark eyes flashed murder at him. "I'll clean your precious seats. Okay?"

"Great."

"Great." Wrenching her gaze away as though she couldn't subject her eyeballs to the torture of looking at him for one more second, she rested her elbow on the back of her chair and propped her chin on her hand. "I can't believe you *kissed* me. You shouldn't have done that. You're *such* an idiot."

Pay dirt. Eric felt a tremendous surge of satisfaction because he'd been itching for a fight, and now here it was, in spades. "*I'm* the idiot? Who's the one who kept pushing me? *'What's wrong,*

Eric? Let's talk, Eric.'" Batting his eyes, he mimicked her in the dead-on impersonation that he knew drove her crazy. Sure enough, her face and lips tightened until he could've bounced a tennis ball off them. "Well, you wanted to talk, so we talked. You should be happy."

"Do I *look* happy?" Jumping up, she marched over. "You and your...your—"

Words seemed to fail her, so she used Fluffles to gesture vaguely and impotently toward Eric's privates. Delighted to be included in the discussion, they remained at attention and awaited further instructions.

"—your little *friend*—"

"Not that little, Iz, surely."

"—won't be happy until you've slept with every woman in the state. I should have known that *you* can't be friends with a woman. You have to ruin everything, don't you?"

Well, now wait a minute. He loved women and sex as much as the next guy—a little more, maybe—but he'd been nothing but a gentleman toward Isabella for all these years and never dreamed of being anything but until he saw her yesterday.

"Don't blame me for this mess," he snarled. "You need to check *yourself*. With your little short skirts and your dimples and your lips, smiling at me and whatnot, what was I supposed to—"

Outrage puffed her up like a balloon overflowing with helium. "Don't you *dare* try to blame *me*. I am the same as I always was."

She couldn't be. It simply was not possible that he'd never seen her for the gorgeous creature that now had his guts tied up with longing. "Well, you can point the finger at me all you want, Iz. The bottom line is that something's changed between us. It doesn't matter whose fault it is. The horse is out of the barn."

"Gee, you think?"

"I could do without the sarcasm, Isabella." Trying to look dignified and affronted with a rock the size of Gibraltar in the front of his shorts was hard, but he thought he managed reasonably well.

"Oh, you could do without the sarcasm." She sneered. *"Jerk."*

It was a sign of her new power over him that, as much as he wanted to grab her by the shoulders and give her a shake, he wanted to lay her across the examining table and make love to her—hot, hard and endlessly—even more.

Through the unfocused haze of his anger at being caught in this dilemma, he saw it all, felt it all, and wanted it all: Izzy naked and writhing beneath him, urging him deep inside her body, scratching his back with her short nails, moving with him.

The glide of his hands over her skin, the smell of her, the taste of her.

He needed it in a way he'd never needed anything before. Shuddering from the force of this unwanted emotion, he rested his palms against the cold metal table and leaned into it because he didn't have the energy to hold himself upright and argue with her at the same time.

"You know what this means, don't you?" she asked.

"Isabella." Beyond drained, he turned his head to look at her and answered with absolute sincerity. "I don't have the slightest idea."

Muttering at his cluelessness, which appeared to be both a tremendous disappointment to her and no less than she'd expected, she told him, "It means we've got to have sex with each other and put it behind us. As soon as possible."

Chapter 6

Eric's jaw hit the floor and stayed there. He was still gaping and blinking at her—what did she just say?—when the door swung open and a man in a white coat strode in. Eric hastily sat in the nearest chair and vowed to remain there until he got his body under control.

"Ms. Stevens?" The man looked amused as he shook Izzy's hand. "I'm Dr. Wu. You've got yourself a sick little dog there. Any idea what all he ate?"

Worry lines creased Isabella's forehead and she wrung the bedraggled Fluffles as she thought about her answer. "I'm not sure, but we saw McDonald's wrappers—I think it was a Filet-O-Fish—and a pizza box, and a few candy wrappers, and…Eric, was that a bag of French onion or barbeque potato chips we saw? Do you remember? The bag was green."

Eric grunted.

"So I think if it was green then it must have been French onion chips." Her recitation concluded, Izzy turned her anxious gaze back to the vet. "Is Zeus going to be okay?"

Dr. Wu smiled. "He'll be fine. But if he ate some rancid fish, well…I don't need to tell you that's not so good."

"It's my fault for being, ah, distracted." For emphasis, she shot Eric the kind of icy glance he imagined she'd give Adolf Hitler if he walked into the room. "I turned my back for a minute and Zeus just went wild."

Dr. Wu consulted his clipboard. "Well, the good news is that the vomiting seems to be tapering off—"

"Thank God for that," Eric murmured, earning himself another death glare from Isabella.

"—but I'm still debating whether to give him an IV or not. To keep him hydrated."

"Whatever you think is best," Isabella said anxiously.

"Let's give it a few more minutes and see what happens."

"Can you give him Fluffles?" Isabella handed the stuffed bunny to Dr. Wu, who looked startled but took it anyway. "It's his transition object."

"Ah…sure." Smiling and flashing Eric a discreet but clearly sympathetic look—*Poor guy, you have your hands full dealing with these two, don't you?*—Dr. Wu left.

The second the door clicked shut behind him, Izzy rounded on Eric again. Wild-eyed and indignant, she waved her arms and read him the riot act in a fierce whisper.

"If Zeus doesn't recover, it'll be *your* fault for not keeping your hands off me. I *never* would've turned my back on him but for you and your little under-the-tree seduction scene. Why didn't you keep your hands to yourself? Huh? How was I supposed to think straight and be a responsible pet owner with you climbing all over me?"

"Isabella—"

But she wasn't finished with him yet. "*This* is why we need to just go ahead and sleep together, satisfy our curiosity, and get back to the way things were before. It's the only way. We'll just do the deed, and then—"

Eric had, obviously, slipped into the nether region between the Twilight Zone and the regular world, a place where down was up and in was out. Holding up a cautious hand, he stopped her, mid-rant.

"Are you telling me," he said, speaking slowly to ensure that there were no dropped syllables, mangled words or other errors of communication, "that you want to have sex with me so you can satisfy your curiosity—"

"Yes."

"—get it over with—"

"Yes."

"—and get on with your life?"

"Yes."

That's what he thought she'd said. It wasn't his imagination making a fool of him. She had, in fact, proposed the kind of exceptionally stupid idea that tended to get a person fired or killed.

Flabbergasted, he stared at her earnest face and wondered what'd happened to the brilliant Izzy he'd always known, the one who'd gotten better grades than him all through their undergraduate careers at Princeton. How could she suggest something this ridiculous? Had she been watching too many *I Love Lucy* reruns? Was that it?

"Are you insane?" he asked her.

"No."

In fact, she looked vaguely hurt, as if she couldn't quite understand why he wasn't jumping on her offer to have no-questions-asked sex with her. He didn't understand, either, to tell the truth. All he knew was that a nasty, sickening feeling was growing in his gut and he had the sudden, near-overwhelming urge to take one of those ugly plastic chairs and smash it through the closest window.

"So we'd be…what? Friends with benefits? Sex buddies?"

"Of course not." Offended now, she drew herself up and crossed her arms over her chest, all wounded dignity and unshakable pride. "I'm not the sex buddy type."

"I know that."

"Our friendship is the most important thing. I don't want to jeopardize it because of our attraction."

"Neither do I."

"So we need to address the attraction and get past it."

Eric was all for addressing the attraction. It was the getting past it part he had problems with. "So…we'd have…what? An affair for a few months and then—"

"Oh, no." She shuddered at the suggestion. "I'm leaving soon anyway, remember? For South Africa? No. I think a night would do it. Two at the most."

A black rage descended on him, so dark he could barely see her through his dimming vision. It only got worse as she watched him, her expression chirpy, bright and annoying as hell, and it took him a good ten seconds to force a response up and out of his tight throat.

"A night…or two? That's it?"

"That's it."

This idea was so repugnant…so inconceivable…so unbelievably freaking idiotic, that he would have laughed if he could have unlocked his throbbing jaw long enough to smile. Worse, a vein was now pulsing in his temple—he could *feel* it—and this…this…*woman* was about to cause him to stroke out or have a heart attack right here in the middle of an animal hospital where they probably didn't even have the equipment necessary to revive him. With his luck they'd probably slap him on a gurney and crack his chest open right next to a collie getting his balls clipped.

A night with Isabella would never be enough, not with the way he wanted to gorge on her body and revel in her. He wanted to make love with her…laugh with her…explore her, in a way he'd never done before.

This was the last thing he'd wanted or expected. Life as a player was pretty good, after all—but there was something so right about deepening the relationship with Isabella, so comforting, so logical that he just couldn't ignore it. He was already emotionally closer to Isabella than he'd ever been to another woman. Why not take it a little further and see what was there?

After several deep breaths he was able to choke out a couple sentences. "How about this." Something in his voice, which sounded hoarse and dangerous, even to his own ears, seemed to pierce Isabella's blithe attitude, and she watched him with a new wariness. "How about we have sex, spend a little more time together and see if we can build a relationship?"

She goggled at him for an arrested moment. Her expression, which hovered somewhere between startled amusement and abject horror, did nothing for his ego, which was already critically wounded and on life support. And that was *before* she emitted a weird hiccupping sound that erupted into full-blown hysterical laughter. Seething, he watched as she clutched her side and doubled over, clinging to one edge of the table for support.

"You?" Gasping, she straightened, wiped her streaming eyes and tried to catch her breath. "In a *relationship?* The man who gets hives if a woman leaves a toothbrush in his bathroom? The man who's never, to my knowledge, been with the same woman for longer than a few months? The man who thinks staying all night at a woman's apartment is a commitment like marriage? *You?* Why would I pin any girlish hopes on *you?* Do I look that s-stupid and self-destructive?"

Laughter bubbled up and overcame her again and she bent at the waist. Cursing, he vibrated with righteous anger, but then it occurred to him that it couldn't really be *righteous* if her little assessment was correct.

It was worse than that, actually. She had him dead to rights.

He should've known all those long talks he'd had with Izzy over the years would one day come back to bite him in the ass. What kind of moron confided relationship details to a *woman?* How could he have forgotten that she was a *them* and he was an *us?* What had he been thinking?

Actually, he knew what he'd been thinking: that it was great to talk to Izzy because she was so earthy. That he could be himself with her. That it was nice to have a female perspective on sex and dating. That she didn't judge him.

Hah.

Well, she was judging him now, wasn't she? Served him right for being such a major jackass as to confide secrets that should remain strictly within the Universal Brotherhood of Players. *Shit*. He should have his membership card revoked.

The funniest thing about this whole discussion, not that any of it was really funny, what with his groin about to explode and all, was the fact that any one of the hundreds of women he'd dated over the years would think that her fairy godmother had granted her fondest wish if Eric indicated just the *slightest* interest in developing a relationship. Any other woman would have been thrilled with this opportunity to be with a rich, handsome and, let's face it, fun-to-be-with CEO like him. Thrilled.

And here was Isabella about to wet her pants with laughter.

Ironic. That was the word he was looking for.

Driven to the limits of his endurance and about a hundred miles beyond, he snapped. With no conscious thought whatsoever, he took Isabella by the shoulders and, ignoring her startled squeak, swung her around until he had her backed into the far corner. Once there, he held her hand to his erection, forcing her to stroke him.

"Here's the thing, Isabella." Leaning in nice and close, he licked and bit her ear as he spoke. "I don't really think this is a laughing matter."

But her amusement had already vanished without a trace, and he found this supremely gratifying. Those dark eyes rolled closed, her head fell back, and she made the most delightful sound of excitement.

Without his encouragement her fingers tightened around him as though she needed this touch between them as much as he did. Even so, he did not let go, but flattened her palm against him, making the caress rougher. *Perfect*. Shuddering now, drunk on her, he murmured her name again and again.

After moments of this glorious torture, though, she came to her senses, which was more than he could do. Opening her eyes, she tried to pull back her hand, but he held tight.

"Eric, please." That sexy voice saying his name drove him wild. "We are in a *vet's office*."

"I don't give a shit."

Lowering his head, he took her delicious mouth, stroking deep, long and hard, and she answered with a ferocity that matched his. Only the sound of a nearby door slamming— probably from one of the examining rooms down the hall— brought any sanity back to the proceedings.

He broke away and cursed. "I want you," he panted.

"You can have me."

Yeah, he could tell. She was soft and pliant and a hot, urgent passion glittered in her eyes. This new thing between them, whatever it was…she wanted it as much as he did.

"I want you for more than one night," he told her, desperate to reach an accord. "I want to see what's here."

Like magic, her body went rigid and the glow in her face died. At the thought of being with him for any extended period of time, she withdrew completely, as though he'd suggested bigamy or murder. When she spoke, her voice was cold, her tone absolute.

"One night is all I'm offering."

That same black anger came back, making Eric feel wild, desperate and unhinged. So she could make love to him and walk away. She could be clinical and detached about what would be a life-changing event for him. She could slam the door in his face, leaving not the slightest glimmer of hope, when he needed her this badly.

"Screw that, Isabella."

Touching her now seemed like a punishment rather than the gift he wanted more than any other. Leaving the building was his only option since he couldn't stay in the room with her and couldn't go out to the waiting room in this condition. Shoving away, he wheeled around to the glass emergency door that led to the parking lot and pushed it open. He was halfway outside when she called after him.

"Eric—"

He ignored her.

In that dark moment he didn't want to see her face again.

* * *

Once in the parking lot, Eric lingered by the SUV. He'd had the vague idea of sitting inside the vehicle and listening to some calming music, but he was much too upset for that right now. There was no way he could sit still. He was just wondering whether a walk down the sidewalk to the corner would cool him off a little when his cell phone vibrated and played *The Imperial March*—otherwise known as *Darth Vader's Theme*—from *Star Wars*. This special ringtone was reserved for this caller only, and normally it gave Eric a private chuckle every time he heard it. Not this time. Cursing—just what he needed right now—he snatched the phone off its belt hook and answered.

"Yeah," he snarled.

"Whoa. What's wrong with you?"

Only one man on earth had that amused, wry voice and the bad timing to call at a moment like this: his cousin Andrew Warner, the yin to Eric's yang, the person who could irritate him like no other, except, maybe, Isabella. They usually spoke several times a week, if not daily, about company and family matters, but Andrew wasn't exactly the guy you wanted around during a moment of vulnerability. *Andrew.* He did *not* have the energy for this right now.

"Shit," Eric said.

"Nice." Andrew's laughter came over the line loud and clear. "What's got your panties in a bunch?"

"Nothing," Eric said quickly, trying to sound more upbeat lest Andrew scent his blood and start circling like the shark that he was. "What's up?"

"We're having Andy baptized in Columbus on Sunday. Can you come?"

"*Sunday?* How about a little more notice? I told you Izzy and I are driving to Jacksonville for a wedding on Saturday."

"Yeah, well, the boy's nearly one. If we put it off any longer he'll be able to drive to his own baptism. So you can come back a little early. Your parents'll be in town this weekend—"

"God help us," Eric muttered.

"—and after that they'll be in Europe until who knows when."

"Is that right?"

Andrew snorted. "They're *your* parents, man. Do you ever talk to them?"

"Not if I have any other option, no."

"Well, we'll talk about your family issues later. Can you come?"

Typical Andrew, expecting everyone to drop everything to be at his beck and call at a second's notice. *Jerk*. Still, Eric wouldn't miss any of the events in little Andy's life if he could help it. At the thought of Andrew's adorable son who, with his smiling face, masses of curly black hair and fat little legs, was the cutest kid Eric had ever seen, some of Eric's tension at last began to slip away.

"Well," he grumbled, thinking of his right-hand man, with whom they could hitch a ride back to Columbus. "Brad's got the jet down in Miami to meet with suppliers this week. I'll have him stop through Jacksonville and pick us up."

"Great. Appreciate it. By the way, Viveca wants you to be the godfather."

"What?" Eric came to full attention, his throat unaccountably tight now and his eyes misty. *"Godfather?* You sure?"

"Yeah," Andrew said, and Eric could almost see him shrug. "It's mostly ceremonial, so you can't screw it up."

Eric snorted. He knew Andrew was only kidding, but still. Teasing from Andrew, which normally would be only a minor annoyance, like a buzzing fly, had, within the last year or so, taken on an irritating new significance.

Maybe it was the absolute change that had come over Andrew since he met his wife, Viveca. Usually smug, arrogant and obnoxious—Eric's greatest joys in life had come from needling the brother—Andrew was now insufferably...happy. Always smiling, always laughing, always sharing secret little looks and touches with Viveca, with whom he seemed to be glued at the hip.

As if that wasn't bad enough, Andrew now had a wonderful family, what with Viveca, baby Andy, and their adopted son, Nathan, who was now nine or ten.

The only good thing about the whole sickening scenario was that Andrew and crew lived in New York City, so Eric only had to endure their excruciating joy once a month or so when they came to Columbus to visit his grandmother, Arnetta Warner.

Why Andrew's newfound happiness felt like such a personal affront to his own life, which was pretty good, all things considered, Eric had no idea. The man deserved it, Eric supposed grudgingly, and he wanted his cousin to be happy. Even so, something about Andrew and Viveca left him vaguely pissed off. Pinpointing a reason seemed to be impossible, so he'd stopped trying months ago. He just knew that Andrew's great life suddenly made Eric's life seem…less. Andrew's happiness underscored Eric's loneliness. Yeah, he was lonely. May as well admit it. That was the nameless ache he'd been feeling for a while now.

Watching Andrew with Viveca, seeing the way they exuded sex and contentment—there'd been one night when Eric saw them emerge from the pool house at Heather Hill, Arnetta's estate, with messy wet hair and shifty looks, as though they'd been skinny dipping and making love—put the strangest thoughts into Eric's head.

Made him wonder, for the first time in his life, if having a wife and children might be as wonderful for him as it was for Andrew. If being married could be nice rather than the cut and dried business arrangement that Eric's parents had maintained for the last forty years. If Eric, too, could be happier—if it was also his time to settle down.

A woman's murmuring voice on Andrew's side of the line cut across Eric's troubled thoughts and stretched his taut nerves. So Viveca was right there with Andrew. *Of course.*

"Hang on a minute," Andrew told him.

Eric rolled his eyes and waited. There was a bumping and a jostling, and then Andrew's voice came back on the line, along with the unmistakable gurgle of Andy, the world's happiest baby.

Something tugged, hard, on Eric's heartstrings.

"How's my boy?" Andrew cooed to his laughing son, whom he was now, obviously, holding. "Huh? How's my boy?"

Eric had a sudden inspiration. "Put Viveca on. I need to talk to her."

"Why?" Andrew's voice lost its new-father softness and assumed the faint growl it always had whenever he thought Eric was showing too much interest in his wife. "What do you want?"

"Just put her on."

"You're lucky I don't hang up on your ass."

Eric supposed that was true. Chuckling, he leaned against the SUV, checked the clinic's front door for signs of Izzy—none yet, thank goodness—and enjoyed the gentle breeze on his face as he waited for Viveca, who came to the phone right away.

"Hey, Eric," she said. "What's up?"

"You got a minute? I have a little, uh, problem." Eric belatedly had second thoughts about confiding personal issues to Viveca, who seemed to be a pipeline straight to Andrew. But she was generally very cool and he was desperate. "It's private."

"Okay."

The new interest in her voice gave him pause, but he plowed ahead anyway. "So don't tell the jackass."

She laughed, reminding him why he liked her so well. "I won't."

"So…the thing is—"

He couldn't quite bring himself to say *Izzy wants to love me and leave me,* so he decided to keep it simple. Viveca would understand because she'd once commented about the possibility of a relationship between him and Izzy. Thinking back on the comment now, he wondered at his own stupidity because he'd thought Viveca was spouting serious nonsense at the time.

Sheesh. Could he have *been* any blinder? Maybe Viveca had seen the writing on the wall before he had. At this point he wanted to award her a million dollars for her brilliance. Taking a deep breath, he laid it all on the line.

"Things seem to be, ah, *changing,* between me and Izzy."

"Oh." There was a short pause. *"Oh."*

"Yeah."

"Hang on."

Eric listened to the sounds of Viveca's footsteps hurrying somewhere in her massive Park Avenue apartment, and then a door shutting. When she came back on the line, her voice was breathless and excited.

"I *knew* it. The second I saw the two of you together, I *knew* you shouldn't be just friends. So what's the problem?"

"Well, this is a little, ah…sudden."

"Right…?"

"And it's going to take some time getting used to. I don't want to ruin the friendship and all. And Izzy's special. Not like the other, ah—"

"Hoochies?" she suggested helpfully.

"—well…yeah, not like the other hoochies I date."

"You'd better not blow it, okay?"

The sudden vehemence in Viveca's voice made him pull back a little. He held the phone away from his ear and looked at it, half-expecting to see Viveca climb out of it and point a finger in his face.

"I don't want to hear about you hurting her, or cheating or anything—"

"Excuse me," he snarled, pacing back and forth next to the SUV. "Before you start ranting about what a terrible person you think I am, let me just stop you right there, okay? *This* is the problem—she's not gonna give me the chance to hurt her. She's already got an end game in mind before the damn relationship even starts."

"What do you mean?"

"I mean she says she'll have sex with me, and that's it. *One time*. And then she's moving to South Africa to teach."

Just then a stooped man and woman, one of those little old couples who look like they've been married since the time of the pharaohs, tottered by several feet away on the sidewalk. Hearing the word *sex*—maybe Eric *had* been talking a little louder than he'd meant to—they glanced around, looking scandalized. Eric smiled, waved, and watched as they clutched each other's arms tighter and hurried off.

"Oh," Viveca said in his ear, and Eric could almost see her

face fall. "Well, I could see why you'd turn down that arrangement, but—"

"Oh, don't worry," he interjected. "I'm taking the sex. Any way I can."

"What?"

"The problem is getting her to stick around so we can see where this thing goes. There's no way I can up and move to South Africa. You know that. But I just don't get what her problem is. Why would she tell me a flat-out *no?*"

"Well…" Viveca sighed thoughtfully. "If she's anything like me, she probably doubts your ability to, ah, commit to one woman. Maybe she's worried about that."

"Maybe," he said doubtfully.

That explanation certainly jibed with what Izzy had said a few minutes ago, in between her bursts of hysterical laughter, but his gut told him there was something else going on. He just didn't know *what,* although he had the persistent and sickening worry that she was still hung up on her ex.

"But if you think there's more to it, and you really want her—"

"I do," he said. "You have no idea."

"—then you need to hang in there with her. Isabella's worth it." Viveca paused and he heard the smile in her voice. "Anyway, I don't think there's a Warner man who ever lived that couldn't, ah, win over a woman he wanted."

Right on cue, Eric heard a door open on Viveca's side of the line, and then approaching footsteps that could only belong to one person.

"Excuse me," Viveca hissed, though her voice was a little muffled now, as if she'd put her hand over the receiver. "I was in the middle of a very important *private* conversation."

"So sorry," said Andrew's faint voice, but he didn't sound sorry at all, especially when he raised his voice for his next sentence, no doubt to make sure Eric heard him. "You need to tell my cousin to get his own wife because I need mine back now."

Viveca laughed and then her unmuted voice came back on the line. "Eric? Sorry. Gotta go."

"Yeah, I know." Eric supposed he should be grateful Andrew had let the poor woman talk on the phone for this long. Turning back toward the SUV, he saw, out of the corner of his eye, the door to the clinic open. Isabella emerged, looking grim, and saw him right away. Once again his pulse went into overdrive.

Lowering his voice, he gripped the phone tighter. "Here she comes."

"Keep me posted." Viveca now sounded breathless with excitement and Eric pictured her bouncing on the balls of her feet, waving her hands, and all but levitating with rapture on his behalf. "Call me any time! Good luck!"

"Thanks," Eric muttered, turning his phone off. "I'll need it."

Chapter 7

Isabella crossed the parking lot and approached him with caution, as though she wasn't sure what kind of reception she'd receive. She stopped when she got within two feet of him, and there was a look of contrition in her dark eyes that went a long way toward soothing Eric's jangled nerves.

"Hi," he said.

"Hi." The breeze brushed one dark strand of hair across her face and she tucked it behind her ear. "Zeus is okay. But they're giving him an IV. We have to leave him for a couple hours."

"Okay."

This would put them behind in their wedding travels—he wondered vaguely whether they'd now have to skip the visit with her family in Greenville—but the wedding was the very least of his concerns right now.

She hazarded a small smile, the one that was warm and sweet and as familiar as the fingers on his right hand, and his life shifted that much more into unfamiliar territory. He was used to seeing that smile and smiling back. He was not used to seeing that smile and wanting…everything. Longing for her tightened its hold on him and sank its fingers deep.

He waited, with absolutely no idea what to do or say.

"Can I tell you something?" she asked.

He nodded.

"I'm really sorry. For…laughing and all. That was rude."

One of the great things about Izzy—and there were a lot of great things about her, like her colorful clothes, free spirit and enormous heart—was her lack of posturing. She didn't jockey for position, wasn't a control freak and wasn't passive-aggressive. She didn't sulk or punish. If she was wrong, she said so, and if she was mad, she vented and moved on.

She was always just…herself. Always irresistible.

"I suppose I deserved it." It was easier to discuss his imperfections when she'd already admitted to one herself. "I haven't exactly been…a monk."

That got him a laugh, one that weakened his knees and reheated his skin.

"I think we can agree on that," she said.

A silent moment passed during which they stared at each other and he heard several cars pass on the street behind him. Other than that they were alone in the parking lot and, as far as he was concerned, in the universe.

Izzy edged closer, looking up at him with the same kind of vulnerability that currently had him in a stranglehold. "Can I tell you something else?"

"Anything." He cleared his throat against its sudden huskiness.

To his astonishment, she took his hand and squeezed it. He clung to this lifeline to Isabella and the things he needed that only she could provide. She swallowed and tried to smile, but her lips didn't turn up all the way.

"This is hard," she whispered.

"Take your time."

A flush crept up her neck and over her cheeks, infusing her with color until she looked as though she'd been kissed and loved by the sun. "I've always had a little crush on you." She paused. "Did you know that?"

"No."

"I didn't think you did. But I saw you the second you arrived at freshman orientation. You wore jeans and a white linen shirt, and you were thinner then, and you had a tan—I think you'd been to the beach or something—and I thought you were so sexy."

"I can't believe you remember all that."

"Yeah, well…I kind of always wondered why—when you pretty much had sex with every other woman who crossed your path—you never even looked twice at me."

"Because I was *stupid*." The desperation-fueled vehemence in his voice startled both of them, but he'd never spoken truer words in his life. "I'm just not that bright, Izzy. You should know that by now. You can't hold that against me."

Another laugh, but then she sobered and continued with her confession, still clinging to his hand. "It doesn't matter now—"

"I'm sorry, Iz—"

"Shh," she said, drawing closer until he could smell the sweet summery warmth of her skin. "Here's what I want. Are you listening?"

His voice failing, he wagged his head like one of those foolish toy monkeys with the clanging cymbals.

"I want to make love. I want this night with you. I don't want to miss this chance and then regret it forever. I want to know what it feels like to have your hands all over me—"

Eric shuddered, his lust making him unsteady on his feet.

"—and then I want us to go on with our lives—"

"Isabella—"

"—and I want to know that we'll still be there for each other, the same way we've been for all these years. Can you agree to that?"

"Is this about…that guy?" Eric couldn't bring himself to say Joe's name, to put the man between them at such a crucial moment. "You still want him? Want to get back together, maybe?"

She crinkled her brow, as though she had to dig deep to figure out who he was talking about, but then her expression cleared and, with a small laugh, she shook her head.

"Joe is the very last thing on my mind. Trust me."

The relief he felt was primitive and fierce. "Good. Then we can try—"

"No," she said flatly. "We can't."

He stared down at her, mutinous and silent. Seconds passed while he fumed with anger and frustration hot enough to burn the clothes right off his body. The sharp pulse of pain up past his ear and out the top of his head told him he'd been grinding his back teeth, and he worked hard to unclench his jaw.

What should he do? Never in his life had he been so stymied.

He looked away, staring at the traffic but not seeing it, and wondered how she thought they could strike a straightforward agreement about something so intimate and important. And then he wondered how he could make love to her without outright lying to her because God knew he had no intentions whatsoever of letting her go.

Finally he looked back in her face and settled on addressing some of their issues but not all. "Don't expect me to happily watch you get on a plane and move halfway across the world."

Her level gaze never faltered. "Can you agree?"

Staring at Izzy, wanting her, needing her, he decided that a small lie, this one time, wouldn't matter for long in the scheme of things. Once they were together, once he'd moved inside her body and made her his, once he'd given her the kind of addictive pleasure he knew she would give him, she wouldn't want to leave him. He knew it. One day they'd look back on this ridiculous conversation and laugh that she'd ever tried to impose such an unworkable condition on him.

"Yeah," he said. "I can agree."

Turning her palm up, he pressed a kiss into her hand, and then she was in his arms and they were clinging to each other, swaying. Sinking his fingers deep into those silky sheets of hair, he thought that he'd do almost anything for this woman, including, probably, kill or die, but the one thing he would not do, could not do, was let her leave him.

Pulling away, determined to make her his before she changed her mind, he led her that last step or two to the SUV, pulled out his keys and unlocked the door.

"Let's go."

"The honeymoon suite?"

Isabella tossed her purse on the nearest end table in the tan, red and black suite and wondered what on earth she'd gotten herself into. After about three minutes using his in-dash computer and cell phone, Eric had selected a luxury hotel in downtown Knoxville as the place for the consummation of their relationship. Now here they were.

Isabella wasn't certain what she'd expected, other than a room with a bed, but this high-rise palace with sweeping city views, kitchen, dining room and…yes…enormous down-covered bed and plasma flat-screen TV was not it.

"Not that I'm not grateful or anything," she continued, "but…it's a bit much, isn't it? You don't have to impress me with your money."

Eric arranged their overnight bags in a corner and, though he'd seemed a little quiet in the last few minutes, flashed the killer smile that was one of the reasons she was here with him now. Her belly did that delicious fluttery thing she'd gotten pretty used to in the last several hours, and she shivered with anticipatory heat.

"Did you think I'd take you to one of those no-tell motels we passed on the interstate?"

She laughed and he laughed, but then the laughter died away and they were left staring at each other across the space of twenty feet with no clear idea of what to do now.

Sexual tension hummed and vibrated between them, enough to power twenty luxury hotels for a year. Isabella was already so aroused she thought she'd probably come if he so much as kissed her cheek. Eric radiated the kind of leashed tension that could be found in a Ferrari idling by the curb waiting for someone to hit the gas. It shimmered around him, hot and bright, and was obvious in his sudden, absolute stillness.

They stood there, waiting…waiting…

His gaze slid over her body, lingering on her breasts and thighs, and there was no disguising the glittering hunger in his eyes. Swallowing hard, he shoved his hands in his pockets as though he needed to stop himself from pouncing.

In response, her body heat ratcheted up another notch or fifty, well into the red zone. It was all she could do not to vault across the room and tackle him to the floor, her need was that great. In her entire life, she'd never wanted anything the way she wanted *this*. And no one had ever wanted her as much as Eric did now; she knew that instinctively. There wasn't even a close second. That was another reason she was here now.

Most of all she was here because she couldn't *not* come. For years she'd wondered, in the dark little corner of her mind she pretended didn't exist, what it would be like to be the focal point of Eric's desire. How it would feel to have those strong hands skim over her overheated skin. How hard that heavy body would be as it slid across hers. How he would sound when he made love. Whether he kept his eyes open or closed. Whether he was tender or wild or both.

They'd been so close in every other way, told each other most of their secrets. He'd confided about his dysfunctional parents; she'd cried on his shoulder about her occasional financial woes. They'd laughed together through college and shared many of life's ups and downs. Taking this last step with him just seemed…right.

Nevertheless, being here was probably a mistake. She knew that, too. Despite all her bravado about them getting each other out of their systems and moving on with their lives, there was no chance—none whatsoever—of her recovering from making love with Eric Warner. He occupied too much space in her life, was the central point in too many of her long-ignored sexual fantasies, was too *much* to ever just get over. It was an impossibility right up there with a polar bear and a seal living together in harmony atop a glacier.

Nor was there any chance of their building a relationship, although it was nice of him to suggest it. Misguided, but nice. No doubt in the thrill of first lust he actually thought such a thing was possible, but it wasn't; she knew him too well.

How many women had come and quickly gone from his life over the years? She could probably name twenty or thirty without breaking a sweat, and those were just the ones she knew about. God knew how many more there were. None had made any impression on him, and he probably didn't even remember all their names. He was a world-class commitment-phobe and that was fine because she knew it going in.

And anyway, she was leaving soon for South Africa.

And of course she was never getting married, not that *that* mattered.

So, no, she wouldn't get over him, but she could insulate herself a little by keeping her vision clear and her expectations low. They had right now, this moment, and that was all. There could never be anything more or anything else. If she gave him the expiration date for their relationship ahead of time, it would spare him the awkwardness and embarrassment of trying to get rid of her nicely, and that was the best thing for both of them. Keeping it short and sweet was the only way they could hope to preserve their friendship— and her feelings—when all was said and done. In the meantime, she had this one moment with him and she would not waste it.

Eric cleared his throat and took a hesitant step closer. "Are you hungry? We can order room service."

"Yes." The answer was automatic because she usually was hungry and was always in favor of room service, but then she realized she didn't need food nearly as much as she needed him. "No."

Her knees trembling now, she took a step toward him. Eric let out a long, serrated sigh, took his hands out of the pockets of his strained shorts and eased closer.

"Did you need a minute or two to relax or take a shower, or—"

"No." She managed a quick smile. "Unless you're trying to tell me something?"

"No." He'd reached her now and was only a foot away, if that, close enough for her to smell the fresh, seductive scent of Oriental spices on his skin. His gaze dropped to her lips and his voice lowered to the merest hint of a whisper. "You smell good enough to eat."

Isabella shuddered. "I was just thinking the same thing about you."

One side of his mouth hitched up and he gave her a slow, heavy-lidded smile that was a seduction in itself. "We don't have to do this, Isabella. You know that, right?"

"Maybe *you* don't, but *I* do."

Something happened to him. She could tell because his eyes rolled closed and a ripple vibrated through his big frame. Maybe it was passion or excitement, or maybe it was just that his grip on his self-control was slipping. It didn't really matter. All she knew was that the sexiest thing she'd ever seen was Eric struggling against the power of his desire for her and losing the battle.

"Isabella-aaa." Taking a deep breath, he opened his eyes and they were glittering, hot and unfathomable. "I'm trying to control myself, but…I'm not sure I can."

"I don't want you to." She tipped her face up, hoping he would kiss her. Touch her. Take her. The excitement and anticipation burning in her heaving chest threatened to knock her flat, and her breathing was just this side of a pant. "Do you feel like we're stepping off a cliff?"

"Yeah." He nodded, looking suddenly anxious. "I feel exactly like that."

"Maybe we'll crash and burn."

The clouds cleared from his expression, leaving only a tender half smile as he raised a hand to her face. "And maybe we'll fly."

It was an easy, skimming caress that started at her temple, slid down to the throbbing pulse between her collarbones, and then around to her nape, the kind of touch that made a woman frantic to claw her clothes off and desperate to feel a man's body atop hers. Her heavy head fell back and her last coherent thought was that she hoped she didn't pass out and miss all the fun.

His fingers tightened in her hair, tilting her head the way he wanted it. Stooping a little, he ran his nose up the column of her throat, soaking her in and torturing her with the hot whisper of his breath but never quite making contact, never touching his lips to her blistering skin.

Shaken and shaking, she reached out, so desperate to feel all of him and to feel it *now* that she didn't care if she whimpered or begged. "Eric, *please*."

"Shhh." Pulling back enough to look down in her face, he linked their fingers and lowered their hands between them. "We're going to take this nice and slow—"

"No." Nice and slow would kill her; she could barely manage him as it was. *"No."*

"—and I'm going to make this so good for you you're not going to know whether you're living or dying."

Isabella froze and stared with no idea what to make of this declaration, which contained none of the male arrogance or cockiness that made it the sort of empty promise every woman in America had heard at least once in her life. Looking at him, she saw only the absolute seriousness and sincerity with which he might have recited wedding vows, and losing herself in his sultry dark eyes, Isabella realized that he meant what he said. Maybe meant it more than anything else he'd ever told her.

"Do you think we could get started on that?" Taking her time about it, she reached up to run her thumb across the plump curve of his bottom lip and was rewarded when his lids flickered and he swayed, as though he was having as much trouble staying upright as she was.

"I think that can be arranged," he said, and lowered his head.

Chapter 8

The first kiss was a taste, the barest stroke of his tongue across her mouth, a polite but insistent request for her to open and give him what he wanted. So she opened, needing him in her mouth and body, needing him hard and deep, but the second their tongues met, he slipped away and pulled back.

She whimpered, protesting.

He shushed her, waited until she'd calmed a little and then leaned in again for a slightly longer kiss that ended too soon when he tugged her bottom lip with his teeth.

Trembling and mewling now, her belly fluttering, her skin burning, she surged again and tried to claim his mouth. She needed to bite, to suck, to gorge, but the more urgent she got, the more languid he became. He eased away for the third time and made a low growling sound of warning even though he looked vaguely amused.

"Isabella." His husky voice, chiding softly as though her writhing inability to control her body was a huge disappointment to him, had the perverse effect of driving her higher. And that was *before* the backs of his fingers inched down the insides of her bare arms, raising goose bumps over every inch of her skin and into her scalp. "You need to learn, don't you?"

This was no time for learning. Not when her body was this desperate and needy. This was a time for speed, for shimmying up his body like an islander climbing a coconut tree, and for slaking the explosive need he stoked deep in her belly.

How could she get him to hurry? What would it take?

Reaching down, she grabbed the bottom of his polo shirt and ripped it up and off. He let her, much to her surprise, and she laughed, feeling triumphant. Now she would feel that skin. Now she would experience the play of all those muscles under her eager fingers.

Now, now, *now*.

And she did. For ten of the most glorious seconds of her life, she ran her hands all over his quivering torso and back, and he wrapped himself around her.

His name poured out of her mouth, unstoppable. "Eric… Eric…"

She reveled in him. Got high on him. He was satin over living marble, heat and strength overwhelming and surrounding her until there was nothing but him, could never be anything but him and the sensations he gave her.

"Isabella." His mouth caught hers in the kind of deep, ruthless kiss she'd needed, and she groaned into him, tasting mints and Eric and *home*. Frantic now, completely outside herself, she scraped her nails over his shoulders, pulling him closer… closer…but then, suddenly, he jerked free and was gone.

"No," she said.

Her protest had no discernable effect on Eric, to her eternal dismay. He stood there looking immensely satisfied for someone who hadn't had an orgasm yet, so cool and aloof she wanted to smack him. A little breathless now but otherwise in perfect and complete control of his body, he watched her with gleaming eyes that held that same trace of amusement but no mercy.

And Isabella realized that she could throw herself to the floor in a kicking, screaming tantrum and it wouldn't matter one bit. He would not take pity on her and move at her pace. He was in charge and he wanted to make damn sure she knew it.

She begged anyway. "Hurry, Eric. *Please*."

That faint hint of a smile gave way to his tightening jaw, and Isabella felt the power shift between them as she watched him shudder. *Well*. Things were suddenly looking up. Maybe he wasn't entirely in control after all. Maybe she should try to push him beyond his limits the way he pushed her.

Watching him from under her half-lowered lids, she reached between her heaving breasts—any second now she'd have to stop the proceedings in order to find a paper bag and hyperventilate into it—and unbuttoned the first tiny button to her blouse.

Eric froze, his flashing gaze tracking the movement.

"You like things slow?" Taking all the time in the world, she peeled the edges of the blouse apart to reveal the tops of her aching breasts in her lacy white bra.

He licked his lips and took a long time to speak. "Yeah."

Standing on tiptoe, she brushed her bosom against his chest as she nuzzled his mouth, and this time *he* groaned. Cupping both sides of her face in an abrupt, jerky movement, he tried to deepen the kiss, but she was too quick for him. Pulling back, she tried to match his reproachful tone.

"What do you think *you're* doing?"

Eric grunted.

In her best stripper impersonation, she undid the next couple of buttons and pulled the edges of the blouse farther apart, down to her belly. Eric stared, mesmerized, as she trailed her fingers against her collarbones to her dark aureoles, which, she very well knew, were clearly visible through the lace. She arched her back and traced slow circles around her nipples, and Eric's eyes widened to the point of bulging. He reached for her.

Feeling more feminine than she'd ever felt in her life, more powerful, she laughed. "*Eric*…I thought you wanted to go *slow*."

"Not this damn slow."

With no further warning, he grabbed the two halves of the

blouse, ripped them apart, and popped all the remaining buttons off with one violent yank.

Isabella gasped and stared at him in astonished silence.

Eric didn't notice. He looked wild as he tossed her blouse to the floor and concentrated on her breasts with the kind of intense focus with which futures traders watched the market reports.

Isabella felt her nipples engorge to the point of pain and honey flowed for him, hot and thick, between her thighs. Her overwhelming arousal erupted as a long, earthy moan, and he glanced up at her face long enough to flash her a look that plainly said he was a starving man and she was the only thing on the menu, the only thing he needed.

In that instant it occurred to Isabella—again—that she didn't know him, not at all. Not one thing about this side of his personality was familiar to her, but it didn't matter. Whoever he was, he could have anything he wanted— *anything*—from her.

He was already taking it. "Enough with the slow." Reaching behind her back, he undid the bra's clasp with a quick flick, slid it down her arms and pitched it to the floor.

His hands went to her wrap skirt, untied it, and sent it to the floor before going to work on his own clothes. His shorts seemed to give him a little more trouble, maybe because the zipper was so strained across his crotch he could barely budge it. Finally it gave way and he slid the shorts past his narrow hips before kicking them off.

Straightening, he locked that gleaming gaze on her, and all of Isabella's breath whooshed out of her lungs.

She'd seen some sexy things in her life. Every movie with Denzel Washington in it, for instance, or the Bulls game for which she'd miraculously scored courtside seats and been close enough to see the beads of sweat trickle off Michael Jordan's glorious chest. And of course none of her boyfriends had been that hard to look at. She appreciated men. Loved men. Desired men.

But there were men and then there was Eric Warner. And the sight of him standing there, watching her with gleaming eyes and wearing a pair of black boxer briefs that barely contained his straining erection, was enough to send her into either immediate cardiac arrest or spontaneous combustion.

She took an involuntary step back and held up a hand to hold him off.

What a fool she'd been to think she was ready.

She licked her dry lips. "Eric—"

But Eric was talking, not listening. "I can't go slow." With the speed of a lion springing out of a crouch and onto an unsuspecting gazelle, he grabbed her under the arms and yanked her closer. His hands, rough and excruciatingly wonderful, ran over her breasts, palming her nipples, circling and kneading.

"What are you trying to do, Izzy? Hiding a body *like this* from me for seventeen years? Did you think I'd let you get away with *that?*"

Did he think she could think right now, much less answer?

Panting and heading straight into hyperventilation territory— *next stop: emergency room*—she clung to his hard shoulders and back and tried to survive this onslaught. "Why didn't you notice me? Why didn't you ever look?"

"I'm looking now. What's *this?*" Isabella's skimpy white panties seemed to be the new focal point of his attention. He stared down at the scrap of lace even as his fingers dug into her hips and his thumbs traced the indentation of her belly button. "Huh?"

Isabella babbled something incoherent.

"What's this?"

In another dizzying burst of movement, he slipped his fingers under the satin ribbons on each of her hips and pulled. The panties came free and rubbed her swollen sex as he pulled them out from between her thighs. The unbearable friction had her crying out again, but he didn't seem to notice or care as he waved the wet underwear in her face.

"Wearing panties like *this* right under my nose for all these years? What are you trying to do to me?"

"I—I'm not—"

But he was already onto her next transgression against him. His long fingers slid down her trembling stomach, scratched across the black thatch of hair, and then delved into the hot river that flowed and flowed, all for him. An approving croon rumbled in his throat.

"Why didn't you tell me you were this wet?"

Ripples began deep in her belly and Isabella cried out, swooning a little. When she swayed, he hooked his free arm around her and held tight.

"I need to know, Izzy." Resting his forehead against hers, he eased two fingers inside her body and made a purring sound deep in his chest. Isabella teetered at the crest of a cataclysm, waiting for it to crash over her and praying for survival when it did. "Do you always get this wet?"

"I don't…I don't…I don't know," she lied.

Eric swore. He withdrew his magical fingers and rested them just half an inch or so from the spot where she needed them to be, leaving her undulating, moaning and bereft.

"Are you about to come?"

She nodded frantically.

"No, you're not. You're going to wait."

"I need you," she whispered.

Her begging seemed to be beneath his notice, or maybe it was that he was so focused on driving her wild that he was incapable of hearing her. Those fingers crept a little closer to her core and his voice lowered to a mesmerizing murmur that was as irresistible as it was seductive.

"Do you always get this wet, Isabella? Tell me."

His would-be casual tone didn't fool her for a minute, not when that primitive light still shone so brightly in his dark eyes, but the force of his will compelled her to answer. They'd be standing here until the cows came home and went back out again if she didn't tell him what he wanted to hear—what he already knew—and she just didn't have the strength to outwait him.

"No."

"Don't lie," he warned.

"I'm not lying," she said, desperation making her voice shake. This reassurance seemed to have no effect because he continued with the relentless questions. "What about Joe, Izzy?" He gently scratched his nails over her clitoris and her weak knees buckled. "Are you thinking of him now?"

"No!"

"No? You don't want him back?"

"I only want you," she gasped. "Only you, only you."

"Only me?" He smiled with immense satisfaction and rewarded her with an exquisite stroke of his wet fingers over her core. Delicious spasms rippled through her belly. *"That's good."*

Good? Not from where she was standing, but now was not the time to worry about his mastery of her body. Sagging with relief— maybe now he would let her come—she raised her lips to his.

He took immediate advantage and kissed her, long and deep, and then, while she was distracted with the taste of him, slid the hand that was holding her down the cleft between the two globes of her butt.

Those fingers—*oh, those amazing fingers*—worked on her from behind now, sliding back and forth and finding hidden spots of pleasure she'd never dreamed existed.

She cried out, bowing her tense body, as frustrated as she was aroused.

"What's wrong, Izzy?" Looking deceptively puzzled and innocent now, he licked her lips again. "Is there something you need?"

Yeah, she needed to smack the smug smile right off his face. She needed to punish him for ruining her like this, for making her ridiculous with the strength of her lust for him.

"I hate you, Eric. *Hate you."*

"Izzy." Those fingers dipped lower, driving her to the edge of insanity and one inch beyond, and she moaned, low and earthy. "That's not very nice, is it? If you want something, all you need to do is ask." He smothered his smile. "Nicely."

More begging? She didn't think so. Reaching down, she ran her hand over his length and cupped him with every intention of returning the balance of power to her side, feeling his size again, testing his hardness.

He clamped his hand over hers and forced her to stroke him roughly as he'd done before at the vet's office.

"Izzy." Her name was a groan, a prayer, a desperate plea. She would not have thought it possible, but he swelled even more, growing longer and thicker beneath her caress. "Ask me. *Ask me.*"

Trembling now, sweating, panting, and more than half out of her mind, Isabella decided that a little more begging wasn't necessarily a bad thing, especially if he was also doing it.

She eased her free hand across the hot satin of his waist, inched his boxer briefs down his hips and off his legs, and, straightening, dug her nails into the hard muscles of that round butt as she pressed herself against him. When she couldn't get any closer, she nuzzled and licked the pulse at the base of his neck, tasting sweat and heat and skin.

"I need you inside me right now," she whispered. "I'll do anything."

A seductive smile inched across his face. "Yeah, you will."

He was already planting his hands on her butt and lifting her. Springing up, she wrapped her legs around his waist and pressed her jiggling breasts to his face. Without missing a beat, he greedily latched on to one of her nipples and sucked her deep into his mouth as he swung her around. By the time he'd ripped the duvet to the foot of the bed and laid her onto the cool sheets, they were both muttering mindless words of encouragement. The only thing Isabella understood was the extreme urgency, his and hers.

Half atop her, he reached for a red foil package on the nightstand—when had he put those there?—looked down at her writhing body, and paused to study her with wide, appreciative eyes. One slow hand stroked her neck...her breasts...her belly. He thumbed and tongued her nipples, torturing her as though the future of humanity depended on how wild he could make her and how hard she writhed. Isabella mewled and tried not to come even though her aching inner muscles pulsed for him. She saw him lift the package to his teeth through her flickering lids.

"Are you ready to let me in, Isabella?" He rubbed the broad head of his penis against her, demanding entry.

Limp with relief, she spread her thighs. *"Yes."*

Trembling now, glistening with sweat, Eric worked his way inside her tight body, half a millimeter at a time. Isabella's eyes flew open and she cried out, long and loud because the sensation was so exquisite. Watching him with open astonishment and parted lips, she waited while he filled her bit by bit.

Eric stared back, looking as stunned as she felt. The shaking in his arms got worse the deeper he went, until finally he'd seated himself to the base and his entire body vibrated with his need.

An arrested moment passed, during which all they could do was watch each other. Isabella tightened her legs around him, digging her heels in to bring him as close as possible, and his hard body vibrated with lust although he didn't move.

She just couldn't believe that she was here with him, making love with him, being possessed by him. *This,* she now knew, was the moment for which she'd unknowingly waited all these years: Eric levered over her, his heavy body pressing hers deep into the mattress, his eyes glittering at her, his body inside hers. The taste of him in her mouth, the scent of him on her skin, the feel of him imprinted on her soul.

Making love with Eric was so stunning, so indescribably beautiful, that she realized one thing with utter clarity: if she died right now she would have no regrets because she'd shared this moment with him.

Clamping her fingers into his hard round butt to absorb the flex and play of his muscles, she pumped her hips once, twice. His trembling increased as they surged and flowed together, and then he paused.

"Now, Isabella." Eric leaned down to nuzzle her lips and swiveled his hips one slow time. "Come *now*."

She did.

It was the slow slide of his tongue into her mouth that did it; she didn't need anything else. Without a thrust of his hips or a stroke of his thumb over her core, with nothing more than the tight, delicious friction of Eric inside her body and the taste of him in her mouth, she came.

Huge, crashing waves convulsed her rigid body and bowed her over backward until Eric had to struggle to keep hold of her. Her frantic hands reached high overhead and scrabbled for something to hold on to, something to keep her from hurtling through space forever, and finally gripped the top of the head-board. With a grasp tight enough to splinter the wood, Isabella rode it out as the endless convulsions wracked her body.

Nothing had ever prepared her for this.

Eric shushed her and muffled her primitive cries with his mouth. His hands, soothing now instead of tormenting, stroked over her skin as though to calm her down. If she'd been capable of speech she would have told him not to bother. If she'd been capable of movement she would have smacked him for trying to gentle her when he'd been the one to get her this worked up in the first place.

A moment's rest was all she needed. With a sudden burst of strength, she flipped him onto his back and straddled him. "Your turn," she said as she began to move.

Chapter 9

Frantic and out of control, Eric bucked beneath her, driving deeper, harder, as though her body could possibly absorb any more of him. He pulled her down and took her mouth and his kisses were long, deep, and wet. *Sweet*. So sweet she could die from them, would happily die from them.

Bracing on her forearms, she watched his face and tried to memorize this moment, to sear everything on her brain because this was all she could ever have of him. She would not forget the way he scrunched his eyes closed as though he was in pain. She would not forget the way he chanted her name. She would not forget the hoarseness in his voice. She would not forget the fact that, one time in her life, Eric Warner had needed her this desperately—that she had once done this to him.

Suddenly his eyes flew open and he skewered her with his bright, fierce gaze. "I'm never letting you go."

"Eric," she said, but his name was only a whimper because the pleasure was building again, the wave retracting and preparing to crash. "We agreed—"

But he only got more agitated. His hips pumped harder, hurting now with the sort of delicious pain that would cause her to have trouble walking later, and the desperation rose in his eyes. "You're not leaving me."

"Shhh." She was full of primitive needs today, all of them incomprehensible: the need to make love; the need to be ruthlessly possessed; the need to comfort Eric. Stroking her hands over his skin, she murmured to him. "It's okay. *It's okay.*"

"You're mine now."

There was no time for more talking, no room for it. Eric went rigid and all his warm flesh turned to stone beneath her hands. Burying his lips in the curve of her shoulder, convulsing with a force strong enough to shake the bed he came with a shout of her name and a final thrust of his hips.

When he dug his nails into her butt and forced her to absorb the full impact of his body surging into hers, she came, too. This time the waves crashed over her with enough momentum to make her first orgasm look like a ripple or two in a child's plastic wading pool, and she cried out with it…cried and cried and cried.

They soothed each other and gently returned to earth.

"Sunshine," he murmured in her ear. "My *Sunshine.*"

They were both still panting a few seconds later when he smoothed her hair, palmed her cheeks and, with a tired smile, kissed her with a tenderness that broke her heart into a million pieces.

Eric went to the bathroom and came back to an unpleasant surprise: Isabella, her incredible body now enshrouded and practically mummified in a white sheet, standing in a corner and muttering as she rummaged through her overnight bag on the chair.

He'd imagined her waiting for him in the tumbled bed with the drowsy smile of a well-satisfied woman and open arms anxious for his return. Also on his mind: a long afternoon getting to know each other's bodies followed—eventually—by a joint shower and a delicious room-service dinner in bed.

So much for that fantasy.

The taste of bitter disappointment soured on the back of his tongue.

His ego, which was still smarting from her ridiculous *let's have sex one time and move on with our lives* proposal, did not take kindly to the sight of her furtively snatching fresh undies and clothes—*my God, how much lace did that woman own?*—out of her bag as though she needed to dress and flee the vicinity of the bed before the Gestapo arrived to drag her away. All the tension they'd so beautifully relieved came slinking back into the room, more nerve-wracking than ever.

"Hey." He fisted his hands on his hips, fighting his irritation.

Shooting him a quick glance over her shoulder, she clutched the sheet tighter to her chest with one hand and resumed rummaging with the other.

"Hey."

Finally she found what she was looking for and fished out a hot pink flowered dress the color of Pepto Bismol but somehow perfect for her because it matched her free spirit. But seeing her with new clothes had the unfortunate effect of reminding him about his catastrophic loss of control earlier when he'd ripped her out of the old ones.

He felt his cheeks heat as he remembered how desperate he'd been to see her body, to touch her, to possess her. Worse, his penis, which really should have been happy if not comatose at this point in the proceedings, perked up hopefully.

The renewed arousal was something he could ignore. It seemed to be something he just needed to get used to as part of his changed relationship with Isabella. What he couldn't ignore was the way Isabella's face fell when she spotted her ruined clothes on the plush carpet beneath her pretty bare feet, or the way she winced when she stooped to pick them up.

Oh, God. His stomach gave a sickening lurch. *He'd hurt her.*

Hurrying across the room, he touched her arm as she straightened. Shame made his head hang low and he couldn't even look her in the eye. When had he become the kind of animal that hurt a woman during sex? When had he ever been that frenzied with lust? What the hell happened to him when he touched Isabella?

"I'm sorry, Izzy." He cleared his scratchy throat and tried to find the words to express how bad he felt. "I didn't mean...to hurt you. I shouldn't have been so...rough."

Two things happened, one good and one bad. The bad thing was that Isabella flinched away from him as though the light touch of his hand on her bare arm destroyed her flesh. The good thing was that her face flamed with the kind of heat that made her appear feverish and she darted a glance at his groin, which was still semi-engorged and achy.

A shy smile turned up the outermost edge of one side of her mouth, and then was gone. For that one second she did not look like a woman who'd been injured by his base impulses. She looked like a woman who'd had the sex of her life and wouldn't mind another round.

"You didn't hurt me."

Relief tinged with hope flared in his chest. Was she telling the truth? He hadn't thought he'd done anything wrong at the time, but of course he hadn't been in anything close to his right mind.

"Are you sure?" he asked.

For the first time she looked him in the eye, and that brief connection was so hot he felt his retinas burn and his heart singe. But then she looked away and there was no connection at all, only an excruciating awkwardness that was the worst torture imaginable after what they'd just shared in that bed.

"Yeah. I'm sure."

She backed toward the bathroom, making a show of shaking out her clothes and folding them over her arm. But he saw her gaze flicker over his naked body again, lingering for just a second on his privates, and she licked her lips. This, of course, sent him over the edge into full-fledged arousal.

"Isabella." He took a step toward her, needing her again and cursing himself for the strength of his lust and weakness in his blood.

A flare of panic crossed over her expression and she edged

farther away, looking as though she'd like nothing better than to sprint to the bathroom, where it was safe, and bolt the door against him.

"I'm taking a shower. And you should—"she swallowed hard—"get dressed."

Like hell he would. He'd never been shy or ashamed of his body and he damn sure wasn't going to start now. Especially since he was just discovering the wonders of making love with Isabella and fully intended to do so again.

Right now.

"Why?" To his further irritation, he sounded like a furious dictator, not a man who had seduction on his mind. "What's the rush?"

Still she wouldn't look at him. Some spot just to the left of where he stood held her rapt attention. "We need to pick up Zeus—"

The *dog?* Was this some sort of a cruel *joke?*

"Zeus isn't going anywhere."

"—and get to my parents' by dinnertime. They're expecting us."

What did she just say? *What?*

Stunned anger left him stuttering and speechless for ten long seconds, and it wasn't just because of his doomed erection. *That* he could deal with. What he couldn't deal with was a distant Isabella who wouldn't look at him, let him touch her or, apparently, change her outrageous position on a relationship with him even after they'd had the kind of sex most people only dreamt about.

Taking a deep breath, he tried to be calm. Tried to sound reasonable.

"I thought we were going to spend more time here, Izzy. This can't be *it.*"

"It is." Above the top edge of that stupid sheet her breasts heaved and he knew that her calm voice wasn't telling him the whole story. "We said we'd get each other out of our systems, and—"

"Am I out of your system already, Iz?" he snarled, losing a good chunk of the little composure he had. "'Cause you sure as hell aren't out of mine."

He waited, daring her to try to lie her way out of this one, but she had the good sense not to go down that road. Instead she tried a diversionary tactic that would've been a lot more successful if she'd had the guts to look him in the eye while she said it.

"*One* time. That's what we agreed to—"

"Yeah?" Fired up with outrage and growing frustration, he abandoned the whole attempt to remain calm which was, obviously, impossible. "Well, I think we should revisit this *agreement*—"

"I don't."

"—because it's *bullshit*."

"Then why did you agree?" she cried.

"I think that's fairly obvious."

For the first time she seemed to get upset. Her brows flattened and her eyes blazed brown fire at him. He took heart, telling himself it was because she was as scared as he was by what was developing between them, but maybe that was just his desperation deluding him.

"You know what?" Her voice rose and cracked at the end, coming dangerously close to a screech. She flapped her free arm in a wild arc. "I don't care why you agreed. The point is that you *did,* and now I expect you to be man enough to keep your word."

"I don't think my manhood is in question at this point. Do you?" He edged closer and, when she didn't protest, put a hand around her waist.

Isabella backed up a hasty step and stumbled when she stepped on the edge of her sheet. Righting herself, she pointed at him as she shouted.

"*You stay away from me.* We agreed to one time, we had our one time, and now it's *OVER.*"

He didn't mean to smirk. Really he didn't. He was furious, she was furious, and nothing about this whole tangled situation was a laughing matter. But there was something so incongruous about her standing there, wearing nothing but a murderous expression and a white sheet, that he couldn't stifle a single bark of laughter.

She made a little growling sound in her throat that reminded him of the warning Zeus made when you tried to take away his chew toy before he was done with it, but he didn't care. If she was angry with him, that was just too bad and she'd have to get over it.

"Do you realize how *ridiculous* this is? We can't un-ring the bell we just rung. The horse is already out of the barn, and—"

"Stop mixing your metaphors," she yelled.

Ah, yes. One always had to be grammatically correct with an elementary school teacher, even during the heat of a passionate argument. The urge was there to laugh again but he tamped it down, figuring that any more laughter would cause her to reach for the nearest lamp and clock him over the head.

"Isabella." Pausing, he shook his head because he just couldn't figure out how they'd come to such a weird point in their relationship. "If you think we're never going to have sex again, you are certifiably *insane*."

"You arrogant son-of-a—"

"In fact, I'd be willing to bet most of my inheritance that we'll be having sex again in—" he checked his watch, calculated travel time and the dinnertime visit with her family, then added an extra half-hour for good measure "—about seven hours."

"In seven hours," she said with a slow emphasis on every syllable, as though she wanted to make sure even someone as dumb as he was understood what she was saying, "we are going to be asleep at my parents' house, and *I* will be in my old bedroom and *you* will be on the sleep sofa."

This time, striving for maximum irritation value, he let the smirk come. Embraced the smirk. "Wanna bet?"

She glared at him for a few seconds, killing him a good twenty or thirty times with her eyes, before whirling and stalking off. Her only answer was the teeth-clacking slam of the bathroom door.

They made it to Greenville by dinnertime after spending the worst afternoon in the history of car travel trapped in the SUV together. A few hours of Isabella's frigid silent treatment made Eric long for the peaceful simplicity of a nice cross-country trip to the Grand Canyon with, say, four or five preschoolers. Several screaming, hitting, yakking kids, surely, couldn't be any worse than what he'd just endured: the glares, the huffs, the cold shoulder. Even Zeus, recovered now to tail-wagging health, seemed pissed off at him and hadn't let Eric scratch his ears upon his return, with Fluffles, to the backseat.

Finally they arrived at the working-class east Greenville neighborhood and small brick home where Izzy's family had lived since before the dawn of time. As usual, the sprinkler watered the lush green grass, which was clipped and trimmed to horticultural perfection, and the top of the hedges beneath the windows was so level that Eric could probably balance a beer mug atop it.

Nothing about the house had changed, at least not as far as he could see. Mama Jo's flowers overflowed from various beds and pots stationed on the porch and up and down the walk to the driveway—impatiens, geraniums and black-eyed Susans, among others, and there seemed to be no requirement that the flowers match or even complement each other. The result was a hodgepodge that would no doubt be the shame of any local garden club, but which Eric thought was beautiful.

Four or five ancient cars lined the driveway, warning him that her brothers were here and he would, therefore, have to endure a fair amount of good-natured ribbing before the night was out.

He grinned, looking forward to it. Other things he looked forward to: seeing Isabella's mother, JoAnn Stevens, known as Mama Jo to all who knew and loved her, which was pretty much everyone she met, gorging on Mama Jo's phenomenal cooking and talking golf with Isabella's father, Ray.

Yeah, life was momentarily looking up. Izzy may be determined to ignore him for the foreseeable future, but her family would welcome him with open arms. Best of all, Mama Jo would be a powerful ally in his quest to win Izzy. The only issue was how to enlist her help, but he'd get that part figured out by dessert. He knew it.

For the first time in hours, he felt some of the heavy tension ease from his shoulders and he sighed with a quiet but deep satisfaction.

Man, it was good to be back here. Really, really *good.*

They trudged out of the car and Zeus, once more at the end of the leash that Isabella would no doubt never drop again, relieved himself before exploring the nearest flower bed. Eric started up the path toward the front door, but Isabella, now looking anxious for some reason, put a hand on his arm.

"Can I, uh, ask you a favor?"

Eric stopped dead, thrilled beyond all reason that she'd acknowledged his existence. Instead of pumping a triumphant fist in the air, which was what he felt like doing, he kept his wits about him and managed a scowl. No need to let her know she'd had his belly tied up in knots this whole time.

"Oh?" he said coolly. "You're talking to me again? This must be my lucky day."

"The thing is," she continued as if he hadn't spoken, "my mother has always liked you—"

"I know." Keeping his brows firmly lowered, he yawned and tried to look bored.

"—and wished we'd get together—"

"Right."

"—and her little drumbeat has gotten worse since I entered my thirties—"

"Uh-huh."

"—especially with all my brothers on their second or third kid by now."

There was a pause during which a lightbulb went off over Eric's head and his heart did a funny little stuttering thing, which he ignored. He thought he saw where this conversation was headed and was already thinking of a way to turn the situation to his advantage, but he let her flounder anyway.

"And this is my problem...how?"

Isabella did a fair amount of fidgeting before she answered, shuffling on her feet, running a hand through her hair, and retracting Zeus's leash. After all that she opened her mouth and said...nothing.

Eric waited impatiently, praying he looked, at best, only mildly interested.

She shut her mouth, cleared her throat, and tried again. "I just want…I just want us to be, ah…*careful* not to give my mother the wrong idea."

"I…see." He hesitated, trying to maximize her obvious tension. "And what, pray tell, is this wrong idea you don't want her to get?"

"You know very well what I'm talking about."

Pulling his best perplexed face, he shrugged and shook his head. "No idea."

She flushed the color of the pickled beets her mother would no doubt be serving within the hour, but plowed ahead, her chin high. "I don't want her to get the idea that there's something going on between us."

"There *is* something going on between us." Enjoying himself now, he walked up the path to the front door. "Why would I pretend otherwise?"

"Eric." Her voice sounded strangled now, and he heard her hurrying footsteps behind him. She pulled him around by the arm, openly desperate now. "Do you want me to beg? Is *that* it?"

Grinning both because she was so funny and, more importantly, because he knew it would infuriate her, he stepped closer and made a big production out of trailing his fingers down the smooth, sexy column of her neck.

To his further amusement, he saw a red patch at the base of her throat that was clearly, even to the untrained eye, a spot where he'd accidentally scratched her with his goatee during the heat of passion. His grin widened. She'd never hide *that* from her eagle-eyed mother.

"Well." Ignoring the sound of excited voices inside the house, he let his fingers glide lower, over that wonderful swell of her breasts. "I do *love* it when you beg."

This reference to their time together in the honeymoon suite did not seem to calm Isabella or allay her fears, much to his continued amusement. In fact, she looked more flustered than ever as she shot a panicked glance at the door and then looked back at him with irritation in her flashing brown eyes.

"Now is not the time for any of your little practical jokes, so don't even think of embarrassing me in there. This is *not* all fun and games," she hissed, pointing a finger in his face.

Yeah, she was right about that. Well, partially right: this *was* fun, but it was no game. Not when he still wanted her so much and she was so important to him. Moving quickly—someone was almost at the door now, he could hear them—he ran his hand around to her nape and gently tilted her head so she could look at him and see how serious he was.

If the neighbors caught him touching her like this, or her parents or brothers, so much the better. He wanted to shout it from the rooftops but kept his voice low because, his desire to be open about their new relationship notwithstanding, he didn't think Greenville was quite ready to hear about his X-rated plans for Isabella.

"I still want you, Isabella."

"Oh, no."

"I wish I was inside you right now, and I plan to get you naked again in the next few hours. We *are* in a relationship and your mother will be thrilled to know it. I'm not hiding *anything*."

Clamping his other hand around her, he pulled her, struggling, up against him, fitted his mouth to her sweet lips, and gave her the kind of kiss that could never be mistaken as platonic.

Just as Eric had planned, they were still fused at the mouth—Isabella stopped struggling, just as he'd known she would—when the door flew open and the sound of her mother's shocked *"Oh, my!"* followed by excited clapping broke the silence.

Isabella tried to push him away, but he was having none of it.

Taking his time about ending the kiss—Izzy's mother had waited years for this moment, so he might as well make it worth her while—he nuzzled Izzy's lips once or twice more, broke away, and waited for the fireworks to begin. Judging from the fury flashing in Izzy's eyes, they were going to be spectacular.

Chapter 10

Reeling from Eric's shenanigans—she should have *known* not to waste her time asking that so-and-so for a favor of any kind—Isabella smoothed her hair with her free hand and stretched her still-tingling lips into what she hoped was a nonchalant smile for her mother's benefit.

No need.

The darn woman was too busy greeting the person she really wanted to see: Eric, Spawn of Satan. Glowering, Isabella folded her arms over her chest and watched the whole sickening display.

"Eric!" Mama shrieked, holding her arms wide, her mouth open in a delighted smile big enough to accommodate a whole McDonald's cheeseburger. "You give me a hug *right now!*"

But Eric caught her hands, held her at arm's length, and surveyed her in a critical appraisal that involved much head-shaking and appreciative muttering.

"Mama Jo," he said, flashing that patented dimpled smile that was fatal to any woman who beheld it. "You get prettier all the time, don't you?"

Isabella snorted at this blatant brownnosing and was generally ignored as Eric caught Mama in a bear hug and swung her around in a circle while Mama kicked her short legs and squealed like a toddler.

After a minute or two of this foolishness, Mama smacked Eric's arm as though she meant business. "You put me down, boy."

"Okay. *Okay.*" Eric gave her a kiss on the cheek and released her.

Mama jammed her hands on her hips and made the angry face that'd terrified her four children over the years but which she'd never really level at her precious Eric. "Why didn't you come see me at Christmas? You know I was expecting you."

"Did you make the sweet potato pie?" Eric asked.

"Yes, I did."

"Man." Eric threw a hand over his heart as though he'd been mortally wounded by this news that he'd missed one of Mama's pies. "I was sick about missing Christmas down here. I was in Hong Kong and I—"

"A-hem." Isabella, who'd had more than enough of this blissful reunion, decided she needed to remind these two of her presence. "Maybe you two can catch up later so *my* mother can greet *me* now. How would *that* be?"

Mama let Eric go at last, looked around, and acted surprised to see Isabella standing there. "Eric!" she cried. "Did you bring Izzy Bee with you?"

"Ha, ha," Isabella muttered. "Very funny."

"Poor baby. Come here."

Mama yanked her into her fierce magnolia-blossom-scented embrace, and the two women swayed together for a minute. Something loosened around Isabella's heart, and she knew that, whatever mess she'd gotten herself into with Eric, and it was a *big* mess, she was home now, with Mama, and Mama wouldn't let anything happen to her.

"How's my baby girl?" Mama murmured before kissing her cheek.

"Pretty good," Isabella lied.

As usual, Mama could detect a falsehood at a thousand paces. More than once Isabella had wondered if Mama could actually smell a lie the moment it hit the airwaves, and this time was no different. Pulling back a little, Mama studied Isabella's face with a critical eye and frowned.

"Hmmm. What's up with you and this boy here?" She nodded in Eric's direction. "Something you want to tell me?"

"No." Well aware that her voice was way too high and sharp, Isabella shot Eric a warning look—he grinned and winked at her, the jackass—and forced herself to smile at Mama. "You do look great. Is it all the golf?"

It was true. Retirement agreed with Mama, who seemed to bloom a little more every time Isabella saw her even though Isabella knew Mama missed the little second graders she'd taught at the elementary school around the corner since time immemorial.

As always, Mama's brown skin glowed with the kind of health and vigor that were the envy of women half her age, and her dark eyes were sharp and bright. Today her short, slightly plump body was dressed in a pink polo shirt and god-awful pink and purple plaid shorts that screamed *Golfer, here!* And there was a telltale flattened ring around Mama's wavy bob that told Isabella Mama had worn her sun visor within the last several hours.

"We played eighteen holes this morning." Mama, as always, recounted her golf adventures with the seriousness and enthusiasm of a cardiac surgeon who'd just performed quintuple bypass and saved a life. "Only nine yesterday on account of the rain. We'll try for eighteen tomorrow. Your father shot a ninety-seven, so he had to do the vacuuming. I shot eighty-nine. Hah!"

"What driver are you using these days?" Eric, wide-eyed with interest, matched and probably exceeded Mama when it came to golf fanaticism. "Did you get that Callaway you were talking about?"

Isabella rolled her eyes. "Oh, for crying out loud."

"I'll tell you later, Eric." Mama patted Eric's arm in a mollifying gesture, and then her piercing gaze swung back around to Isabella. "Right now I want to know what's going on with you two."

"Nothing."

Isabella had never been a good liar, especially not to her mother. Worse, she *knew* she wasn't a good liar, which only added to the awkwardness when she needed to tell a little white lie on occasion. Like now. That telltale twitch began in her right cheek, and she bit her lip, trying to stop it. This, of course, made it hard to talk, but she somehow managed to babble anyway.

"I already told you nothing is going on. *Nothing*. Eric and I are *just friends*. Same as always."

Eric clicked his tongue and gave her a reproachful look that did nothing to hide his amusement. "That's not *exactly* true, is it, Izzy?"

"I am talking to my mother now," Isabella snarled.

Mama cocked her head, narrowed her eyes, and put her hands on her hips. "Nothing, eh?" she asked, all business now and reminding Isabella of a bloodhound on the scent of an escaped convict. "What was Eric doing with his tongue down your throat just now if nothing's going on? Checking to see if you still had your tonsils?"

Isabella cringed and felt her face all but burst into flames. Eric choked back a startled snort of laughter, which both the women ignored.

"That was…nothing," Isabella said with rising desperation as she felt the tide turn against her. *"Nothing."*

"Uh-huh." Mama huffed, vibrating now with the kind of indignation that would accompany a false accusation of murder. Her lips managed to be both pursed and tight. "I'm guessing that hickey on your neck is also *nothing*."

What? *What?* She had a *hickey?* No. Please, God, *no*. Anything but that. Why couldn't lightning just strike her dead on the spot and save her from this inquisition? Isabella clapped a hand to her neck.

"Oh, this? This is a…a little scratch, from, ah, Zeus. Not a hickey. *Please*. Hickey. *As if*."

Mama raised one eyebrow, the picture of motherly exasperation. "Other side."

Fuming, Isabella moved her hand to the other side of her neck. Eric laughed at her obvious discomfort, but the smile was sucked off his face when Mama turned in his direction and fixed him with that no-nonsense look that only Southern mothers can truly manage.

"Uh-oh." Eric snapped to attention like a Marine during inspection.

Mama crossed her arms over her chest and glared up at Eric, barely five feet of determined elder-womanhood ready to take down Eric's six-plus feet if it proved necessary.

"Since I am getting nowhere with my daughter, I expect *you* to tell me the truth, and I expect you to do it right now."

"Yes, ma'am." Over the top of Mama's head, Eric shot Isabella a furtive glance that communicated about a paragraph's worth of information, namely that he was sorry to put her on the hot seat like this, but not sorry enough to miss this chance to gain a powerful ally in Mama Jo, and he hoped that Isabella forgave him one day but didn't really care if she didn't.

Isabella glowered at him.

"What's going on with you and my daughter, Eric?" Mama asked.

"Well," Eric began, but was interrupted before he could get any further.

"Woman," bellowed a gravelly male voice from inside the darkened depths of the house on the other side of the screen door. "Are you going to let my daughter in this house *or not?* The food is getting cold."

Mama, looking furious at this unwanted interruption, turned her head over her shoulder and hollered back. "We are talking. *Talking.* And you had best not interrupt me again if you know what's good for you."

"We are *hungry.*"

Daddy's voice sounded forlorn now. Pitiful even, as though he hadn't eaten in a good three weeks or more. But Mama was on a righteous mission and wasn't about to let trivialities like food and supper sidetrack her. Muttering darkly, she wheeled around, marched up to the screen door, opened it and stuck her head inside.

"Did you hear what I said?" As always, Mama repeated herself, louder, as though she wanted to rule out the twin possibilities that Daddy actually hadn't heard what she'd said and/or had a hearing problem. "I said that we are *talking* and you had *best not interrupt me again.*"

Silence from inside the house.

Mama withdrew her head. Now wearing an expression of grim satisfaction, she let the screen door bang for emphasis. Isabella, meantime, cringed from embarrassment and wondered whether it was too much to hope that she'd been adopted and did not, in fact, belong to this uncouth family. But no. She looked much too much like her mother for that to be a possibility, alas.

What Eric thought about the whole tacky Stevens clan, Isabella shuddered to think as she shot him a veiled look from under her lashes. His family, in their genteel estate, Heather Hill, never yelled, never bickered and probably never called any of the women *woman.*

She'd always wondered what had brought him back here for visits so many times over the years. No doubt it was fierce loyalty to Isabella—Eric was good like that—that kept him from openly laughing at the eccentrics she called parents. But Isabella's cringing and fretting were abruptly cut off by Mama's purposeful throat-clearing.

More determined than ever, Mama marched right back up to Eric, replaced her hands on her hips, drew herself up and resumed her interrogation.

"What is going on with you and my daughter? Answer me now."

"Well, ma'am," Eric said with utmost sincerity, "I'm crazy about her."

"Of *course* you are." Mama nodded with obvious impatience, apparently wanting him to stop wasting her time with the little details she already knew and get to the important part. "Who wouldn't be? The question is: what do you plan to do about it?"

Eric opened his mouth to answer, but Isabella, who was seriously considering taking off down the street at a dead run and hoping the neighbors on the corner were home and would take her in for the night, decided it might be worthwhile to register a protest.

"Excuse me," she said, "but I don't need my *mother* to manage my—"

Mama turned the full might of her withering glare on her and Isabella shut up mid-sentence. "If you were so good at managing your personal life, you'd be married by now and settled down instead of making plans to traipse off to the ends of the earth."

She paused, giving Isabella the chance to argue if she dared, but Isabella, being no fool, opted to keep her mouth shut and seethe in silence.

"Now I want you to stand right there—" Mama pointed at the walk beneath Isabella's feet, as though there were some confusion about precisely where Isabella should stand "—and hush up while I talk to this boy."

Isabella fumed and pretended she didn't see Eric's encouraging wink.

"Eric?" Mama turned back to him.

"I want to let nature take its course, Mama Jo, but Izzy says no." Eric, to Isabella's surprise, now lost his smirk and managed to look serious, almost sad, as he paused. "She won't even think about it. And she won't tell me the real reason why."

Much as she would have loved to make a joke—something about needing a violin to accompany Eric's tale of woe—there was something in his forlorn expression that touched Isabella deeply and kept her quiet.

Mama seemed to see it, too. She stared, unblinking, up into Eric's eyes, and Isabella wondered if the poor man knew he was having his soul analyzed and mapped by the world's most intuitive woman. She'd've warned him if she wasn't so angry with him for tattling.

And then, abruptly, it was over. Mama blinked, nodded and patted Eric's cheek with so much affection it was difficult for Isabella to watch. Then Mama bent and picked up Zeus, who'd been snuffling hopefully around her feet. For a minute she scratched him behind the ears and then she adjusted his bandana and pressed a loud kiss to his fuzzy forehead, beaming as though she'd never seen anything as amazing as this one little dog.

"I've got some *bacon* for you," she said in a stage whisper.

Zeus, hearing the magic word, yapped once and squirmed happily.

"Oh, no," Isabella said. "He's got a sensitive stomach."

Ignoring this warning, Mama turned and swept through the screen door into the house. "Let's go," she called over her shoulder. "People are hungry and supper's getting cold."

Isabella and Eric gaped after her, both startled by the sudden end to the interview. After a minute Isabella felt the heat of his gaze on her face, but her churning emotions were too raw for her to look at him now and she was too much of a coward to risk letting him see how ambivalent she felt.

What had he meant, telling Mama he was crazy about her? Why did he sound like he meant it, like there was more to his feelings than the heat of new lust? Why did that possibility scare her so much? Above all, *what* had he done to her in bed this afternoon?

Deciding it was best not to be alone with him—not now, not *ever*—Isabella reached for the screen door, which had banged shut behind Mama.

"Tattletale," she muttered as she brushed past.

"You better believe it."

To her dismay and unwilling pleasure, Eric reached out and touched her forearm, holding her in a warm grip she could easily have broken if only she'd had the necessary willpower. She didn't.

"You of all people should know I don't give up without a fight, Izzy," he murmured, serious in a way she'd only seen a handful of times during all the years they'd known each other.

"If your mother can help me keep you here, so much the better. I'll take any help I can get."

Yeah. She knew he never gave up, and the knowledge scared her.

Only one thought remained clear in her overwrought mind, and she clung to it. She must not let this man steal any more pieces of her heart. He did not belong to her and never would. Great sex didn't change anything. Well, it made her care more deeply for him, but it didn't work the same way for men like Eric, who got what they wanted and moved on. She'd seen it happen a thousand times since she'd known him.

So, yeah, her eyes were clear. Eric was a player, born and bred, and he wouldn't be changing for her any more than a leopard could unzip his spotted suit and slip on a striped one. Once his lust wore off, he'd realize the same thing, but by then she'd be firmly in love with him and her poor heart would be broken. That was something she meant to prevent at all costs. Only by setting firm limits could she salvage their friendship, and that was her goal.

If he would just *cooperate.*

Anyway, she was moving to South Africa, where it was safe, and nothing would stop her. And who in the history of life had ever maintained a long-distance relationship between Columbus, Ohio, and Johannesburg?

"You're wasting your time," she told him.

A tender smile hitched up one corner of his mouth and then disappeared, leaving only that unfamiliar gleaming intensity in his eyes and a corresponding terror deep in her belly.

"I don't think so, Sunshine."

God, she wished he wouldn't call her that. It killed her every time.

He paused, and whether he was struggling with his own fears or deciding how much he should hold back for strategic reasons, she couldn't tell. In the end he laid it all on the line.

"I think this is the most important fight of my life," he said.

Chapter 11

After supper, the entire group—Isabella thought there were about twenty-five people there, but she couldn't get an accurate head count because the kids didn't stand in one place long enough—migrated into the living room and sprawled across the various weathered sofas and chairs.

Daddy, as usual, took his place of honor in the brown leather La-Z-Boy recliner Isabella and her brothers had gotten him when he retired from his job as an electrician, and picked up the remote to the wall-mounted flat screen TV they'd gotten him for his seventieth birthday. Soon the noise from a Braves game added to the general chaos.

Daddy rocked back in his chair, kicked his feet up, twisted open the cap on his current bottle of Miller Lite, and rubbed his swollen belly. "Shoulda worn stretchy pants."

"I agree," Isabella said.

She was wedged on one of the love seats between her oldest brother, Bobby Joe, and his eternally pregnant wife, Sarah. Crossing her legs and trying to make her hips smaller, she eyed

Daddy's garish plaid golf pants. They were—she shuddered again—yellow, green and orange. No one appreciated bright colors and patterns more than Isabella, but this was ridiculous. She could only imagine what he and Mama had looked like out there on the golf course together. The other golfers were probably still seeing spots before their eyes, poor things.

"Stretchy pants would be better than those," Isabella continued. "*Anything* would be better than those."

Daddy laughed, taking no offense, and scooped up two-year-old Joey, Bobby Joe's middle son, as he toddled past. Joey squealed and patted his grandfather's bald crown, earning himself a wet raspberry on the cheek.

"Stop that." Joey squirmed and laughed for a minute, and then hopped down. Racing across the room and through the back screen door, he escaped to freedom on the screen porch, where about five or seven of the other grandchildren were playing a game that involved a lot of shrieking.

"You haven't lost your touch, Mama Jo." Eric, sitting in one of the straight-backed chairs across the room from Isabella, his long legs taking up far more than their fair share of the limited space in the cramped house, raised his own beer in a toast. "That was the best dinner I've had since the last time I was here."

There was a general chorus of agreement, but Mama, who was shuttling dirty plates between the dining room and kitchen, paused only long enough to wave a dismissive hand. "Those ribs were a little too dry this time and I—"

Everyone shouted her down. Flushed with pleasure at the compliment, Mama disappeared around the corner.

Isabella, forgetting she was upset with Eric and trying to keep him at arm's length, made the mistake of catching his eye and laughing with him. *Typical Mama Jo,* the look said.

It felt wonderful. *Right.* For a few delicious seconds, it was just the two of them, their laughter and that connection between them, and then it all changed. That naked heat surged anew between them, threatening to incinerate Isabella and leave only ashes where she had once been. God, it scared her. Looking away quickly, she tried to get control of her thundering pulse, to think, to breathe, but it was impossible.

Sarah stirred beside her, pressing a hand to her enormous belly. "Baby's kicking," she announced happily to the group at large.

"Wow." Isabella looked around, nodded and smiled. Since her sister-in-law was now on her fourth child, this hardly seemed to be a noteworthy event, but Isabella tried to look interested anyway. "That's great."

Sarah beamed and slid her hand around to a new position. "Feel."

"Oh, no," Isabella said quickly. "I don't think—"

Too late. Sarah had already grabbed Isabella's hand and clapped it to the enormous tight mound of her belly, and, sure enough, there was a strong spasm that felt like Muhammad Ali was trying to get out.

Isabella forgot all about Eric, the uproar he'd caused in her life, and the yakking family all around her. There was a baby in there and Isabella felt a sharp and unexpected pang of longing. She snatched her hand away.

"Oh, sorry," said Sarah.

Isabella forced a smile. "No problem."

"Isabella?"

Eric's worried voice cut through her sudden misery. Blinking furiously, she raised her head and plastered a smile on her face. "Yes?"

Their gazes locked and her expression must have given her away. It usually did with Eric. She hadn't yet had an emotion he couldn't read.

Frown lines developed between his heavy brows. "You okay?"

"I'm great," Isabella said, but her voice sounded high and false and Eric didn't look at all convinced. When the concern in his eyes became too intense, she looked away and prayed for enough grace and composure to get through the rest of the evening.

Just then, a new distraction arrived. Isabella's youngest brother, Randy Lee, and his wife, Norma, appeared from down the hall, each carrying a year-old twin. Norma held the hand of their third child, Becca, a four-year old diva-in-training wearing a cute little leopard-spotted dress that was more fashionable than anything in Isabella's closet.

"The twins have clean diapers now," Becca announced in a voice that would do any local town crier proud. "They don't stink anymore."

"Good to know." Mama hurried through with another armload of dishes.

Becca, who'd been in love with Eric pretty much since birth, rocketed over to him and settled onto his lap, resuming the position she'd held throughout dinner. Eric smoothed her braids and kissed one of her fat cheeks.

"Did you help change them?" he asked her.

"Ewww!" Becca's button nose scrunched down until it seemed to sit directly on top of her pursed lips. "That's *gross*."

"Isn't that a big sister's job?" Eric wondered.

"No. But I can give them a bottle."

"Well. As long as you help." Eric kissed her cheek again.

"Oh, she *helps* all right," Norma said.

She put the twin she was holding, Randy Jr., on the floor and hovered nearby as he balanced on his chunky but shaky legs. Randy Jr. stuck his arms high overhead and stumbled a wobbly three steps or so before collapsing to his bottom. Beaming with a proud smile that revealed a vast stretch of gums and a single tooth that looked like a grain of rice, he glanced around the room to make sure everyone had noticed his accomplishment.

Norma clapped for him and continued her recitation. "Yesterday Becca *helped* by eating the twins' mashed bananas. Isn't that right, Becks?"

Becca grinned, unabashed. "Mashed bananas are *good*."

"Mashed bananas?" Eric frowned at her. "Do you drink their bottles, too?"

"No!" Affronted, Becca crossed her arms over her chest and glowered up at her hero. "I'm a big girl."

"I'm just saying," Eric said mildly, shrugging. "If you'd eat *mashed bananas…*"

Watching Eric and Becca with their heads together and seeing the absolute worship on the girl's tiny face did the nastiest things to Isabella's insides; her throat dried out and her stomach knotted. Worse, tension squeezed her chest, as though someone had eased a belt around her torso up under her arms and tightened it.

Don't look, Isabella told herself, but she didn't take her own advice. It didn't matter how much the sight hurt, or that she could barely see them anyway through the sheen of unshed tears coating her eyes. She couldn't stop staring and thinking about the beautiful children Eric might produce.

"Do you have kids?" Becca was asking Eric now. She patted his cheeks gently—Isabella saw the glimmer of the girl's chipped pink sparkle nail polish—as she spoke, as though she needed to touch him and just couldn't help herself. Isabella certainly knew how *that* felt. "Any little girls like me?"

"Oh, *Lord.*" Norma was now sitting cross-legged on the floor and supervising while Randy Jr. clumsily petted Zeus. The shameless dog was rolling around on his back, exposing his belly like a Vegas stripper and hoping for any affection that might come his way. "There she goes with the personal questions. Ignore her, Eric. If you don't, she'll be asking about your underwear next."

But Eric just laughed and kissed Becca's forehead. "No little girls like you, Becca. Maybe one day. I need to get married first."

"I'll marry you!" Alight with happiness at this glorious idea, Becca clapped her hands together and bounced on Eric's lap. "I'll be a *good* wife!"

"Yeah. I know you will, cutie," Eric told her. "But you should probably finish kindergarten first. And I might need a wife before that."

"Oh." Poor Becca's face fell and Isabella could almost feel

the weight of her four-year-old despair. "But you can wait for me, can't you?"

"Becca," chided Norma softly, shooting Eric an apologetic look.

Eric didn't notice. Neither did Becca. They stared at each other, he with affection and tenderness, she with so much breathless hope she seemed to quiver with it. Finally Eric delivered the bad news.

"I don't think I can wait that long, cutie. Sorry."

Becca took it like a woman. Nodding wisely, she shot an annoyed but resigned look in Isabella's direction. "I knew it. You're going to marry Aunt Izzy, aren't you?"

There was a moment's arrested silence followed by generalized tittering by the adults who weren't watching the game. Isabella cringed—could this night *get* any worse?—but Eric froze.

"Bec-ca!" Norma had finally had enough and mouthed *Sorry!* to Isabella. Lunging to her feet, she grabbed Becca's hand and yanked her off Eric's lap. "You come with me right now. I think it's bedtime for you. How would that be?"

"Noo-oo." Becca's wail echoed down the hall as they disappeared.

"That girl." Daddy glanced up from the TV for the first time since he'd assumed his position in front of it and stared affectionately after his departing granddaughter. He caught Isabella's eye and winked, but then his gaze seemed to snag on something just south of her face.

Isabella winced. *Uh-oh.*

"What's that on your neck, girl?" he asked loudly. "A hickey?"

All activity ceased and every pair of eyes in the place swung around to Isabella's neck. Even Randy Jr. paused in his playing with Zeus and stared up at her. Clapping a hand on the spot—the correct side this time—Isabella managed a laugh and carefully avoided looking at Eric.

"Of *course* not, Daddy. Zeus scratched me."

"Scratch?" Daddy shook his head. "That don't look like no scratch to me. That looks like a *hickey.* I've seen enough of 'em to know."

Isabella's unconcerned smile slipped a little but she managed to hang onto it. "Get your eyes checked, Daddy. It's a *scratch.*"

Daddy didn't look like he believed her for a minute, but luckily a commercial ended just then and the game came back on. With the siren's lure of the big screen calling him, Daddy forgot all about his daughter's neck issues, rocked back in the recliner, sipped his beer and lapsed into silence.

Normal activity resumed after a few people cast curious glances Isabella's way. Isabella was vaguely aware of Mama coming to stand in the doorway, but she was more interested in Eric.

With every intention of apologizing for her niece's flights of fancy—*the girl's only four,* Isabella wanted to say, *she doesn't even remember to flush the toilet half the time*—she tried to catch his gaze, but he stared vacantly at the spot where Becca would have been if she was still on his lap. He looked as though he'd been turned to stone; Isabella couldn't detect the slightest flicker of his lids or even the rise and fall of his chest as he breathed.

Poor Eric, she thought vaguely, even as that stupid invisible belt tightened again around her heart. *It takes him ten minutes to recover from hearing himself and marriage mentioned in the same sentence.*

But then something funny happened. Eric looked in Isabella's direction in a process that seemed to take forever, as though he could only turn his head a quarter of an inch at a time, and their gazes connected with the force and power of two bullet trains colliding.

There was something so thunderstruck, so troubled, so *unfathomable* in his expression that it hit Isabella like a jolt from a car's battery cables and almost knocked her out. Warning bells of all shapes and sizes clanged in her brain, but she ignored them while she and Eric stared at each other.

She didn't know what was behind the look on his face, only that it was about a lot more than a player recoiling at the ridiculous thought of marrying a woman with whom he'd had sex only once. *A lot more.*

As much as that terrified her, she still couldn't look away.

"Isabella Grace."

Isabella blinked once, then twice. On the third time she was finally able to peel her gaze away from Eric and look around to see who was talking to her. Looking was unnecessary, though, because of course only one person in the universe called her by her full name.

Mama stood in the doorway to the kitchen, watching her with sharp eyes as she wiped her wet hands on the flowered towel slung over her shoulder. To Mama's eyes, if no one else's, Isabella would look exactly the way she felt: like a deer caught in the headlights and waiting to get smashed by a Mercedes SUV barreling in her direction.

"Isabella Grace," Mama said again, "are you planning to sit there all night or are you gonna help me with these dirty dishes?"

Isabella snapped out of her Eric Warner stupor, a little late, true, but better late than never.

Bless that woman. Wonderful, wonderful mother. Bless her.

Seizing eagerly on this excuse to get away from Eric, Isabella squeezed her way to the edge of the love seat, out from between Sarah and her enormous belly on the one side and Bobby Joe on the other.

"Sorry, Mama." She surged to her feet. "Here I come."

Well aware of Eric's scorching gaze on the side of her face, Isabella ignored it... Tried to ignore it... Wished she could ignore it. As she crossed over into the relative safety of the kitchen, she heard Billy Jack's voice rise above the murmur of the rest of the crowd.

"Let me ask you something, Eric," her brother said. "How many crunches are you doing these days?"

The kitchen wasn't as much of a mess as Isabella had feared. Most of the dishes had already been rinsed and stacked, and only a few leftovers remained on the counter to be bagged and refrigerated. She looked around the tiny space with its avocado walls, outdated countertops and ancient appliances, and awful, though pristine, floors. She'd joked on more than one occasion that the kitchen was a graveyard, the place where linoleum came to die.

How one woman in one minute kitchen—without benefit of a Wolf stove, Cuisinart food processor or KitchenAid mixer, by the way—could have produced so many lip-smacking, belly-busting, diet-ruining meals for four kids and countless others over the decades was something Isabella would never figure out. But Mama was the indisputable heart of this family, and this room was the nerve center of the entire Stevens operation. This place, with this woman, was *home*—and comfort.

Which was good, because Isabella needed about a million barrels of crude comfort right now. Her stomach was tied in so many knots she could probably make a nice embroidery sampler out of them. That being the case, food was probably not the answer, but she didn't let that stop her.

Glancing around, she reached for the first flowered bowl she saw: baked beans. Isabella had never been proud and now was not the time to start. Using the enormous serving spoon, she scooped a huge bite of the dark beans—molasses was the secret ingredient, along with some barbeque sauce—and shoveled it in her mouth.

Mama watched her with hands on hips and eyes narrowed and speculative. Her mama's Spidey sense seemed to tell her that Isabella needed a minute or two because she kept quiet through Isabella's first four bites. When Zeus trotted in and yapped once at Mama's feet, Mama stuck her fingers into Isabella's bowl, extracted a tiny piece of nicely-browned bacon—Isabella frowned because she'd been planning to eat it on the next bite—and slipped it into the Yorkie's mouth.

Zeus yapped his thanks and trotted out again.

Isabella glowered at her mother. "That dog has a sensitive stomach."

"Hush now," Mama said. "A little bacon never hurt anyone."

Snorting, Isabella thunked the now empty baked beans bowl

on the counter and started in on the remnants of Mama's mustard potato salad.

That seemed to be the last straw for Mama. Turning on the faucet to muffle the sounds of their voices, not that anyone was listening anyway judging by the dull roar coming from the living room, she snatched the potato salad from Isabella and placed it on the other side of the counter, well out of reach.

"What has that boy done to you, Isabella?" Mama whispered, aghast.

Isabella, thinking of Eric's hands sliding over her overheated body, his tongue gliding into her mouth and his penis thrusting deep inside her, shuddered with renewed longing. "You don't want to know."

"You're in love with him."

Isabella froze, refusing to meet her mother's eyes. It took her a minute or two to work up a respectable splutter of outrage. The astonished laugh took a little longer.

"*Love?* What on *earth* are you talking about, Mama?"

Mama made a dismissive noise, turned toward the bubble-filled sink, and plunged her hands in among the crusty pots and pans. "Well, you've always been in love with him, of course." She paused in her muttering long enough to shake her head. "I've seen this coming for years. I'm surprised it took this long, to tell you the truth. And sleeping with him now, too. *Goodness gracious.*"

While Isabella knew that lying at this point would be a waste of time, she still wasn't quite ready to discuss her newly-thrilling sex life with her mother. Instead she snatched a deviled egg off the platter and wolfed it down, hoping that Mama would attribute her silence to a full mouth.

No dice. Mama rinsed the pot, placed it upside down in the rack, and looked over her shoulder to fix Isabella with that look.

"What about Joe?" Mama asked.

"I told you all the Joe details when I called. I'm over him. Kindly don't mention his name again."

"Good," Mama said flatly. "I never did like him. Too arrogant."

"Now's a fine time to mention that."

"Well?" she demanded. "What have you got to say for yourself about Eric?"

Isabella took her time about swallowing her latest mouthful, using the delay to construct a careful answer that would, hopefully, satisfy her mother and end this whole dangerous conversation.

"Eric and I have, ah, recently decided to, ah, explore our attraction—"

Mama emitted a hiccupping little laugh that further shredded Isabella's frayed nerves. "*Explore your attraction?* Is *that* what they're calling it these days?"

"—but it was a one-time thing and it doesn't matter anyway because I'll be moving soon and we'll just go back to the way—"

The look of abject horror on Mama's face stopped her cold.

"*Moving soon?*" Mama pressed a hand to her heart. "Good Lord, you're not still talking about teaching in Johannesburg?"

"Of course I am," Isabella said, feeling distinctly prickly now. "Why wouldn't I?"

"Eric can't leave his job, Isabella Grace. He runs the whole company."

"Haven't you been listening?" Realizing she was raising her voice, Isabella lowered it. "It was a one-time thing and we are *going on with our lives.*"

Mama's eyes widened to the point of bulging. When her jaw dropped, too, Isabella braced herself, knowing she was really about to get it with both barrels.

But a new diversion appeared in the form of Daddy's head poking around the corner. During the seventh inning stretch or halftime, depending on which season it was, he liked to move around a little, get a fresh drink and find a snack. Otherwise his butt remained firmly in the recliner.

"Woman?" Daddy rubbed his belly and surveyed the counters hopefully. "You got any coconut cake left?"

Mama recovered from her stupefaction and nailed her husband with an annoyed look strong enough to make him shrink like a punctured beach ball.

"We are talking here. I don't have time to get you any *cake*."

Daddy paused, apparently battling with both his fear and his hunger. The hunger won. "But I am hungr—"

"Here." Mama flung open a cabinet with a bang, rummaged around, and produced a bag of pork rinds, which she thrust at Daddy's chest. "Have a snack to hold you over."

Daddy's doleful expression cleared into utmost joy and happiness. With a broad smile, he disappeared back around the corner.

"What are you doing with *pork rinds?*" Isabella hissed. "Are you *trying* to give that man a heart attack? I didn't even know they still made those things."

"Oh, hush," Mama snapped. "I keep them around for emergencies."

"Wonderful."

Having dispatched with this unwelcome distraction, Mama resumed her interrogation with the kind of zeal that made Isabella wonder if the woman had been a CIA operative in a past life.

"Isabella Grace," she said, "how on earth do you think you and Eric can go on with your lives and live on two different continents? Why would you want to?"

There was something about her mother's urgency, as though she needed to talk Isabella out of throwing herself in front of a herd of rampaging elephants, that was more than Isabella could deal with right now. All kinds of unwelcome emotions churned in her gut and overflowed to her tight chest, and she felt dangerously agitated, borderline crazed. Why was Mama making this so hard? Why was she refusing to understand the obvious? Why did they have to go through this excruciating exercise?

"Why?" Isabella cried. "Why would I derail my career plans for a relationship that'll never go anywhere?"

"Never go anywhere?" Mama floundered, apparently undone by her daughter's stubborn refusal to acknowledge that which was already, in her opinion, crystal clear. "Isabella, you're in love with each other. Why *wouldn't* your relationship go anywhere?"

Isabella had the sudden urge to brace her hands on the

crowded counter for support. *"In love?"* she echoed. "Eric's never been in love in his life."

"Isabell-aaa."

Mama's wry, pitying look was salt to Isabella's already bleeding wounds. "I didn't raise any blind children, so you need to open your eyes, girl," Mama said. "That boy has always been in love with you just like you've always been in love with him. He just wasn't ready for it. Until now."

This was not true and wishing it was wouldn't change anything. "It's only lust," Isabella said, weary now to the depths of her soul. "It'll pass and then he'll go on to the next woman, just like always. There's nothing special about me."

Mama's face contorted with a sudden ferocity. She didn't bother being gentle as she clamped her fingers around Isabella's chin to hold her in place.

"As long as you live, Isabella Grace Stevens, you better not ever let me hear that kind of nonsense come out of your mouth ever again. You hear me?"

Duly chastised, Isabella opened her mouth to answer, but Mama didn't give her the chance. "Eric Warner would be lucky to have you and he knows it. Any man would be lucky to have you. Do you understand me?"

Isabella meant to nod but something stopped her, and it wasn't her mother's hard fingers gripping her face. It was because, in her heart of hearts, she didn't believe any man would be lucky to have her, least of all Eric. In her heart of hearts she knew no man would want her once he knew the whole truth.

Especially not Eric.

Mama seemed to read her mind. Her expression softened and, letting go of Isabella's chin, she patted her cheek with the utmost affection. This, naturally, made things worse. Isabella had the sudden and irritating urge to cry but she swore to herself that she wouldn't. Not here, not now.

"Does he know about what happened with Al in college?" Mama asked.

"Most of it," Isabella said, unhappy with the conversation's turn.
Mama stared at her. "Does Eric know…"

"That I can't have children? No."

Isabella blinked against those hot tears, jolted by her own
mention of her biggest heartbreak in life. Her infertility was the
very last thing she needed to think about now; wasn't she already
conflicted enough tonight dealing with a pregnant woman,
children and Eric? "No. And it's not relevant anyway."

"It's relevant to any man who loves you and wants to support
you."

"Yeah?" Isabella said. "Well, I told Joe, who supposedly loved
me, and he showed his support by freaking out and cheating on me."

"Eric's not Joe."

Exasperation now battled with frustration, and Isabella didn't
know which was worse. "Eric doesn't *love* me. He *wants* me.
There's a difference."

"You love him, though."

Isabella remained upright even though it felt like the tacky
linoleum floor—hell, the whole earth—had dropped out from
under her feet. Stuck in a limbo where she couldn't acknowledge her love for Eric and couldn't deny it, there was nothing
to do but look away from her mother's sharp gaze and focus on
the awful flowered wallpaper.

Mama said nothing, letting Isabella flounder in her own confusion. From the next room came the sound of raucous male
laughter and clapping. Maybe the Braves had hit a grand slam.

Zeus, as though sensing she needed him now, toddled in and sat
at Isabella's feet, staring at her with the expectant look that Isabella
had never been able to ignore. She scooped him up and rubbed her
cheek against his soft little face, taking comfort where she could.

Finally she was ready to look back at Mama. "I'm so stupid,"
she whispered. "I thought I'd be able to control my feelings for
him. Now things are worse than ever."

Mama scratched Zeus's ears. "You're not stupid, baby. Eric's
a hard man to get over. He's special."

Ain't that the truth. The only good thing about this whole unfortunate scenario, at least as far as Isabella could see, was that she had a plan, something on the horizon to take her mind off Eric.

"It'll be better once I move. I'm really excited about my new job, Mama, and I—"

Impatience erupted out of Mama and spewed like lava. She flapped her arms and made a strangled sound that had Zeus looking around in alarm.

"Isabella! What are you thinking, girl? You think you won't love each other if he's *here* and you're *there?* You think you won't take this problem with you to Johannesburg or Greenland or the planet Jupiter if you could get there?"

"What problem?" asked a deep voice.

Chapter 12

Cringing, Isabella turned to discover Eric leaning against the doorframe with his ankles crossed, taking up most of the space in the tiny kitchen without even coming all the way into the room.

As if it wasn't bad enough that he'd heard part of their conversation—Isabella prayed it wasn't much—he held Randy Jr. in his arms. The toddler had one tiny hand clutched on Eric's shoulder. In the other he held the mushy remnants of what looked like Zwieback toast.

"Ric!" said Randy Jr., waving the toast. "Ric!"

Eric grinned down at him. "Er-ic. Er-ic."

"Ric!"

Randy Jr. laughed at his own brilliance and then resumed gnawing on his toast. This, unfortunately, freed Eric to look around at Isabella and continue with his questioning, concern darkening his eyes until they looked black.

"What's the problem?" he asked. "Maybe I can help."

Not bloody likely, Isabella thought, especially since he was the cause of all the major problems in her life. Shooting a warning glance in Mama's direction, she worked hard and managed to come up with a fairly convincing smile.

"The only problem you need to be worried about," she told Eric, pointing to the disgusting smear of wet cracker on his shirt, "is how you're going to get that yucky mess off your shoulder."

To her surprise, Eric, the most annoyingly fastidious person she knew, looked down at the smudge and laughed. "That doesn't matter, does it, buddy?" he said to the grinning, gnawing Randy Jr. "What's a little mess between friends?"

"Ric! Ric! Ric!"

When Eric laughed again and planted a kiss on Randy Jr.'s fat cheek, Isabella had to look away because it was too painful to watch them together. Examining why it was painful was also painful, so she tried not to do it.

Wasn't it best to delude herself into thinking that she couldn't stand the sight of any children at this vulnerable moment? Yeah. She'd pretend that was her problem. It wasn't seeing *Eric* with children that caused the ache in that dark corner of her heart. Not that. Never that.

Moving reflexively, she reached for the bread basket and grabbed one of Mama's now-cold but still obscenely delicious yeast rolls. A bite of the spongy, buttery goodness made her feel better but had the perverse effect of causing Eric's troubled gaze to latch onto her face and linger.

The roll also caught Randy Jr.'s attention. He pointed and his foot-kicking enthusiasm made him bob up and down in Eric's arms. "Peese?" he said. "Peese?"

Isabella swallowed her mouthful and all her gloomy thoughts along with it. It was easy to smile at that angelic little face as long as she didn't think about the fact that she'd never have her own angelic face to feed.

"*Please?* Did you say *please?* Aren't you a polite boy! Randy Jr. wants some roll, *please?*" She offered him a piece. "Is that what you're saying?"

"Yeah!" Randy Jr. dropped the Zwieback on the floor and

reached for the roll, practically snatching it out of her hands. "Yeah!"

The adults laughed and watched with indulgent smiles as he gummed the bread, making a further mess, but when the boy opened his arms to Isabella and leaned toward her, her amusement dried up and died.

There was no way she could hold that precious child right now, feel his warm, solid weight in her arms, smell his sweet scent of powder, lotion and *baby,* and not fall apart. She just couldn't do it.

Isabella took a hasty step back before she caught herself and recaptured her smile. "Oh, no you don't." She tried to talk in her best baby singsong, but her voice was one big croak. "You keep those yucky hands over there with Eric. *You keep those hands over there.*"

That seemed to be fine with Randy Jr., who had no particular loyalty and just wanted to be where the food was. But Eric kept staring at her and there was only so much ignoring she could do before she just looked ridiculous.

Feeling a weird combination of dread in her heart and butterflies in her stomach, she met his intense stare while Mama, feigning blindness and deafness now, grabbed Randy Jr. and took him to the sink to wash his grubby hands. Eric steered Isabella into the far corner of the kitchen and Mama obligingly turned the water up high.

"You okay?" he asked, his voice low, sexy, and unhelpful at this vulnerable juncture.

"Of course," Isabella lied.

"You don't look okay." Hesitating, he reached up and stroked her cheek. Isabella soaked up the warmth from his hand and wanted more even as she cursed herself for her absolute weakness where he was concerned. "I'm worried about you."

Good sense finally prevailed and Isabella stepped back out of his reach. Cold descended on her, as though someone had extinguished the sun. "You probably shouldn't touch me like that."

Eric let his hand drop and a light went out behind his eyes.

"Come on, Randy Jr.," Mama announced loudly as she walked out. "Let's go find Mommy."

Neither of them glanced at her.

"I've always touched you, Iz." Eric's chin had a defiant set to it now, as though he was gearing up for a fight. "You can't expect me to just stop."

"It's different now."

"Yeah. Better."

Being the ineffective liar that she was, she decided to just keep quiet on this point. Better to change the subject altogether. "We should go back out, don't you think? They'll be wondering what happened to us."

"Isabella."

Isabella stilled while the butterflies swarmed in her belly. The challenge was gone from his eyes now and there was only vulnerability and, worse, need. If only he didn't pull so hard on her heart strings. If only she could shield herself from the powerful ache of longing he created.

"Yes?"

"Let me touch you." His cheeks colored and his voice turned hoarse. "Please."

After a beat or two of hesitation, Isabella took his hand and he reeled her in until they stood toe to toe. Instead of pulling her all the way into his arms, he rested his forehead against hers and sighed long and deep.

"That's better," he murmured.

Yeah, Isabella thought, *it was.*

They stood like that, lost in each other, with only the sound of the crowd and the TV in the other room intruding upon their solitary universe. Finally Eric spoke.

"I know we're moving a little fast," he said, "and I know this is a little intense." He laughed, the sound bewildered and humorless. "Who am I kidding? This is scary as hell."

"I'd noticed."

"But this isn't a sex buddy thing, Isabella. The way I'm feeling about you, I—"

"You *what?*"

But whatever it was, he couldn't bring himself to say it. Shaking his head, he paused. "Stay with me tonight," he whispered. "I know I gave you a hard time earlier, and I teased you about this and I probably sounded cocky, but it isn't a game. Stay with me. Let's give this thing between us a chance."

The *no* she needed wouldn't come; there was no sign of it. The idea of spending the night in his arms, laughing and making love with him, was wonderful and seductive. But she couldn't quite get to *yes,* either. The best she could manage was...

"I'll think about it," she told him. "Give me a little time."

He smiled, looking relieved and hopeful. "You've got it, Sunshine."

The night wore on and wound down.

One by one, her brothers left, taking their drowsing children and wives with them, until finally only Mama, Daddy, Isabella and Eric were left to watch the Braves win in extra innings.

Inside the warm cocoon of her parents' house they talked and laughed, and Isabella drank a little wine. Daddy finished off another beer or two, rocking in his chair and absently scratching the ears of Zeus, who sprawled across his lap and was as content as a four-legged friend could ever be this side of heaven.

Isabella had a second slice of coconut cake, sank into the love seat, and, somewhere between the tenth and eleventh innings, fell more deeply under Eric's spell.

It was because her defenses were down, she told herself. The mellow evening, the wonderful food and wine, the quiet joy of being home with the people she loved best. But the same wine that relaxed her so beautifully wouldn't let her lie to herself, no matter how much she wanted to. Any maybe it was time that she looked the unwanted truth in the face:

She'd probably always been under Eric's spell.

Daddy, his attention span restored to full power now that the Braves had won, turned from the TV and looked around with mild surprise to see them still there. Taking a pull from his beer, he regarded Eric with fatherly interest.

"So," he said. "How do you like being top dog? They running you ragged?"

Eric shifted beside her, as though she needed the reminder of his presence. At some point during the evening, with all the getting up and sitting down again as people departed, they'd re-arranged themselves. At first she'd been on the loveseat and he'd been on a chair across the room, watching her with intense eyes, but now he sat next to her, his arm flung across the back of the loveseat behind her shoulders.

He didn't touch her and didn't need to. Though her body was relaxed, it vibrated with awareness—of his heat…the faint spice of his scent…his desire. Everything about him surrounded her, filled her. He was the focal point of her existence even if she didn't dare believe she could ever be the focal point of his.

Eric shrugged and gave Daddy a good-natured grin. "I can't complain. The pay's pretty good."

Isabella had to smile at this colossal understatement.

"They *are* working him too hard, Daddy." Isabella shot Eric a sidelong glance, daring him to contradict her. "He just got home from Hong Kong, and before that he was in Rio. There's no telling when he last spent a whole week at home."

"You're not worried about me, are you, Izzy?"

It was an innocuous question and nothing about Eric's inflection hinted at…anything at all. To her parents' ears, no doubt, this sounded like a routine conversation. But Isabella heard the rough edge of lust in his voice and her nerves prickled with awareness.

"Of course I'm worried," she said. "You're working your-self to death."

One of Eric's heavy brows rose infinitesimally and she did not take this as a good sign. But to her surprise and relief he merely looked away and gave Daddy a wry, reassuring smile.

"I'm a big boy," Eric said. "I can take a little hard work."

"There's somethin' to be said for hard work, o' course."

Daddy, relaxed and philosophical after a few beers, his Mississippi childhood evident in every drawling word, rocked back in his chair, linked his hands over his belly, and stared up at the ceiling across the room. "Lord knows I worked my fingers to the bone to support this fam'ly—'specially with those boys tryin' to eat me outta house and home—"

"Lord, yes." Mama nodded from the sofa, bearing witness like always.

"—but there's more to life than work." Daddy waggled an arthritis-knotted index finger at Eric. "You keep up like this, son, and one day you'll look up to see that the best part o' life's done passed you by."

"What's the best part of life?"

"The best part of life," Daddy said, "is fam'ly. Childrens." Here he paused to shoot Mama a fond look, which she returned. "You won't never go wrong spendin' more time with your fam'ly."

"Yeah, well, everyone doesn't have a great family like this one, Joe." Muscles in Eric's jaw tightened down, making his profile look harsh and unhappy. Isabella, who was apparently born without the gene that would have made her impervious to his emotions, shifted closer, offering comfort in the only way she could at the moment. "You know what I mean?"

"Yeah, Daddy." Isabella smiled and did her best to keep her voice light, tried to make a joke before Eric's dark thoughts took root and grew. "Poor Eric here didn't have enough siblings to put together a basketball team like we did. And I've heard rumors that he didn't have to share one bathroom with five other people. Had his *own* bathroom. Fancy that."

The teasing worked. Eric snorted with laughter and the brilliance of his smiling gaze, as it connected with hers, was enough to strike her blind. Her heart skittered and, unless she was much mistaken, stopped altogether.

Daddy grinned, too, but he wasn't finished delivering his message. "You just remember," he told Eric as he leaned across the side of his chair, reached down, and pulled the lever to lower the foot rest, "that it don't matter what kind of fam'ly you come from. It's the kind of fam'ly you *make* that matters."

Eric went utterly still. Just like that, his smile froze in place and even his breathing seemed to stop for several long beats.

They'd always been attuned to each other's moods, but now that they'd become lovers it felt like Isabella was thinking his thoughts. And she knew he'd just had a colossal *Aha!* moment because he'd realized he wasn't doomed by fate or a Warner family curse to have a miserable marriage like his parents'. He'd realized that he, like Andrew, could break the cycle.

After several long seconds, he seemed to recover from his shock and shot her an indecipherable sidelong glance.

"I never thought about it like that, Joe."

Daddy nodded with satisfaction, looking like a wise old owl behind his bifocals. "And what's this I hear," he said, pinning Isabella with a fierce gaze that wasn't the least bit unfocused or cloudy despite his seventy-five years, "'bout you up and moving to South Africa? Your Mama don't want you to go."

Isabella had expected this. As the only daughter, she'd always been a daddy's girl and didn't expect that to change at this late date no matter what he claimed about *Mama* not wanting her to go.

"Is that a *congratulations* I hear?" Unfortunately she infused her voice with a little too much cheer, and it sounded forced. Clearing her throat, she tried to act a little less manic. "This is a great opportunity."

Daddy looked unimpressed. "There's great opportunities in the United States, girl. Mebbe you ain't up on the news, but there's prolly childrens in Cincinnati that needs your help."

Isabella shifted, uncomfortable now and fully aware of Eric's keen interest in this topic. Though he kept still and said nothing, she felt the tension of waiting in his body, as though he was stretched through with piano wire that had just been tightened half a turn.

"Well," she said carefully, "I do know that, but I'd like to travel a little. Help where I'm most needed. And I think a little change and a little adventure might do me good. And it's only for a few years."

Daddy wasn't buying it any more than Eric had; she should have known. The old man's weathered brown face twisted into the kind of derisive look he'd given her a thousand years ago when she broke Mama's crystal lamp, one of the family's few valuable possessions, and tried to convince him that the dog had done it. And then, just to add insult to injury, he snorted.

"Isabella," Daddy said, "I didn't raise no fools. And you know darn good and well that this here's nothin' more than you tryin' to run away from your problems. And you oughta know that your problems'll be right there with you in South Africa, same as if you'd packed 'em in your suitcase with your toothbrush."

This time Isabella was the one who froze. The heat of embarrassment rose up from her neck and crept across her cheeks until she no doubt glowed like lava flowing down the side of a volcano.

No one could strip away the frills and expose the truth in all its brutality the way Daddy could. He was right, though it killed her to admit it, even to herself. First she'd thought she'd go to South Africa to immerse herself in the needy children and the culture and to recover from Joe's betrayal, and then she'd seen it as a handy escape from falling too far under Eric's spell. Either way she looked at it, though, she was running away.

Maybe the thing she was really running from was her own fears.

"I'm going to think about that, Daddy."

"See that you do, girl."

The topic turned to golf and Eric and Daddy began an enthusiastic and hyperbole-filled discussion of their latest exploits on the links. Isabella's thoughts drifted back to Eric and what he'd told her in the kitchen.

This is scary as hell.

The way I'm feeling about you, I—

Let's give this thing between us a chance.

He's asked her to stay with him tonight, and they both needed her answer.

What was her answer? If only she knew. An epic struggle was going on in her heart, body and spirit and she was afraid she'd lose no matter what she chose.

If they stayed here tonight, she'd have the empty pleasure of knowing she'd made the sensible decision and a long, excruciating night without Eric to think about what a clever, self-disciplined, self-protective woman she was. She'd stay away from Eric and take that first, crucial step toward stopping him from breaking her heart.

On the other hand, she could leave with him now and spend the night in his arms. She could spend hours making love with him, exploring his wondrous body, and best of all, talking with him. And in the morning she could pay the piper when she had to get up and acknowledge, as she inevitably would, that she'd fallen deeper in love with him than she already was.

So that was the choice: lonely self-preservation or ecstatic self-destruction. Either way, through, her heart was already his to break because she loved him.

That being the case, why not enjoy tonight with him? Did she have to address all her fears and concerns tonight? Of course not. It wasn't like he'd proposed marriage. Why not enjoy this time with Eric? This paralysis she'd been feeling was ridiculous; it wasn't as if another round of lovemaking with Eric would lead to her death within twenty-four hours. Why be such a coward?

Taking a deep breath, she chose.

"Mama," she said into the temporary pause in the conversation, "Eric and I need to get going. We've got more driving to do tonight, so we'll spend the night at a hotel along the way."

Chapter 13

Though she focused on her mother, Isabella could feel Eric's vibrating stillness, his rapt gaze on the side of her face. Still she didn't look at him.

Mama fixed her with a knowing mother's gaze that conveyed both concern and exasperation.

"I hope you know what you're doing, girl."

The best Isabella could manage was a wry grin and a one-shouldered shrug. "So do I, Mama."

"Eric." Fierce now, Mama rounded on Eric and pointed her finger at him. "You be careful with my girl. You hear me?"

The casual observer might have thought Mama meant to drive safe at this late hour, but Isabella knew better than that. So, apparently, did Eric. When she worked up the nerve to glance his way, he looked Isabella straight in the face, and in his un-blinking eyes she didn't see any signs of triumph.

What she did see was some sort of inner glow, a glittering excitement, and the kind of solemnity that usually accompanied a swearing-in ceremony of some sort. Swallowing hard, she wished she could regulate her thundering pulse and wondered how they would make it to the nearest hotel without tearing each other's clothes off in the car.

"Mama Jo," Eric said, staring at Isabella, "the one thing you never need to worry about is me being careful with your daughter. I promise you that."

They found another hotel with another honeymoon suite, this one with pale mint walls and sleek black furniture.

Pausing only to unhook Zeus from his leash and find Fluffles for him, Isabella crept up behind Eric, wrapped her arms around his waist, slid her hands up under his shirt and across that silky-hot skin, and let the relief flow. It consumed her—wiped her out, a tidal wave of dangerous emotions that she would, just this once, indulge.

His reaction was powerful and immediate: his skin quivered under her fingers and then he wrapped his muscled arms across hers and pulled her closer, until she was flush against the hard wall of his back and the high round curve of his butt.

"I'm addicted to you now," she told him. "I guess you're feeling pretty cocky, huh? Are you going to tell me you told me so?"

"Cocky? No. *Happy?* You better believe it."

Isabella could hear it in his hoarse voice. The pulsing excitement, the need, the straining passion that would break free just as soon as they got a few things straightened out. She knew him well enough to know that, as desperately as he wanted her, he would hold himself in firm check until he was satisfied that they'd reached an understanding.

Understanding, she knew, was impossible. What middle ground could there be between a man who couldn't love and the woman who loved him? Under what circumstances could the woman emerge from the relationship unscathed? None that Isabella could see.

Still, she pressed her cheek to his back and breathed him in, absorbing those intoxicating Oriental spices, his fresh musk and the faint scent of deodorant and fabric softener. *God, he felt good. Right*.

But her doubts lingered. Not enough to make her stop sliding her hands up his torso to lift the shirt over his head and throw it to the floor, but still there.

"This is *such* a bad idea," she murmured, pressing her lips to his bare back and tasting the faint salt of his skin. "So bad."

"No, it's not," he said, some of his restraint slipping. There was another shudder, violent this time, a groan, and then, in one swift movement, he pivoted and wrapped her in his arms.

Emotions were running high and she knew it, but there was no preparing for the wild gleam in his dark eyes or the contained power that rippled through him. With a hoarse groan he clamped both of his large hands on her butt and brought her up against his raging erection.

She cried out, undone on so many levels she couldn't even begin to count them. As though he knew he'd scared her a little, he loosened his grip and lowered that too-bright gaze to stare at her lips rather than her eyes. He did not, however, stop his hands from sliding up under the hem of her skirt to cup her butt, which was bare but for the negligible strip of lace between her cheeks.

Looking wry and rueful now, as though he just couldn't believe how she affected him or how much he needed her, he shook his head. "Damn, girl." One of his fingers slid experimentally under her panties, savoring the lace and her skin at the same time. "You're killing me here."

Her need ratcheted higher, climbing slowly to the ultimate destination like one of those old wooden roller coasters mounting that first, tallest hill. "You like my undies, I take it?"

His quick, wolfish grin sucked the little bit of remaining breath right out of her lungs. "You could say that, yeah."

Waves of sensation shook her and she undulated against him, helpless to control her reactions. "I'm so glad."

She wanted to drive him wild—to the outer limits of his control and beyond. So she backed out of his arms, trailed her hands up her parted thighs, made a slow show of sliding her skirt up to her hips and shimmied out of the panties, rubbing herself as she did. Once she'd kicked the panties off, she ran her hands back down her thighs and let the skirt fall into place, hiding her curly black triangle from his feverish gaze.

Eric unraveled right before her eyes. Eyes bulging, arms trembling, he gasped and pulled her by the upper arms until she was flush against him, molded from shoulder to hip.

His frantic hands stroked up and down, up and down, rubbing her butt until the entire bottom half of her body felt pliant. She thought he would kiss her and she knew it would be a crazed, rough, biting kiss, but he surprised her and held back, refusing her parted lips and denying her what she needed. But his face inched closer until his mouth was a scant breath away and his eyes were nothing but a glitter of brown crystal.

With a harsh breath, as though it cost him a large chunk of his soul to be patient, he whispered the one question she'd fervently hoped he'd never ask.

"Why are you so scared, Izzy?"

She froze.

Why wouldn't she be scared? Because he was such a good prospect for a long-term relationship? *Puh-lease*. Falling in love with a player was right up there with scaling the Empire State Building without a rope in terms of self-destructiveness. She might as well go out and play in interstate traffic and be done with it; it'd be safer in the long run than spending more time like this with Eric when he was guaranteed to break her heart.

"Tell me," he said.

All the reasons were right there on the tip of her tongue but she couldn't say any of them:

You're a world-class player.

You've broken the heart of more women than I can shake a stick at.

I love you and you've never loved anyone.

And the biggie, the one she could never, ever tell him:

You wouldn't even want me anymore if you knew my real truth.

In the end, she settled for an umbrella answer, one that encompassed everything and revealed nothing:

"Because this is too intense," she said. "It's too much."

There was a long, pregnant pause during which only their harsh breathing broke the silence. "Yeah," he agreed finally with sorrow on his face and regret in his voice. "It's a lot."

"Gee. You think?"

This excruciating conversation would never lead them anywhere. Deciding that distraction was probably her best tactic at this point, Isabella dug her nails into his nape, pulled his face down and, standing on her tiptoes, kissed him.

For thirty seconds he went wild. His hot mouth slanted over hers, frantic and greedy, and they drank each other up with the kind of desperation that drove people to primitive acts like murder or suicide. But he didn't stay distracted for long and she felt foolish for thinking he would. He broke away and in his eyes she saw the kind of ruthless focus that made him a world-class CEO.

"What's the real reason you're so scared, Izzy?" Letting her go entirely, he went to work on her top. "Tell me. Is it because of my track record with women? Is that it? I know it's not good."

"*Not good?* I think the word you're looking for is *abysmaaaal.*"

The last word died on a low, earthy groan as he tongued a nipple through the white lace of her strapless bra, but if he could stay focused, so could she.

"Y—you're not a very good prospect, are you?" she asked.

"No."

His honesty on this point was a sickening surprise. Disappointment washed over her, chilling some, but not all, of the heat in her blood, but she didn't have time to reflect on it. In a dizzying flash of movement he scooped her up—as though she was a doll—and slowly swung her around to the bed.

Once there he pulled the duvet out of the way and laid her down on cool white sheets. Then he straightened and slid and kicked his way out of his shorts to reveal more boxer briefs, black this time, but not black enough to hide the size of the erection that strained almost to his belly button for her.

Isabella's mouth went dry and her head went light, but he didn't give her the chance to reflect on the pleasures waiting in store for her in the next few minutes. His hands smoothed up her thighs to her hips and slid her skirt off, as careful now as he'd been frenzied the first time they made love. Naked now but for her bra, shameless and needy as a mare in heat, she spread her legs and arched her hips, using her body to beg him to hurry.

His hot gaze, brighter than Arctic snow in the sunshine, skimmed over her, lingering on her thighs, wet sex and breasts, and then he saw the faded marks. Low on her belly.

"What's this?" He frowned and smoothed his fingers over the faint lines.

Isabella hesitated and then said, "Nothing. I need you."

The words had the desired effect. He swallowed so hard she saw the distinct bob of his Adam's apple in the strong column of his throat. He licked his lips and tried to speak, but...nothing.

After several long beats he seemed to get his wits about him and finally looked up into her face. To her surprise, his expression was imploring and vulnerable, almost sad.

Time slowed as he climbed onto the bed and straddled her, his muscular thighs rippling with sinew. Reaching between them, he skimmed his fingers over her sex, slowly...slowly...slowly homing in on the hard button that wept for his attention.

Isabella fought hard to remain lucid but couldn't silence her cries.

"Can I tell you something, Sunshine?"

"Yes," she breathed, arching her back and rubbing herself against him, beyond care, beyond pride, beyond anything other than accepting the gift of pleasure that only this one man could give her.

He watched her with heavy-lidded eyes while a faint, lazy smile crossed over his face and then was gone. "You're right," he whispered. "I'm a—*what was your word?* Oh, yeah. I'm an *abysmal* prospect for all the other women I've dated. And you know what? That doesn't have a damn thing to do with *you*."

Isabella, hovering on the edge of an obliterating climax, flung her arms over her head and squirmed, but then his words sank in with a jolt. Quieting down as much as she could, she tried to pay attention because this was important.

"What—what do you mean?"

"I mean," he said, those fingers never pausing in their relentless stroking, "that there's never been another woman in my life like you and there never will be. If you weren't so busy being scared, you'd see that."

There was a pause while the words slowly penetrated her fuzzy brain.

"Oh," she said.

"Yeah, *oh*."

Inching forward, he leaned over her until he could nuzzle her lips, keeping it light and easy when she would've drunk deep. After a few seconds, when she was nearly blind with lust, he pulled back and gave her another slow grin of such unbearable sexiness she wondered dimly whether he could make her come one day just by looking at her across a crowded room and smiling.

"Can you do something for me tonight, Izzy?"

"Absolutely," she told him in a hoarse whisper.

"That's the kind of thing I like to hear."

Sliding his hands underneath her back, he undid the clasp of her bra and slid it away, freeing her breasts with a bounce. His breath caught and his eyes rolled closed. For a minute or two he couldn't seem to do anything and the wait was excruciating, but then he bent again and cupped a breast in each palm.

Squeezing them together, he flicked his tongue across one nipple, then the other. Back and forth he went, over and over again, licking and then suckling hard and then licking again, and the whole time she felt the tension building between her thighs and her sanity slipping away.

She'd forgotten all about her name, much less the threads of their conversation, but he hadn't. Panting now, his wonderful pink tongue running over his bottom lip, he raised his head and stared up at her with glittering eyes.

"Can you stop thinking so much, Izzy?" He paused. "For the rest of our trip can you just…see what happens?"

She hesitated.

"That's all I'm asking, Iz. *Please*. Can you do that for me?"

As if there'd ever been any doubt about it. "Okay," she said, praying he never asked her to jump off the Suspension Bridge into the Ohio River because she'd probably be foolish enough to agree to that, too.

"Good."

Triumph flashed over his face and then he bent low, a man on a mission from which nothing could deter him. Before she knew what'd happened he'd run his tongue over both nipples again, inched it down to her belly button and then gone lower, to where honey flowed hot and thick for him, and she was keening and coming…and coming…and coming.

Chapter 14

Eric made the mistake of looking up to see Isabella's expression as she climaxed, and the beautiful, half-smiling contortions of her face and pouty lips nearly did him in. He couldn't take his eyes off her. The arched back, the sweet straining column of her neck as she threw her head back against the pillows, the engorged dark nipples, her endless cries were all too much for a mortal man like him. Was he supposed to witness her ecstasy—knowing he'd caused it—and not come in his draws like a twelve-year old with his first wet dream? How much could he take?

More, as it turned out.

Isabella opened her eyes and a slow, seductive smile eased across her face, the kind that made a man's belly do flips and his skin break out in anticipatory sweat. He swallowed hard, his gaze riveted to her, and watched as she rose up on all fours, her heavy breasts dangling like delicious fruit.

"Lie back." Her eyes glittered with what looked like eagerness—excitement.

Eric's heart nearly stopped. "I don't—" he began, but Isabella was in charge and she was having none of it.

"Lie back," she said again, and this time she pushed his chest until he complied.

Panting now, he gripped the sheets and told himself to hold on as she slid lower.

But then she cupped him and her tongue stroked up the length of his overheated flesh and he cried out, his back arching off the bed of its own accord, and there was no holding on.

Isabella seemed to like this reaction. Tilting her head to look up at him with those gleaming, knowing eyes, she smiled again and sucked him all the way into her mouth. Those plump lips wrapped around him was the sexiest sight he'd ever seen and he gasped, every muscle in his body strained to the breaking point.

Gripping her silky head as it bobbed over him, he watched her for a few seconds and felt the excruciating pleasure tighten deep in his belly, but then she began to make thrilling little humming noises that vibrated through him—as though she'd never tasted anything as delicious as him—and the heightened sensation was too much. He broke free, desperate to thrust inside her now.

Shaking now—there was no other word for it—sweating, trying to hurry, hurry, *hurry,* he reached over the side of the bed for his shorts and caught sight of Zeus. That silly dog was sitting there watching him with rapt interest, his little teddy bear head cocked to one side as though he was trying to learn from Eric's technique. Eric would have laughed if he hadn't been so close to catastrophic heart failure caused by his lust for this one woman. Muttering, he tossed the shorts in Zeus's direction and the dog scampered off.

Eric's hands wouldn't function. It felt like he was wearing twelve pairs of leather garden gloves, and he just couldn't manage things that required fine motor skills, like getting a condom out and slipping it on. After the longest delay of his life—he couldn't get his lungs to expand, couldn't think, couldn't move fast enough and his body was going to *explode*— he worked the damn thing on.

Isabella, now on her back again, watched him with her bright brown eyes half closed, and when he caught her gaze she smiled and opened her arms for him.

His heart threatened to burst.

Beyond desperate now, barely capable of a coherent thought, he wanted to grab her, take her and never let her go, but he forced himself to slow down.

But then she whispered to him. "Come here."

That was it. Game over. With a cry he rose up over her and drove home, into that delicious body that was so hot and wet, so unspeakably tight and, better than that, *right*.

Isabella went wild, writhing beneath him…meeting him… matching him…stroke for stroke, surpassing any dream he'd ever had, any fantasy, any hope. Those thighs he'd drooled over tightened around his waist, pulling him deeper, and her hands searched and roamed, digging her nails into his nape, shoulders and butt, hurting and pleasing him. He'd be a mess of scratches later and he didn't give even half a damn.

And the noises she made. She was destroying him with those choked, breathy sounds that were music to his ears and heart, Mozart for his soul. He'd never be right again after this. Not even close to right.

Yeah, it was all over for him.

Much as he wanted to prolong the pleasure until he passed out from it, he just couldn't hold on. Five strokes, six tops, and that was it. The hot squeeze of her body was too much, and she did it to him every single time.

He'd slide out to the very tip, until they'd nearly separated, and try to work her, just a circle or two to make sure she was as crazed as he was, but she was in charge the whole time and she was having none of it. She'd rise up to claim him again, and he'd have to plunge in again, harder…faster…stronger.

On that sixth stroke he felt the eruption coming and there was nothing he could do as the wave retracted, gathered strength and hurtled out of his body. Sinking his fingers deep into the fragrant silk of her hair, he whispered her name—it was all he could manage, a lame, half-choked whisper. After that there was only time enough for him to slide his tongue into the sweet depths of her mouth and hold on before the blinding sensations crashed over him.

And he was flattened. Ruined in the best possible way.

He went rigid, paralyzed and helpless with ecstasy.

On and on it went, like nothing he'd ever felt before or likely ever would again, and she was right with him, chanting his name on breathy sighs. Listening to her, feeling her, absorbing her, he wondered—even before his spasms had died away—how soon he could take her again, how many times tonight he could have her before his body gave out, how much was too much to need her.

Finally it was over and they clung to each other, stroking hands over damp skin, sweaty and exhausted. *Changed.* Nothing could be the same after this. This time was different from the first time, although he wasn't yet sure why. He would damn sure figure it out, though.

Disentangling himself inch by reluctant inch, he slid off the bed. Zeus, who was now settled, with Fluffles, on top of Eric's shorts, looked up hopefully, but he didn't have time for that dog right now.

After a step or two away from Isabella, Eric had to glance back and make sure she was still there. She looked wonderfully rumpled, a sensual mass of wild hair, swollen lips and flushed skin—more than good enough to eat, and he intended to hold that thought until he got back from the bathroom.

Waiting until she arranged the white sheet around her body and glanced up at him, he fixed her with a warning look. Her drowsy eyes widened with surprise and wary anticipation and he was fiercely glad that he had her full attention as he issued his warning.

"You're not allowed to leave this bed tonight, Isabella."

A sexy smile, the kind that scrambled men's brains, made them saddle up armies and ride out on crusades, curved her tender lips and knocked the breath right out of his lungs.

"I know."

"Good," he said after a lengthy pause during which he tried

to remember what the hell they'd been talking about. He paused again, feeling half-witted at best, no-witted at worst. "Great."

They stared at each other, neither moving.

Well, it was nice to have her assurance, but he still felt unsettled. Partially because of her little *leap-out-of-bed* routine earlier and partially because he knew they still had mountains between them and a lot of things to resolve. Since she was being so agreeable, though, he decided to toss a few more concepts out to her and see how she reacted.

"And we're going to spend tomorrow night together, after the wedding."

"Okay."

Her easy agreement, perversely, made him all the more agitated and greedy. "And then we're flying back to Columbus for Andy's baptism on Sunday. I'll arrange to have my car sent home later."

She opened her mouth.

"No arguments," he added quickly.

She probably wanted to protest the use of the Lear, but being environmentally conscious was the very least of his concerns at this critical juncture. He'd make a donation to Save the Penguins or some such later, when the fate of his personal life wasn't hanging in the balance.

"Fine," she said after a moment's hesitation.

He could tell from her pursed lips, which were always a dead giveaway, that she didn't like it, but that was just too bad. There was one more thing—the *big* thing, the only *important* thing—that they needed to discuss, a card he needed to lay on the table, and he was anxious to get to it.

"And I'm not going to be nice and stand by and quietly watch you move to another continent." He paused for maximum effect because there wasn't going to be any negotiating on this point, and she may as well realize it now. "You know that, don't you?"

He hadn't expected a quick agreement this time, and he sure didn't get one. A shadow darkened her face and it was as unwelcome to him as a castration or lobotomy. He held her gaze, watched her struggle with his pronouncement, until finally she gave her reluctant and unhappy answer.

"I know," she said.

In the awkward—no, painful—silence that followed, one thing became utterly, undeniably clear to him: she still wasn't his. His fight was still far from over and, for all he knew, was just beginning. Maybe she would never be fully his and the worst thing about it was that he had no idea what kept Isabella from belonging to him the way he belonged to her.

A shiver ran up and over him, chilling his bare skin and driving away the last of the feverish heat he'd felt in the bed with her, only minutes ago. The magnitude of his problem hit him, making him feel like a thin sheet of ice, brittle and easily shattered.

He was flying blind here and it scared the hell out of him. He was hers and he knew it, but, even though he'd just loved her the best way he knew how, given her every ounce of feeling he had to give, she still wasn't his.

The knowledge cramped in his gut, sickening him, and he wanted to rage at her, to make her tell him what was really going on—and there *was* something, he could taste it—but he eased back, forced himself to turn away and continue on to the bathroom.

Tonight was for loving. There was plenty of time for fighting later.

And anyway…nothing made him work harder than a challenge.

"I guess we should get ready for this wedding, huh?" Isabella asked.

Exhausted and sated, glistening with sweat and happier than she'd ever been or could have ever hoped to be, Isabella stroked the rough silk of Eric's short hair. He lay with his head on her bare breasts, his thumb skimming across her nipples every few seconds and stoking the fire that burned so brightly for him even now, seconds after he'd made her come.

Again.

True to his word, Eric had kept her in bed all night and no actual sleeping was involved. When she'd put her feet on the floor this morning, she felt like a new person.

It was a ridiculous cliché, so trite she was embarrassed to think it, even to herself, but it was true. Eric had worshipped her so thoroughly, touched her so tenderly and listened to her so intently, that she felt like a queen. As though she could climb any mountain, swim any sea, or cure any illness. As though no unhappiness could ever find her, much less touch her, as long as Eric stayed close.

They'd gotten up, driven the last few hours to Jacksonville Beach holding hands but talking very little and arrived at their third hotel together. The second they got up to their room, Eric pulled her into his arms and gave her a kiss so feverish, so desperate, that she wondered how they'd managed to keep their hands off each other while in the SUV and, worse, how she could possibly put half the world between them when the time came for her to fly to Johannesburg.

And even though they'd made love all night and she was sore and they were running late for the wedding, they tumbled to the bed and made love again because she was addicted to him.

But now it really was time to get dressed.

Groaning, he raised his head, one heavy brow quirked. "What wedding?"

"The wedding," she said, palming his face because she needed to touch him at all times, "that is the reason we drove to Florida in the first place."

A wicked smile inched across his face and tied her stomach in the kind of delicious knots she didn't ever think she'd get used to. "I thought we came down to Florida to make love, Iz," he murmured.

She flushed until even the ends of her hair felt like they were glowing. Repressing her simpering grin was impossible. "That's only the side benefit."

His killer grin widened. "Helluva benefit."

Knowing they'd never get out of bed—*ever*—if they continued like this, she decided to ignore his commentary. "Do you want to shower first, or should I?"

"We can't share?" He gave her a bewildered look, all wide-eyed innocence. "Think of all the polar bears we'll kill with two showers instead of one."

As if she'd say *no* to an activity that let her help save the environment while spending naked time with Eric. *Please*. "Come on."

They lingered in the shower and raced through the reapplication of clothes—white linen pants and tunic for him, fluttery yellow flowered sundress—her favorite because it was so bright and cheerful—for her. Isabella threw on Zeus's little black tie and grabbed the leash and then they were off.

They made it downstairs, through the lobby and out the hotel's back doors to the enormous seaside deck just ahead of the first bridesmaids. The pianist was striking up the first notes of Luther Vandross's "Here and Now" when they settled Zeus under a shady palm tree and ducked into the last row of white folding chairs on the bride's side of the aisle.

Isabella took a minute to enjoy the balmy breeze and tang of salt in the air. There were probably more beautiful settings for a wedding, but none came to mind. Up front, against the backdrop of the white sand, rolling sapphire waves and aqua sky, stood an arch covered with pink and white roses, and more explosions of roses edged the seating area and aisle.

The anxious-looking groom, his attendants and the minister, all very handsome in their white suits, waited under the arch, and the air hummed with the excitement of waiting.

Isabella's body, on the other hand, hummed with the thrill of Eric's attention. She arranged the filmy skirt of her dress and pretended she didn't feel the heat of Eric's gaze on her face and bare legs or the warmth of his adoration shining in his eyes. If she looked at him now, with her heart so full and light, she would... she would...

"Isabella," he said on a sigh so quiet she doubted she'd really heard it.

The stroke of his fingers across the base of her neck derailed her thoughts and renewed the quiver deep in her belly. A bolt of intense pleasure shot through her, as stunning as an orgasm but somehow more devastating because of his unspeakable tenderness.

She tried to pay attention to the proceedings. The smiling bridesmaids, most of whom were classmates of theirs from Princeton, filed by in their pink slip dresses and tried to look dignified and not squeal when they spotted Isabella and Eric. Next came the little flower girl and ring-bearer—Isabella had no idea whose children they were, but they were adorable—and then, finally, came Terri.

The glowing bride glided down the aisle in a white slip dress and short veil, her feet barely touching the path strewn with rose petals. When she made it to Frank, the groom, he took her hand and kissed it. The two of them giggled like children on the playground and then turned to the minister, who grinned indulgently and opened his prayer book.

The ceremony was quick, easy and casual, not much more than the vows and a song or two. It was over almost before it had started, and then Terri and Frank were rushing back up the aisle in a shower of pink and white flower petals.

Cheering and laughing, the crowd followed them to the pool area, which was decorated with ten or twelve candlelit tables set for dinner. Isabella was still laughing when she and Eric found a quiet spot near the rail and waited for their friends to catch up with them.

"That was sooo beautiful!" Feeling very effusive and emotional, Isabella stared out at the water and brushed her hair back out of her face. "I was a little worried about it raining or sand blowing or something, but I really think that was one of the—"

"I'm in love with you," Eric said.

Isabella gasped and whipped her head back around to stare at Eric, her hand frozen by her ear, not at all certain he'd said what she thought she'd heard.

But the second she looked at him, she knew. His face had acquired a ruddy flush that she didn't think had anything to do with the sun, and he looked utterly serious and utterly vulnerable, as though he didn't want to be in love with her, much less tell her about it, but just couldn't stop the words from coming.

Oh, my God, she thought, feeling miserable and ecstatic and every variation in between all at the same time. *Oh, my God.*

When she said nothing, he took one step closer and smoothed that flyaway curl behind her ear for her. Then, with absolute attention, he trailed his fingers across her cheek, down her neck, and across the tops of her heaving breasts. Still she couldn't move. Finally his gaze flickered back up to her face and she saw the hint of moisture in his crystal brown eyes and heard the depths of his emotion in the hoarse whisper of his voice.

"You're everything to me, and I can't...I can't breathe with wanting you so much." He paused and pressed a lingering kiss to her forehead. "I didn't mean to tell you like this, and I don't know why it happened or how it happened so quickly and I know you're not ready to hear it, but, yeah..."

Overcome, he paused to clear his throat.

"I'm in love with you, Isabella."

Chapter 15

Once the initial euphoria of telling Isabella how he felt had subsided a little, Eric's heart fell with the kind of sickening thud that made people reach for the phone to call 9-1-1. Her expression wasn't the *I love you, too, Eric* look he'd foolishly been hoping for, and her ongoing speechlessness could only be attributed to one thing: horror.

Stupid idiot. Why did he tell her? *Stupid, stupid, stupid.*

Well, he knew why. It was because he *did* love her. Probably always had on some subconscious level that he was only now recognizing.

In seventeen years he hadn't made a major decision, suffered a loss or defeat, or celebrated an emotional high without sharing it with Isabella. For his entire adult life he'd relied on her common sense, wisdom and humor. He'd needed her smiles, advice and presence, needed her reaction to events in his life so he'd know how he should react. She'd been the first person he called when he got into business school, the first person he told when he became CEO, the first person he consulted for advice when his parents drove him crazy.

She was his touchstone, his rock. Had been since college.

So yeah, he loved her. Wanted her. Needed her. Would marry her, if she only said the word, and to hell with his fears about marriage and disaster going hand in hand. With Isabella as his wife, he couldn't fail.

But…it didn't look like she'd be agreeing to marriage anytime soon.

The moment stretched between them, bypassing awkward and heading straight for excruciating. He was just beginning to wonder if he should launch himself over the rail and hope the fall to the beach below was enough to at least knock him unconscious for a couple of hours, when the bride distracted them.

Terri, newly married and floating with happiness, had picked this moment to play the gracious hostess. *Lucky him.* Back at Princeton she'd been the biggest yakker on campus and Eric thought it was pretty unlikely that the years had changed her any.

Not picking up on any social cues whatsoever despite his desperate subliminal message—*We're talking here!*—she shrieked and opened her arms.

"Eric! Izzy! Oh, my GOD, I can't BELIEVE it's you!"

Yeah, Eric thought. *Still a yakker.*

He cringed but at this point there was no avoiding her or any of their other friends and they had, after all, come to the wedding to give the happy couple their best wishes. So he dredged up a painful smile, submitted to the woman's hug and kissed her cheek.

"Here's the beautiful bride. How are you, Terri?"

"Well, one of the caterers bumped into the cake and smashed one side of the bottom layer, but they covered it up with some flowers. Oh, and my cousin's flight got delayed—weather out of Chicago, can you believe it?—so I think she's sitting on the tarmac somewhere. But I'm fine other than that—" here she paused long enough to pull free of Eric, take a deep breath and hug Izzy, who still looked shell-shocked "—and you two look GREAT! Wasn't the wedding BEAUTIFUL? Could we have PICKED a better day?"

Isabella finally recovered her voice although she now had two enormous patches of color on her cheeks. "It's so good to see you. You look *gorgeous*. I'm so happy for you."

"And YOU!" Terri snagged Isabella's hand with her left one and Eric's with her right. Taking one step back, she surveyed them like a proud matchmaker. "Finally got together, didn't you? I KNEW it! I saw you during the ceremony!"

If and when he and Izzy got married, Eric thought, the last thing he'd be doing would be watching the guests in the pews to see who was getting with whom.

"Well," Isabella began uncomfortably.

"Did you finally put away your playa's handbook, Eric?" Terri winked at him.

Eric wondered if it would be wrong to wring a bride's neck on her wedding day.

"I don't want to hear anything about you stepping out on this girl, okay?" Terri asked. "You know what? I'll be expecting some VERY GOOD NEWS from you VERY SOON."

Terri looked over her shoulder to signal Frank, who was greeting other guests a few feet away. Dropping Isabella's hand, Terri flapped her arm at her husband, looking like half a bird trying to take flight. "Frank? FRANK!"

Poor Frank, Eric thought. If the brother was having second thoughts about spending the rest of his life with this black Edith Bunker, it was too late now. But Frank just smiled happily and hurried over to his wife's side.

"These two finally got together, Frank." Terri angled her face for Frank's kiss, the epitome of newlywed bliss. "I'm betting they're going to be the next ones to get married. Izzy, you stand right up front when I throw the bouquet, OKAY? I'm throwing it RIGHT to you, for luck."

"Good idea," Eric murmured on impulse, serious. "Throw it to Izzy."

Astonished silence surrounded him on all sides.

He didn't know what had made him say it and at this point it didn't matter. All he knew was that if he was in for a penny he was in for a pound, so why not raise the stakes? He wanted Isabella. Wanted all of her and wanted her for the rest of their lives. Why stammer and hedge?

Three surprised gazes swung around to look at him, but Isabella's was the only one he saw. She looked flushed and stunned—breathless. Most of all she looked unhappy, and that almost killed him.

But it didn't deter him.

He would get to the bottom of her issue. Come hell or high water he would figure it out and nothing would keep him from her. Not South Africa, his unfortunate Warner legacy of unhappy marriages nor Izzy's own fears.

Nothing.

Satisfied that he had Isabella's attention and had put her on notice, Eric realized that he was hungry and thirsty. Goodness knew he needed to keep his strength up to deal with the fight to come. Looking around, he found the bar in one far corner of the deck and saw that it was fully stocked. *Thank goodness.*

"Champagne anyone?" he asked, walking off. "I'm parched."

The reception passed in a blur of crab cakes, mahi-mahi and mango chutney something-or-other, none of which Isabella tasted even though she put it all in her mouth.

All she knew was that someone—probably Eric—steered her to their table, sat her in the chair in front of the place card with her name on it and pointed her to a fork. After that she ate blindly and mindlessly, made lame small talk with the couples on either side and tried not to stare across the table at Eric.

At the first possible opportunity, just as the servers were clearing the dinner plates, she fell back on one of her favorite excuses—walking the dog—left the table, and took Zeus down to the beach where she could think.

Leaving her strappy stilettos at the bottom of the steps from the deck, she walked along the water's edge and watched the pink sunset, too upset even to stop Zeus from splashing in the waves and ruining his little bow tie with the salt and spray.

Eric was in love with her. Eric had hinted that…he wanted to marry her.

And she'd never been more terrified in her life.

Her emotions had developed multiple personalities on her, wavering between devastation and elation with devastation winning by a mile. Because she could never marry—not anyone and *especially* not Eric—and now she would have to tell Eric why. Once she did, she would lose his love. It was inevitable.

To her surprise, there were a lot of doubts she didn't have; somewhere along the way, probably after his absolute tenderness and worship last night, her fears had evaporated. He said he loved her and she believed him.

Maybe she was just flat-out stupid—Eric wasn't exactly the ideal candidate for a long-term, monogamous relationship, after all—but she took him at his word. There had been too much adoration in his eyes and his touch for the last few days, too much emotion for her to doubt his feelings.

True, he'd never been in love before, but so what?

That didn't mean he couldn't love *now*.

She, on the other hand, had been in love, or what she'd *thought* was love, twice before, and she'd been wrong. No other experience in her life, no relationship, no lover, compared in any way to her feelings about Eric. There wasn't even a close second.

Nor did she doubt that he wanted to marry her, or that he'd be a faithful husband. Eric didn't do things halfway and he wouldn't promise anything he couldn't deliver. Yeah, she'd have to fend off the constant onslaught of hoochies trying to hit on him if she married him, but the thought, strangely, didn't bother her.

Eric was too handsome, too special, too incredible for other women not to notice. But he loved Isabella and, if she married him—which she *wouldn't,* she would make him so happy there'd never be an opening for another woman to creep through. Isabella would make sure of it.

But…children of his own.

Eric wanted them. How many kids had she seen him cuddle

and play with over the years? Baby Andy, all her nieces and nephews and countless other kids—Eric welcomed them all, loved them all.

He deserved his own family and that was the one thing she could never give him. And regardless of how much she loved him and how lonely she'd be without him, she could not doom him to life without holding his own child in his arms. She just couldn't do it.

Zeus, who'd been splashing several feet out and yapping at a few seagulls who were foolish enough to fly low overhead, came back, shook his coat dry and sat at her feet. As always when she was feeling bad, he studied her with those soulful brown eyes, looking concerned.

Emotions choked her throat and pooled in her eyes, threatening to bubble over in a sob because this one silly dog would soon be all she had left and was the closest thing she'd ever have to a child of her own.

"Isabella?"

Startled, she swiped her eyes and turned to see the poorly-timed arrival of the one person who could make this night worse. Alphonso Grant, her college love approached with a hesitant half smile on his face.

Her first surprised thoughts were that he'd changed, and not for the better. He was unpleasantly plump now. His fair skin had that sunny flush that everyone acquired when they visited Florida, but the dimples that framed his mouth when she last saw him all those years ago had turned to grooves.

Maybe it was catty of her to notice, but his dark hair had thinned through the temples and would soon be a full-fledged bald spot. He'd shaved his mustache and she had the uncharitable thought that his thin upper lip needed it back, but, really, she'd long stopped caring enough about him to think any thoughts about him, charitable or otherwise.

"Al." Years of Mama Jo's politeness training kicked in and Isabella dredged up a welcoming smile when what she really wanted to do was ask him to leave her alone. "How are you? Terri didn't mention that you'd be here."

He hesitated and then leaned in to brush her cheek with his dry lips. She wasn't quite sure what the protocol was for greeting first loves—somewhere between a handshake and a hug, she supposed—but this seemed appropriate. He gave her the full smile and it tugged at something deep inside her, something long-buried and nostalgic, but mostly she felt surprise that she'd ever thought this man was so handsome. Compared to Eric's prince, Al was definitely the frog.

"We got a cheap last-minute flight, so here we are."

"We?" she asked out of faint curiosity. "Are you married?"

"Yeah." At the mere mention of his wife, he began to glow. This, too, tugged at Isabella's heart, but not the way she'd thought it would years ago when he left her, heartbroken and alone, to wonder why he didn't love her. "We live in Boston now. I'm a day trader. She's a dermatologist."

"That's wonderful," she said, meaning it.

"And you're with Eric, huh?" Something in his expression tightened, grew darker. "I knew that would happen sooner or later."

There was no way she'd discuss Eric with him. "I should get back."

"Izzy." Urgent now, he put a restraining hand on her arm even though she hadn't yet moved away. His voice dropped, becoming choked and husky. "I think about…*everything,* and—"

"Don't." Alarmed, she backed away because she absolutely could not deal with this now.

"—I think about it a lot and I want you to know that I'm *sorry.*"

Isabella gaped at him, sudden anger almost blinding her, and let him have it the way she should have back then. Then, she snapped.

"Sorry? *Sorry?* Well. How nice. Doesn't that just make everything okay after all these years? You decide you're *sorry* so now everything's magically supposed to be right with the world? Is that it?" Her voice was low and deep, wounded.

All the old anger rose up, making her cheeks hot and her vision blurry. There'd been times, over the years, when she'd imagined this scene, pictured herself slapping him, spitting on him or sweetly telling him to go to hell when he begged her for a second chance. The thought of him suffering and feeling one-millionth as bad as she'd felt had gotten her through many long nights of crying all those years ago.

"I'm sorry," he said again.

"You hurt me," she whispered. "Do you get that? Do you have any idea how long it took me to recover from what you did to me? You weren't there for me. You didn't support me. I couldn't lean on you for one damn thing. Do you even care that you said you loved me and then abandoned me?"

"Yes, I care. I'm ashamed of myself. Please forgive me, Izzy." He passed a hand over his wet eyes and she was surprised to see it tremble. "I need you to forgive me."

No, she wanted to snarl. *I don't forgive you. I can't have children practically because of you. I'll never forgive you.*

But then she thought: what was the point? He was sorry, she was sorry, and it was over. Life went on and she couldn't waste any more time being bitter. Nor would she introduce her infertility into this already painful discussion. Al didn't know and he felt bad enough as it was. And she couldn't handle everything else.

"It's okay." The words were out of her mouth before she could stop them, but she didn't want to take them back. *Surprise, surprise.* Her sudden anger was waning, as fleeting as a tropical summer storm now that she'd had the chance to vent. *This was good,* she thought. This was right. This was unfinished business from her old life that she needed to address. She could do this. "*Really.* It's okay. I just needed to say my piece, and I needed to hear you apologize and mean it."

A choked sound—half laugh, half sob—rose up out of Al and he grabbed her hand. "Thank you." She resisted the urge to pull away even though she felt lighter and better. "Thank you."

This wasn't so bad, really. They'd been close once and, although they'd never be close again, she didn't want to hate him or even feel nothing for him. All of her intimate conversations with her mother had led to this.

"I mean it," she said. "I wish you and your wife the best—"

He started glowing again, brighter this time. "You're not going to believe this, Izzy, but—"

A sickening pit opened up in the depths of her belly because she somehow knew what was coming: agony of the worst kind. The one thing she couldn't deal with—not now, not with this man, not with the yawning emptiness inside her that would never be filled with Eric's child.

"No," she said, feeling dizzy.

There was a limit to how much she could absorb…how much she could forgive…how much Al should expect of her. What he was going to say would push her well past that limit, possibly all the way into insanity.

No, no, no. Please, God, no.

Snatching her hand free, she shook her head to stop him but it was too late because the words were already coming and her ears were already listening.

"—Lana's pregnant. We're going to have a little girl next month."

"Oh, my God."

The unstoppable words spewed from her mouth in an awful screech and she struggled to keep her legs under her and hang on to Zeus's leash. For one awful second her heartsickness crossed over into light-headedness and she bent at the waist, certain she would faint.

She had a distant awareness of Al's cry of alarm and his hands wrapping around her, holding her up. And then there was a shout from a new voice followed by a splash.

Her dimmed vision cleared enough for Eric, looking wild eyed and frantic, to come sprinting into view. She had the non-sensical thought that he must really be upset to run through the waves and get sand and salt water on his expensive shoes and pants because Eric hated messes, especially on his clothes.

"What did you do to her, you son of a bitch?" Sneering and growling, Eric shoved Al out of the way, looking as though he'd like nothing better than to dismember the smaller man with his hands and teeth.

"I didn't do *anything*." Al's jaw flapped helplessly. "We were talking—"

But Eric had already dismissed Al and pulled Isabella into his arms with surprising tenderness. "Izzy. Are you okay, Sunshine? What happened?"

Isabella was feeling stronger now, and with the strength came embarrassment. What just happened here? She was making a scene because Al could have children and she couldn't? What was wrong with her? And now Al would go back to the reception and tell everyone what'd happened, and soon all her friends would think she was cracking up. Maybe she *was* cracking up. But they didn't need to know that.

"I'm okay." Pulling free of Eric's resisting arms, she swiped at her eyes and was dismayed to discover that her cheeks were wet. She hastily blotted her face with her palms. "I just…I'm a little tired—we've had a long trip—and I have…you know, a migraine. But I'm fine. Please don't make a scene, okay? I just need a little rest."

Al nodded, looking relieved, but Eric wasn't so easily convinced.

"Izzy," he began.

"*Fine*," she repeated, more firmly this time. "Why are you here?"

Eric's expression cooled and hardened. Closed off and locked her out. He held up his cell phone, which she'd been too upset to notice until now. "The jet's coming for us in about an hour. We need to get to the airport if we want to make it back for Andy's baptism in the morning."

A *baptism*. Isabella looked skyward in desperation, praying for the strength to get through a baptism and wondering how many more pregnant women and babies God was going to send her way this weekend.

"Yeah, okay," she said. "Give me a minute."

Eric muttered something she couldn't quite hear, although she caught the gist and shot him a glare, which he ignored. Turning to Al, she smiled and spoke with sincerity because a precious new baby was coming into the world and Al seemed to have grown into a man who would make a wonderful father.

"I'm really happy for you and your wife. Please give her my best wishes."

Al leaned in to kiss her cheek and she stiffened, teetering on the edge of a full crying jag. "And you have my best."

"And you're going to have my foot up your ass if you touch Izzy or make her cry again," Eric told Al, baring his teeth in a snarling abomination of a smile.

"Eric." Isabella reached for his hand lest she needed to keep him from tackling Al to the ground and pummeling him to dust.

Eric tensed and jerked free.

Al, who should have known better than to provoke Eric at this dangerous juncture—Eric was obviously holding himself in check only by the thinnest margin—shook his head and tightened his jaw.

"You never liked me, man. Did you?"

"No," Eric said flatly. "Never did, never will."

Al glared and lingered, as though he wanted to state his case for not being as big a jerk as Eric thought he was, but then Al's one ounce of good sense finally kicked in and he left well enough alone.

Muttering darkly, he turned and walked off toward the reception, and Eric focused all his considerable energy on Isabella.

"What happened, Izzy? What'd he say to you?"

Staring up into Eric's worried face, hearing the husky urgency in his voice and feeling his tentative touch on her cheek, Isabella couldn't.

She just…couldn't.

There was no way she could explain things to Eric right now, pretend that she was okay when she wasn't or even reassure him that she would soon be okay. All those things required much more effort than she could muster.

"I…can't." She stepped away from his touch. "I can't do this now."

"We have to do it."

"But not now, Eric."

These words got exactly the kind of negative reception she'd expected. Eric stilled except for a telltale darkening of his expression and the rhythmic pulsing in his jaw. For several endless beats he stared past her at the surf, apparently collecting himself. When he looked back at her, his voice was soft but his eyes were fierce.

"You spend five minutes with that guy, and now I can't touch you?"

"Not right now, no."

"When?"

"I don't know."

"Are you still in love with him? Is that it?"

"No," she cried. *"God, no.* Why would you think that?"

"Because the only other thing that could've upset you this afternoon is me telling you I love you." His strangled voice dropped until it was barely audible over the waves. "And I can't stand the thought of you crying because I want to marry you."

The need to reassure him when he was so hurt and vulnerable was too powerful for her to ignore. "That's not it."

"What is it then? I know you're hiding things from me. Don't deny it."

The long list of things she needed to explain scrolled through her brain and it was all she could do not to sink to her knees in the sand and howl like Zeus did when she put him in his crate.

It would be a relationship-ending conversation. She knew that. Eric would look at her with new eyes and want nothing to do with her. Maybe the best thing to do would be tell him tonight on the plane and have him stop in Cincinnati so she could go straight home. He wouldn't want to take her to the baptism after this.

"We can talk on the plane and then you could drop me off in Cincin—"

"No," he said flatly, his face turning to stone. "You said you'd come to the baptism. And anyway we'll be sharing the plane with some of my execs so we won't have any privacy."

"Okay." Tears burned the backs of Isabella's eyes, but she would not let them fall. She was Mama Jo's daughter and she was strong and could get through the baptism and dealing with Eric's family and telling Eric. She had to get through it. "Can we talk tomorrow, then? After the baptism?"

"*Tomorrow?* Is it that bad?"

She couldn't bring herself to add to the flare of panic she saw in his face, so she said nothing.

He seemed to glean the worst. "You're scaring me to death, Isabella."

"I don't mean to."

They stared at each other, time suspended. Zeus played at their feet, frantically digging in the sand looking for a scurrying yellow crab. Above them, on the deck, lanterns glowed and the faint strains of music—"Unforgettable," she thought—began.

Finally Eric let out a long, harsh, serrated breath. "We have to go."

"Okay."

He didn't move and in his dark eyes she saw emotions as changeable and turbulent as the crashing waves ten feet away. It hurt to see him so upset and know she'd done this to him, but she couldn't—*simply could not*—tell him her deepest secrets and then spend all day tomorrow with his family pretending nothing was wrong.

"Please." Swallowing hard, he held out a hand. "I need to touch you."

Isabella hesitated, but not for long. She needed his touch and needed the illusion that their trip was still fun and they were still lovers. Even if it was just an illusion, she needed it.

She stepped into his open arms.

They clung to each other and she didn't know whose need was greater or whose touch was the most desperate. All she knew was that for these last few seconds, on this beautiful beach under this exquisite sunset, she wanted to gather a little of his strength and imprint what it felt like to have his love on her memory and body.

His hands settled up under the hair at her nape, anchoring her him while he kissed her cheeks and whispered fiercely in her ear.

"I love you, Isabella. *Love you.* There's nothing you can't tell me. Whatever it is, I'll understand. I promise you. *Promise* you."

Poor Eric, she thought, digging her fingers into his shoulders to keep him close and teetering between hysterical laughter and hysterical sobs. He'd never make such a futile promise if he had any idea what she needed to confess.

Chapter 16

Early the next morning, Eric was standing in his grandmother's library at Heather Hill, staring out the glass doors at the pool—seeing nothing and wallowing in his miserable thoughts and fears—when a voice spoke behind him.

"What are you doing here?"

Andrew. Eric winced because he hadn't heard any footsteps and it was too damned early to deal with Andrew, especially considering the horrendous night he'd had. After saying a quick goodbye to the newlyweds, he and Izzy had left the reception, sped to the airport, hopped on the Lear and shared the flight back to Columbus with a couple of WarnerBrands executives. There'd been no opportunity to talk even if he'd been able to convince Izzy to abandon her clam routine and open up about what was troubling her.

Then, to his further dismay, she'd refused to go back to his house with him even though she always stayed there when she visited, insisting instead on spending the night at the cottage here at Heather Hill. Her obvious need to get away from him was a sickening blow to his ego from which he hadn't recovered.

What the hell had happened? Eric's disoriented brain still whirled with confusion, as though he'd just stepped off one of those stupid spinning carnival rides. Ten minutes alone on the beach with Al, and Izzy had become a different person. Aloof, quiet, hurting…walled off in some dark place where Eric couldn't reach her. Unwilling even to spend the night under the same roof with him, much less let him make love to her.

And he, whipped punk that he was, had elected to sleep in his old bedroom here at the mansion rather than travel the five minutes to his own house and sleep in his own bed. *What if Izzy needed him?* he'd thought. *Hah.* There'd been no peep from Isabella, no whimper, no sign of her continued existence other than the warm glow of a lamp visible behind the closed shutters at the cottage. For all he knew she'd escaped to Mexico during the night.

Now here he was, running on fumes from another sleepless night. Oh, but there was more. On top of everything else, he now had to deal with his family, starting with Andrew. Scowling, Eric turned away from the view of the sparkling aquamarine waters of the Olympic-sized swimming pool.

"What am I doing here?" he echoed. "You might recall that *you* asked me to drop everything I was doing and cut my Florida trip short so I could be here for *your* son's baptism."

But Eric's irritation died as soon as he saw who Andrew had with him. Baby Andy, who was about a year old now and as adorable as ever, was slung over the shoulder of Andrew's navy suit jacket, chomping on one of those colorful chewy toy things that he held in his chubby little hand.

The poor child wore the unfortunate starched white suit of a baby about to be baptized and Eric wondered if they'd be able to keep it clean long enough for the ceremony. Behind Andrew trailed his adopted son, Nathan, who was now about ten years old.

Nathan wore a miniature version of Andrew's dark suit, and his black shoes were shined to a sleek finish. Instead of a red power tie like Andrew's, Nathan wore the bow tie with the *Star Wars* logo on it that Eric had given him at Christmas.

The boy had his head bent low and his face scrunched up over his beeping, chirping handheld computer game. Without watching where he was going, Nathan wandered to the nearest sofa, stopped when he bumped his shins against it, turned, and collapsed on it. Never once did his fingers stop flying over the game.

Eric grinned, his bad mood dissipating.

The kids were really something. Eric had always liked children, but these two were clearly exceptional. *His* children— God willing and assuming he had a major breakthrough with Izzy and convinced her to marry him—would be like this: smart, adorable and irresistible.

All his life he'd known that one day he'd have children and add to the Warner family tree, unfortunate though it was. But for the first time he felt that ache of longing in his chest. That raw need to make love with the woman he loved, to watch her belly swell and see her nursing his child. That primitive desire to hold his child in his arms and teach it, protect it.

Eric could even see the blurry outline of his and Isabella's future baby. She'd—he didn't know how he knew their first child would be a girl—have Isabella's pretty brown skin and eyes and the same lush pouty lips. Maybe his height, but maybe not, and it didn't really matter either way.

All those platitudes he'd always heard from expectant parents—*We don't care what the baby looks like, we just want a healthy child*—now seemed like the wisdom of the ages. A healthy child and a loving wife was all Eric wanted or needed from his life. Could the universe offer a man any greater blessing? For the first time he felt impatient and realized he was ready for the adventure to begin, ready for that next, and most important, chapter of his life.

So, yeah, he wanted children. In the meantime, he'd enjoy these two.

"What's up, man?" Eric rubbed his hand across Nathan's skull trim, shaking the boy's little head until it wobbled. "What's the good word?"

"No good word." Nathan didn't tear his gaze from the game

but raised one hand long enough to receive Eric's high five. "Andy can pull himself up now. And he tried to eat my baseball mitt." Nathan stuck his tongue out in a disgusted scowl. *"Gross."*

Laughing, Eric shook Andrew's hand and reached for the baby. "Come here, little guy. *Come here.*"

"What I meant was," Andrew said, passing the baby along and then sitting on a loveseat, "what are you doing here *now?* I thought you were meeting us at the church in an hour."

"Yeah, well. Change of plans."

Big upsetting change of plans, but Eric didn't want to dwell on that, especially with little Andy in his arms. He balanced the baby's sturdy weight on his hip and Andy stopped chomping on his rubbery toy long enough to give him an intent blue-eyed stare that was a miniature copy, down to the heavy straight brows, of his father's.

No need for any paternity tests here, Eric thought; Andy was his father's son, no question. The baby studied Eric with the keen intelligence that was to be expected of any child of Viveca's and Andrew's, and then, apparently deciding that Eric was, in fact, okay, gave him a wide, dimpled smile featuring four tiny but perfectly square teeth—two on top, two on the bottom—like Chiclets.

Some answering chord of emotion squeezed Eric's heart hard. Laughing, he leaned in to kiss Andy's fat cheek, and Andy seemed to think that was the funniest thing that had ever happened in his young life. Giggling and delighted, he offered his toy to Eric, who pretended to take a loud bite. Andy screamed with laughter.

The drumming of high heels in the hall announced the coming of a woman, and they all looked around to see Viveca stride in looking beautiful, as always. She'd done something with her hair and it was longer and straighter now, but that wasn't the only different thing about her. Her blue dress emphasized the generous curve of her bosom and, below that, the small but unmistakable curve of a baby bump.

Seeing the direction of Eric's gaze, she grinned and

shrugged—*What can you do?*—and they both laughed. Eric
pulled her in for a hug against his baby-free side. Viveca was
one of his favorite people in the world and unmistakably the best
thing that had ever happened to Andrew in his life.

"Another boy," she told him.

"For crying out loud, man," Eric said to Andrew over the top
of Viveca's head. "Can't you give this poor woman a chance to
catch her breath?"

"That would be a negative." Andrew gave Viveca a swift pro-
prietary glance—the look was filled with immense satisfaction,
like a cat that'd jacked a milk truck—but had the grace to flush.
"And that's enough of you hugging my wife. I told you to get your
own."

"I'm working on it," Eric muttered before he could stop
himself.

Andrew looked around with surprise.

"Uh-oh," Viveca murmured, perching on the arm of Nathan's
sofa. "You've done it now, Eric."

Eric had already figured that out from Andrew's laser-sharp
gaze, which was now riveted to his face. Eric tried not to fidget
although he couldn't stop his cheeks from heating. Andrew's
eyes narrowed and a shrewd, sly smile, the kind that was always
a precursor of trouble, crossed his face.

"Oh no," he said on an annoying laugh. "So *that's* what the
two of you were yakking about on the phone."

Eric and Viveca shot each other furtive glances, saying
nothing, and then Eric concentrated on Andy, who was now
purposely dropping his toy on the nearest side table so Eric re-
peatedly had to pick it up. None of this deterred Andrew, who
now looked positively gleeful.

"Isabella making you jump through a few hoops, is she?"
Andrew shook his head in a mock-regretful way that made Eric
want to tackle him to the floor and acquaint the side of his face
with the antique Persian rug. "Want me to talk to her for you?"

"No," Eric said, making a rude gesture. "I want you to go—"

"*Children,*" Viveca quickly interjected, clapping her hands over an oblivious Nathan's ears. "There are *children* in the room."

Andrew laughed and held out a hand to his wife, who got up and moved to his love seat. The two of them settled together until they were practically in each other's laps, with one of Andrew's hands around Viveca's shoulders and the other on her belly.

Eric felt renewed irritation. "Why don't you two get a room?"

One of Andrew's heavy brows rose with smug amusement. "Given your rotten mood," he drawled, "I can only assume that things are not going well with you and the lovely Isabella. Did you blow it already?"

"No," Eric snapped. He supposed this was karma coming back to bite him in the ass since Andrew was teasing Eric the way Eric had teased Andrew last year, when he and Viveca had hit a rough patch. "We've just got a few things to work out."

This time it was Viveca who narrowed her eyes at Eric. "You didn't—"

"No." Eric glowered, not bothering to hide his annoyance. His increased volume earned him a perplexed and vaguely worried frown from Andy. Eric soothed him by rubbing his back, and then lowered his voice. *"I* haven't done *anything,* so don't start accusing me."

"She's not still leaving…?" Viveca asked.

"Leaving?" Andrew looked from Viveca to Eric. "Where's she going?"

There was a long pause during which Eric wished he'd cut out his own tongue with pinking shears rather than open this whole topic for discussion with Andrew. "Johannesburg. To teach."

This, finally, seemed to kill Andrew's amusement. "Shit, man," he said, pity creeping across his face. "You've got a serious problem."

"Who's got a problem?"

They all looked around to see the owner of this new voice, Arnetta Warner, the family matriarch, sweep in from the hallway. Today the Silver Fox wore a bright blue suit along with her usual strand of fat gumball pearls, and held a pair of white gloves and a hat that seemed to have a peacock's worth of feathers hanging from it.

Close on her heels came Franklin Bishop, the man who'd started out a thousand years ago as the butler and was now concierge, personal assistant, manager and occasional confessor to the entire Warner clan.

"Good morning, Grandmother." Eric balanced the baby, leaned in to kiss the cheek Arnetta tilted up for him and shook Bishop's hand. "Did you sleep well?"

"Yes-I-did!" Arnetta, who lost all sense of decorum whenever her great-grandson was in the room, grinned at Andy, shook his chubby little hand, and spoke in the singsong voice that people couldn't help adopting when addressing a baby. "Yes-I-did-sleep-well! *Yes-I-did!*"

Andy laughed and reached for Arnetta, who happily, though gingerly, took him. "Andrew," she said, her voice crisp now, "where is this boy's blanket? I don't want to get drool on my suit before—oh, here it is."

Bishop passed her a yellow blanket. Arnetta sat next to Nathan, kissed the top of his head, and then arranged Andy on her lap. Andy immediately twisted at the waist, reached for Arnetta's pearl necklace, and tried to put it in his mouth. Arnetta pulled the pearls away and turned to Eric.

"If the problem you were referring to is Isabella's dress for church," she said, "I'm happy to loan her one of my suits. That dress she had on last night when you got here was a little, ah, colorful, dear."

Eric tried not to be too irritated at this doting grandmother, but he just couldn't manage it. *What was it with this family?* Appearances were always far more important than anything else. Better to be a couture-clad witch, for instance, than a kind soul who shopped the sales at Macy's. Better to maintain a miserable fifty-year marriage than put the family through the scandal of a divorce. The content of your character didn't matter around here as long as you looked like you belonged.

"I loved that dress," Eric said flatly. In dire need of fortification, he headed for the granite-topped bar in the corner. "I love it that Isabella always dresses like a flower garden exploded on her. I love Isabella. I want to marry Isabella. Bloody Mary, anyone?"

"Eric." Too scandalized to maintain her baby voice, Arnetta turned to track his progress across the room. "You can't drink before *church*—"

"With the kind of morning I'm having?" Eric splashed vodka in a tumbler and topped it with tomato juice and hot sauce. Normally he drank very little and never in the morning, but on a day like this, such measures seemed basic and essential. "God will understand."

"—and what's this nonsense about marrying Isabella? Why on earth would you want to marry a kindergarten teacher from Greenville, North Carolina, when you can do so much better?"

"Better than what?" Eric snarled. "Marrying a wonderful free spirit who makes me happy? There's something better than that?"

"Who's getting married?" asked a new voice.

No, Eric prayed as he glanced over his shoulder. *Please no. Not them.*

He froze, wholly unprepared for this kind of horror so early in the day. He'd known his parents were in town, of course, but that knowledge didn't prepare him for hearing his mother's voice, which had exactly as much warmth and emotion as the voice of Hal the vengeful computer in *2001: A Space Odyssey,* or for seeing her walk into the room on the arm of Eric's father, the man who'd hated her for the bulk of their forty-year marriage.

Recovering in what he thought was a reasonable period of time, all things considered, Eric raised his glass, toasted the massive oil painting of his late unlamented grandfather, Reynolds Warner, which frowned down at the proceedings from over the mantel, and, with a flick of his wrist, downed the entire Bloody Mary in two hard gulps.

Spicy and coppery, the drink burned his throat and cleared his sinuses, but did nothing for the red anger clouding his vision at having to deal with his parents. Still, a quick drink was better than nothing and he was glad to have it.

Thus armed, Eric made the slow turn to face his parents, Gifford and Della Warner, the poster children for Passive-Aggressives Anonymous.

They were the same, of course. Spending part of the year in Phoenix would never change their core nastiness. Mother was still tall, thin and sleek, with perfect makeup highlighting her Botoxed face, and her hair perfectly done in that same French twist she'd been wearing since the Nixon administration.

Someone seeing her for the first time might have an initial impression of a black Grace Kelly in her tailored gray suit with wide belt, but that quickly passed because Della gave new meaning to the term cool elegance.

Her eternal lack of human warmth, her complete inability to smile, and her unwillingness to engage with people on any kind of personal level made her, as far as Eric was concerned, a human mannequin. It was a constant surprise to him, whenever he kissed her cold cheek, like now, to realize she was made out of flesh rather than marble.

As for his father, well, Gifford Warner was no more a man than a neutered bovine was a bull. From the day of their marriage all those years ago, Della had grabbed the poor guy by the balls and held them, twisted, in the fisted grip of her manicured hand.

From his stooped shoulders swimming inside the seersucker suit that Della had no doubt picked out and told him to wear, to his hesitant voice and distant, usually vacant expression, Gifford, the second, usually forgotten son of Arnetta and Reynolds, screamed that he was a man who'd checked out of life years ago and saw no need to check back in.

"Mother. Dad." Eric mustered what he thought was a passable smile as he shook his father's hand, but apparently it wasn't up to snuff because Della managed to unfreeze her Botoxed forehead long enough to frown at him.

"It's been six months since we came back home to Cincinnati, Eric." She sat in a tall-backed chair, crossed her legs and smoothed her skirt while her husband escaped to a chair in the farthest corner of the room and disappeared behind a newspaper. "You could look a little happier to see us."

Eric almost snorted. Why would anyone ever be glad to see *them?* They brought a cold front with them wherever they went, like a traveling iceberg.

Already everyone in the room was looking distinctly uncomfortable. Andrew shot Eric a sympathetic glance and tightened his arms around Viveca as though he needed to protect her and their unborn child from nuclear fallout. Arnetta and Bishop exchanged worried looks and Baby Andy made a fretful noise.

Even Nathan, who'd been engrossed in his own little world this whole time, looked up from his game and squinted at Della and Gifford through his wire-framed glasses. No doubt the negative energy emanating from Eric's dysfunctional parents was now interfering with the game's batteries. If things kept up like this, the electricity in the mansion would flicker and die.

"Mother," Eric said with utmost sarcasm, "who wouldn't be glad to see *you?*"

To no one's surprise, she ignored this barb. "What did you say about getting married? Or was I hearing things?"

"Nope." Eric figured he might as well jump in with both feet and get the whole ordeal over with. "I was just saying I want to marry Isabella."

Gifford peered out from around his newspaper.

"Isabella?" Della's dramatically lined cat eyes narrowed with obvious dismay. "Your little friend from college? The one with the tie-dyed dresses? Isn't her father an *electrician?*"

This dismissal of the woman he loved on the basis of her clothes and father's occupation left Eric speechless with rage, but a new voice joined the conversation.

Nathan put his game down and spoke with a child's earnest conviction. "I like Isabella. I think Eric should marry her."

Viveca and Andrew smiled at Nathan. "You know what, son?" Andrew said. "I agree. I like her, too."

"Of course *you* agree," Della murmured in her silkiest voice as Gifford disappeared back behind his paper. "You seem to have picked a wife on the basis of her, ah, obvious breeding skills."

This comment, which was nasty even by Della's standards, elicited an outraged bark of laughter from Viveca, but Andrew was already on his feet, his face purple with rage.

"You know what, Della?" Andrew forced the words through his throbbing jaw and tight lips. "If Isabella can make Eric a fourth as happy as Viveca has made me, then he'll be the *second* luckiest man in the world." Here he paused and turned to address the far corner of the room. "Gifford, you didn't make the luckiest-man-in-the-world list, but then you probably already know that."

There was a faint cough from behind the newspaper.

Della sprang to her feet and wheeled around to face her husband. "Are you going to let Andrew talk to me like that, Gifford?" she said to the newspaper.

"Of course he is," Andrew said with relish. "The poor man's just grateful someone stood up to you for a change—"

One of Gifford's bespectacled eyes peered out from around the paper. Eric thought he saw a hint of a smile on his father's face, but he wasn't sure.

"—and since he won't keep you in line," Andrew continued, "*I* will."

Della spluttered.

"If you ever talk to or about my wife that way again," Andrew finished, "I will make you sorry for the day you were born."

Della clamped her jaws shut, not daring to speak for once in her life.

Eric, who suddenly and unaccountably had the first strains of "Ding Dong! The Witch is Dead" from *The Wizard of Oz* running through his brain, wanted to clap Andrew on the shoulder but satisfied himself with winking instead.

Andrew winked back.

Everyone else seemed stunned. A shocked silence descended over the room and Andy, who'd obviously heard the anger in his father's voice, let out an experimental cry, looking as though he couldn't decide how upset he needed to be. Arnetta patted his back and tried to sooth him, but Nathan took over.

"You scared Andy," he accused the room at large. Standing, he picked up his baby brother, who gratefully opened his arms for him, snuggled against his shoulder, and peered out at everyone in a clear attempt to determine whether the room was safe or not. "He's only a baby," Nathan continued. "You can't yell around babies."

Holding Andy with surprising tenderness, Nathan turned on his little polished heel and marched out of the room looking furious. Abashed, they all stared after him until Bishop, muttering, got to his feet and hurried after them.

"I better make sure those two don't get into trouble," he said.

Della, of course, recovered first and resumed her rant. "Eric," she said, her voice rising until it could probably be heard in every far corner of the mansion. "Why can't you have an affair with this girl? You don't have to *marry* her. I *mean*—" she paused, at an apparent loss as to how to explain something so obvious "—don't you want the mother of your children to come from a nice family—"

"A nice family?" Eric interjected. "What—like this one?"

"I just don't understand why you'd want to rush into marriage with—"

"Good morning, everyone," chirped a new voice. "I hope I'm not late. The limo's waiting out front."

Isabella breezed into the room bringing sunshine and light with her as far as Eric was concerned. Though he could see the faint dark smudges under her eyes that were a sign of her sleepless night, she had her game face on and was more than ready for a morning swim in this shark tank called a library, which was good because she'd no doubt heard every word his poor excuse for a mother had just said.

Isabella wore exactly the kind of colorful flowered dress— mostly orange this time—that Arnetta had probably feared, but Eric thought she was the most beautiful thing he'd ever seen, or ever would see.

Her gaze briefly met his and mischief sparkled in her eyes. Eric had a clear glimpse of her wicked smile—he could see it even if no one else could—before she walked up to Della and, throwing her arms around her, locked her in the kind of bear hug that made ice cubes like Della recoil in horror.

"It's *so* nice to see you again, Della." Isabella held on and swayed with the woman, ignoring Della's rigidity and staunch refusal to participate in the hug. "My parents said to tell you hello." After a long ten seconds or so, Isabella pulled free, stepped back and held up the hem of her skirt. "I hope my dress is okay for church. I wasn't sure if it was bright enough or not."

Here she blinked up at Della, all innocence and earnest hope. While everyone else in the room struggled not to laugh, Della stammered and flushed.

"Well, I—" Della began.

But Isabella had already turned and walked to Gifford, who put down his newspaper, stood and grinned at her.

"*Gifford,*" she cried, sincere, Eric knew, but with a thick layer of Southern charm added to her greeting. "Aren't you a handsome devil in seersucker? Give me a kiss."

Oblivious to his wife's wintry glare, Gifford laughed and hugged Isabella, breaking away only after he'd given her a smacking kiss on the cheek. "How are you, girl?"

"I'm great. My mama sent me with some peanut butter fudge 'specially for you. You still eat it, don't you?"

Gifford's face went slack with rapture. "Do I still eat it? Is the pope Catholic?"

"Good." Beaming, Isabella linked her arm through Gifford's and steered him toward the door. Eric fell in line after them.

Gifford, grinning and happy, as though thirty seconds with Isabella had trimmed thirty years off his age, turned to look at Eric as they passed through the door. "I don't care what your mother says, son," he said in a stage whisper. "You don't want to let this one get away."

"I don't plan to," Eric said, as he saw a shadow crossing Izzy's face.

Chapter 17

A luncheon on the terrace followed the baptism, but as soon as they could reasonably break away, Isabella and Eric went back to the cottage where she'd spent the night. She'd stayed there several times before over the years, and nothing much ever changed.

The curtains still fluttered in the open windows, the weathered country antiques were still covered with more pillows than a sultan could use for his harem and glass bowls of roses from Arnetta's garden still dotted most flat surfaces. The cottage was, as always, a warm little slice of heaven tailor-made for lovers. It was not the place where Isabella wanted to tell Eric everything he'd never known about her life.

Things between them had been strained all morning and they now sat on an overstuffed sofa in the kind of awkward silence they'd rarely shared before. They watched Zeus—today wearing his orange and black Cincinnati Bengals jersey—bring Fluffles in from the bedroom and settle with him on the floor under the coffee table, but then that tiny bit of entertainment was over and there was nothing to do but start talking.

"I missed you last night." Eric's expression was dark and subdued, his voice husky. He'd gotten rid of his suit jacket a while back and rolled up the sleeves to his starched white shirt. Isabella could see the flexing tension of his heavy forearms as he gripped his knees. "I couldn't sleep at all without you."

Denying her feelings at this point never crossed Isabella's mind. "I missed you, too."

A flare of hope lightened his features, and he took one of her cold hands between his warm ones and held it tight enough for her to feel some of his strength flow into her. "I love you, Isabella."

Isabella paused because this was a big moment, one that had been fourteen years in the making. Today was a day for telling the truth and she was past the stammering denials and half lies she'd told her mother about her feelings for Eric. Today she owed him the entire story—all of her feelings and all her secrets.

"I love you, too."

He let out a bark of startled laughter but then quickly swallowed it, as though he'd been caught joking at a funeral. "You do?"

"I've been falling in love with you since I saw you at freshman orientation. I fell a little more every time you smiled at me, a little bit more every time we laughed together or you talked me through a hard time in my life. I fell a lot this weekend. Didn't you know that?"

Another laugh, relieved this time. *"No,"* he said. "I didn't know *anything.*"

Raising her hand, he pressed fevered kisses to it and then, as though he couldn't help himself and needed to indulge before the worst came, put a hand to her nape and claimed her mouth.

For those few precious seconds, Isabella kissed him back and pretended that there were no limits on this blinding happiness. That her heart could soar as high and free as it wanted because she wasn't about to smash it. That Eric would always love her this desperately—no matter what she ever told him.

The warring emotions were too much and erupted out of her

tight throat, half sob and half laugh. But then Eric held her face between his palms and rested his forehead against hers and he was laughing, joyous.

"I would never cheat on you, Isabella. You know that, right?"

"Yes."

She *did* know and his potential future infidelity, despite his unfortunate history with countless other women, was the least of her worries now. He'd loved her so thoroughly for the last few days that she no longer had room for doubt, on this one point at least. Eric would be a good and faithful husband but the problem was that in a few minutes he'd no longer want to marry her.

"I can make you happy if you give me the chance."

"I know you can," she said.

"Good girl."

He flashed a thrilled white smile and then took her mouth again in another kiss that was ravenous, deep and filled with endless possibilities. Finally he broke free and a new stillness fell over him until the only sounds in the universe were Zeus's gentle snores and Eric's labored breathing.

"Stay here," he said. "Marry me."

This time, for the first time, she held back the answer she wanted to give. Hot tears burned her eyes and some of them refused to be blinked back. After a long minute, she shook her head.

"Isabella." A new desperation roughened his voice and made his eyes wild. "I know you want to. Don't you?"

"Yes," she said helplessly. "But I can't."

With a growl of frustration, he turned her loose, flung himself against the back of the sofa, rested his head on the pillow and covered his eyes with his forearm. It took him forever to speak and when he did his voice sounded shaky. She couldn't tell whether it was from anger or fear.

"Why can't you?"

Here it was at last—the moment she'd dreaded for what seemed like half her life.

"Because when I tell you, you're not going to want to marry me anymore. You're not even going to love me anymore."

"I'll always love you," he said tiredly, pulling his arm down so he could see her.

"I doubt it."

"Tell me, Isabella."

Yes. She would tell him and she wouldn't be a crying mess when she did. She had made this bed and she would lie in it. There was time enough to cry later. Then she would move on. Clearing her tight throat, she scooted around until she sat on the coffee table facing him. After another deep breath or two, she was ready.

"That summer in college, when I went to South Africa? Remember that?"

"Yeah." Eric looked startled and wary. "For an internship, right?"

"No," she said quietly. "There was no internship. I never went."

There was a pause while Eric digested this lie, the only one she'd ever told him. "What happened then? You were gone for a whole semester. Where were you?"

"Home in Greenville. I needed time—"

"Because that SOB Al dumped you, right? And you were upset?"

"No. Well, that was part of it. But not all of it."

They stared at each other.

Something subtle in his expression shifted and hardened, and she realized then that he'd put two and two together and was beginning to understand. He didn't want to understand, wanted to believe he'd jumped to the wrong conclusion, but he *knew,* deep in his gut, where this was going.

"What's all of it, Isabella?" he asked quietly.

Isabella got up and slowly walked to the chair where she'd tossed her purse when they first arrived. Inside her wallet she found the picture she was looking for and pressed it to her heart for a minute. And then she turned, walked back to the coffee table, sat on it and handed the picture to Eric.

He didn't take it. Obviously didn't want to take it. His lip twisted and his jaw tightened and his cheek throbbed, but he didn't take the picture.

Though it was one of the hardest things she'd ever done in her life, Isabella held his hurt gaze and watched while moisture collected in his beloved brown eyes. When a single tear fell and trailed down his smooth skin, she saw that too and it tore her to pieces.

Finally he swallowed hard, blinked, took the picture and looked at it.

There was no point to her looking along with him because she'd memorized every detail long ago. A fourteen-year-old girl smiled out from that picture, with her shiny black hair in a riot of long twists. She had Isabella's chubby cheeks, bright eyes and dimpled smile, and she wore adorable tortoiseshell glasses that were just right for her face. It was the face of a happy, well-cared-for child who couldn't wait for life's next great adventure.

"My God," Eric whispered, his head bent low. "This could be you."

"Her name is Andrea Jacobs. She lives in St. Louis and she's in the ninth grade. She really likes math and science. She has a yellow Lab named Smiley and she's a Girl Scout. Oh, and last year she got her black belt in Tae Kwon Do."

Keeping her mother's pride out of her voice was impossible, so Isabella didn't even try. Eric, shell-shocked though he was, heard it, too. Raising his head, he worked at a smile but couldn't quite manage it.

"She's beautiful," he said. "Have you met her?"

"No." Isabella pressed a hand to her heart to hold back some of her misery and longing. "I held her for an hour when she was born, and her parents send me a picture and a letter every year on her birthday, but that's all. If she wants to meet me at some point, they'll support that, but so far she—" her voice broke and she had to pause to regroup "—she hasn't asked."

The weight of the picture in his hand seemed to be too much for Eric. He put it on the table, rested his elbows on his knees and dropped his head in his hands. Those forearms flexed again as he rubbed his eyes. When he next spoke it was with the weariness of a man who'd lived a thousand years and was tired of the world and all its problems.

"Why didn't you tell me?" he asked. "Why did you have to lie?"

A harsh laugh, bitter and ugly, rose up out of Isabella's throat. Even now she couldn't forgive herself for the foolish youthful mistakes she'd made. Even now she refused to grant herself absolution for ruining her young life so thoroughly.

"What?" she asked. "Tell you how foolish I was for falling for some idiot and getting pregnant after my parents took out a second mortgage and worked two jobs apiece to send me to an Ivy League school they couldn't afford?" Renewed shame flattened her, the way it always did when she remembered this dark portion of her distant past. "Hell, Eric. It was hard enough to tell *them*."

Eric looked up and his expression was fierce and unyielding enough to startle her. "Yeah, but they understood and I would have, too, if you'd given me the chance."

"I couldn't do it," she said simply, coming as close to an apology as she could get. "I wanted you to think better of me."

"Why are you being so hard on yourself?" His voice rose with obvious frustration at her intransigence. "What college kid alive hasn't gotten in some kind of trouble? Why should you be different?"

"I couldn't do it," she said again. "I just couldn't."

Silence fell. She welcomed the quiet and gave him a minute or two to absorb all this information. He sat staring across the room for a long time, as still and silent as a forgotten grave, without even the flutter of his lashes or the rise and fall of his chest to tell her he hadn't turned to stone.

Slowly he came out of his thoughts, blinking first and then turning to look at her with eyes that were wounded but still, miraculously, loving. One corner of his mouth hitched up in an unsuccessful attempt at a wry smile.

"I'm almost relieved," he told her. "Thank you for telling me."

"Eric," she began quickly.

Cupping her face in his warm palm, he stroked one thumb over her cheek in a gesture of extreme tenderness that ripped her heart right out of her chest and tore it to bits.

"Eric—"

"But you had to know I would never judge you. One day when you have six or eight hours, I'll tell you all the stupid things I did in college." He laughed ruefully and she loved him for trying to ease her mind, as though getting pregnant and having a child out of wedlock was no worse than a drunken frat party or two. "It's the kind of stuff we won't tell our kids until they're grown—"

"No, Eric—"

"And now that I know your terrible secret, we can get married, right? There's no reason why we can't—"

"There *is* a reason," she said, and they were the hardest words she'd ever uttered in her life, four verbal knives sharp enough to maim.

The renewed brightness in Eric's face died and his smile disappeared.

Isabella didn't want to look at him but couldn't look away. In his eyes she saw glimpses of the raw, debilitating wound she'd just given him, and she wondered if it would comfort him to know that she was hurting herself just as much. Beyond his pain was a hint of anger, of reproach, as though he just couldn't understand what would drive her to devastate him like this.

"How many times today," he asked, low, "are you going to rip my guts out?"

This was too much. Despite all her resolve to get through this conversation with dignity and grace, a tear or two fell and she couldn't stop them.

For the first time ever, Eric didn't comfort her when she cried. He sat still and waiting, and he handed her a tissue from the side table, but he did not hold her hand, pat her shoulder or take her in his arms. Maybe he knew no comfort was possible now, or maybe he was too angry to touch her. Either way, she felt completely alone and knew she would have to draw on her own strength to get her through this next, worst part.

She wiped her eyes, calm and strong again.

"There were complications," she told him. "After Andrea was born."

Eric said nothing. For ten long seconds—longer, probably—

he stared at her and she felt the wheels turn in his mind and knew the instant that they arrived at the right conclusion.

"No," he said. "No, no, *no*."

"Eric."

She reached for his hand but he was too quick for her. Aghast, he shook his head, jumped to his feet and wheeled away, an animal trapped in a cage he was desperate to escape.

"Don't say it," he warned. *"Don't say it."*

"I had a massive hemorrhage and almost died. My uterus just about ruptured. I had an emergency hysterectomy. I can't have children." She paused.

"I told you not to say it," he roared.

This pain—*his* pain—was worse than anything else she'd endured in her life. She'd give up a hundred children for adoption if she never had to see this kind of agony on his face again.

"Eric," she said, trying to remain calm while she killed his dreams, "I'm sorry."

Isabella hurried to him but he turned away, bent at the waist as though the weight of his grief wouldn't let him stand up straight, and rested his palms on his thighs. She put a tentative hand on his back and then, when he didn't jerk free, both hands. Shudders rippled through him, one after the other, over and over, and she wondered if he might hyperventilate.

But then he straightened and faced her and his eyes were dry. A little manic and a little desperate, but dry.

"I need time."

"Let's talk this through, Eric—"

"Not now."

He needed time. She understood. But there was one more thing she had to tell him, and maybe that would make a difference. "If I'd known I was only going to get one child in this life, I'd've saved her for you."

"I asked you what that scar was and you said *nothing*." Eric stared at her with distant eyes as he reached for the knob. "I thought I knew everything about you, Isabella." His chin trembled for a moment but then his jaw tightened and it stopped. "Now I'm realizing I didn't know anything about you."

Without another word he wheeled around and left the screen door banging shut behind him.

Chapter 18

Eric hurried out of the cottage and staggered down the steps, feeling as though his knees would give out soon and each stride could therefore be his last. Clammy sweat trickled between his shoulder blades and nausea hovered in his throat, refusing to go either up or down. For the first time in what seemed like a thousand years he thought he might really cry. Not the embarrassed tear or two he'd wept when he'd watched *Schindler's List*, either, but the sobbing, roaring, throwing-things-at-the-wall kind of meltdown that grown men usually didn't have.

The pain was beyond anything he'd thought a human being could endure in the absence of a death or mortal injury. A bottomless emptiness that would circle to the moon and back if he took it out of his aching chest and stretched it out. He couldn't breathe or think. His only goal was to survive until some of the misery eased back a little.

Isabella had lied to him.
Isabella had a daughter.
Isabella couldn't have any more children.

These three things formed a straight line and marched through his mind over and over again, brutal in their relentlessness. *Isabella had lied to him… Isabella had a daughter… Isabella couldn't have any more children… Lied… Daughter… No more kids… Lied-daughter-no more…* On and on into infinity it went, and he'd foolishly thought Isabella would be the mother of his children.

He stumbled down the path, simultaneously numb, pained, blind and hyperaware of everything around him.

Above him floated a rabbit-shaped cloud, but he and his daughter would never lie on their backs in the grass and identify cloud shapes.

Down there was Grandmother's rose garden, but the rose petals from that garden would never be strewn down a church aisle as his daughter marched off to get married.

Straight ahead was the enormous weathered greenhouse where he would never plant tomatoes with his son. Nor would he ever see his own eyes, nose or smile reflected back at him from a tiny face. And he'd never pass his sarcastic nature on to another human being, but maybe that was a good thing even if it didn't seem like it right now.

Instead of the endless possibilities he'd felt only a few minutes ago, when Isabella had told him she loved him, he saw only lost opportunities and brick walls. An endless stream of things that could never be, no matter how much he wanted them or how desperately he needed them.

Blinking against the sun's glare and the moisture in his eyes, he turned into the greenhouse and sank onto the nearest bench, figuring this was as good a place as any to nurse his bleeding wounds. After a few deep breaths his mind cleared a little and he tried to *think* rather than just *feel,* but thinking was impossible because his emotions were running so high and so many of the things he'd thought he'd known about his life had turned out to be houses of cards.

Isabella wasn't a liar. He knew that. Yet she'd told him a huge lie, the kind that ruined families, tore marriages apart and was hard to forgive. Logically he understood that she'd done the best she could and had her reasons, but he still felt betrayed.

The worst part—well, not *the* worst, but one of the worst—was that this whole time he'd thought he'd known everything significant about her. *Hah.* He hadn't known her central secret, so he supposed that meant he'd known nothing about the woman at all. *Nothing.*

It wasn't just that she'd had a daughter, although that was enough to absorb. He had nothing but admiration for Isabella's strength and the loving choices she'd made. She'd decided to bear a child as a young unmarried woman, to risk her parents' displeasure, and then, knowing she couldn't give the child the best possible life, had given her to a family that could. And then Isabella had returned to school, graduated and become the strong woman he'd always known she would be.

Good. Great. Wonderful.

But *he'd* wanted a daughter with Isabella. *He'd* wanted to be the man who had a daughter who looked like Andrea, who was a Girl Scout and a black belt. *He'd* wanted to change Andrea's diapers, rock her to sleep at night and wait up until she came home safe from her first prom.

And he'd never have that chance, he thought, the bile rising again in his burning throat. He anchored his elbows on his knees, buried his face in his hands and tried to think of it another way, tried to give it a better perspective, but he couldn't find one. His frustration and desperation grew, heating and chilling him at the same time, crowding his flesh under his skin until he felt like an overstuffed sausage that would burst at any moment.

Isabella couldn't have children and therefore *he* couldn't have children. Never for one second did he consider any other options. He and Isabella were in this together and their fortunes rose and fell as one even if she didn't accept that yet.

He didn't want some other faceless woman, even if that woman had a functioning uterus that could produce a new generation of Warners. It was Isabella or nothing, and since Isabella couldn't give him the children he wanted, it was nothing.

But it *could* have been something. *If only* she hadn't fallen for that idiot Al, who was the kind of jerk that other men recognized on sight even if he managed to fool the occasional unsuspecting woman. *If only* she'd protected herself better. *If only* he hadn't taken years to realize that she was the only woman he could ever love—he could have claimed her before Al did.

But none of that had happened.

So she'd blessed Al with a child, the most precious thing a woman could give a man. And what had Al done? Had he worshipped her? Cherished her? Hell, no. He'd dumped her. Broken her heart. Signed his child away. Wasted a gift—squandered it.

And what would Eric do if he had a chance for such a gift from Isabella? Drop to his knees and thank God, that's what. Give his fortune to charity, no problem. Adore the child and Isabella. Protect them every day of their lives. He would have been happier than any man had a right to be, but that wouldn't happen now, would it? It would never happen.

He'd never have the primitive pleasure of making love to Isabella and knowing that the act, which was already the most beautiful thing he'd ever experienced, could result in a child. Never see her belly swell, never feel the flutter of the baby's first movement inside her and know that he'd been part of the creation of such a miracle. *Never, never, never.*

All the nevers were suddenly too much for him and he lurched to his feet as a hoarse cry erupted from his throat. Glancing wildly around—he didn't know what he needed, only that he needed *something*—he saw potted orchids and ferns and every freaking kind of flower in the universe, but he didn't need a flower, he needed—

There. A stack of empty terra-cotta pots. *That's* what he needed.

Roaring like a lion with his tail mangled in a trap, he grabbed the pots and heard the satisfying crash of the bottom one sliding out of his grip, hitting the bricked path beneath his feet and shattering.

Yeah. He needed more of that.

Wheeling around, he hurled the next pot at the glass wall ten feet away and it smashed through it with the force of a greased bullet. *Crash.* Glass flew everywhere, skittering and pinging across the nearest tables.

That was for the baby girl he and Isabella would never have. *Crash.*

That was for the ridiculously expensive wedding he'd never have to grumble about paying for.

Crash.

That was for the catcher's mitt his son would never need.

And these—these next ones were for the times he'd never make love to Izzy to try to get her pregnant. *Crash-crash-crash.*

He was out of pots now but he wasn't done smashing things. Panting with savage satisfaction, he pivoted and looked for something else to destroy and take the top edge off his pain, but there was nothing. He cursed because he needed *something,* needed—

"What are you doing?" asked a quiet voice.

Jerking with surprise, Eric froze, pots and destruction forgotten. Nathan. *Shit.*

The poor kid stood there, wide-eyed behind his glasses, gaping up at Eric like a deer that needed only the slight flicker of the grass beneath his hooves to take off at a dead run and disappear. The boy held a basket of ripe red tomatoes and Eric had the distant memory that Viveca—or maybe it was Bishop—had helped Nathan plant a bunch of stuff a while back.

Eric floundered.

This was the kind of moment that a parent would know what to do with, but he wasn't a parent—*ha-ha*—never would be a parent, and had no damn idea what to do now. A calm word or two would be good, one of those *don't-worry-everything-will-be-okay* speeches that reassured kids, but Eric's mouth was dry and his mind was empty. The only thing he could do was swipe the back of his hand across his damp face and pray he didn't look as wild and out of control as he felt.

They stared at each other for several excruciating beats and then Nathan furrowed his brow, opened his mouth and spoke in that same soft voice.

"Are you throwing a temper tantrum?"

Eric was so startled he let out a bark of something that would have passed for a laugh if the sound hadn't been so infused with the pain from his broken heart.

"Yeah," he said. "I suppose I am."

"You're making a big mess."

"Yeah." Eric looked around, realizing, for the first time, the extent of the destruction he'd caused.

"You'll have to clean it up," Nathan warned with no hint of compromise or mercy in his voice. "You can't make a mess like this and leave it for someone else to clean up. Bishop'll be mad."

"Yeah." Eric swallowed hard, imagining the old man's horror. "Right."

Nathan cocked his head, studying Eric with a narrowed gaze and obviously looking for clues as to what could cause this kind of maniacal behavior from an adult.

"What's wrong with you?"

"I, ah…" Eric paused, trying to sum up his misery in twenty-five or less G-rated words. "I'm really disappointed about something."

"Oh." Nathan scrunched up his face, rubbed his nose, and finally nodded with understanding. *Disappointment.* That was something he could get behind. "You should plant something."

"Huh?" Eric said.

"*Plant* something," Nathan said, louder this time. "Mama Viv—

Something in Eric's heart swelled and ached. He'd wondered what Nathan had chosen to call his adopted mother. *Mama Viv.* He liked it.

"—and Bishop both say that if you're upset you should plant something. Because it makes you feel better. It's good to dig in the dirt."

"Really?"

"Yeah." Nathan held up the basket so Eric could make a closer inspection of the bright red tomatoes. "So I planted some tomatoes. But I wasn't upset when I planted them. I just planted them." He pointed to a pot of black-eyed Susans in a pot on a table ten feet away. "But I planted those when my basketball team lost every game." He pointed in the other direction, to a pot of what looked like a vine of some kind. "And I planted that squash when I broke my ankle last year."

"Wow," Eric said. "Did that make you feel better?"

"Well." Nathan tilted his head thoughtfully. "My ankle still hurt, but it did make me feel a little better when I couldn't go on a hike with my summer camp."

Eric grinned. It was hard to feel too sorry for yourself with this kind of sage advice and comfort coming your way. "I guess I'll try it then. I'd like to feel better."

"Here." Nathan selected a tomato and thrust it at Eric. "You can have one of these until you plant your own."

Eric reached for it, touched to the soles of his feet by the boy's kindness, but just as his fingertips skimmed the tomato, Nathan snatched it back. "Oh, wait." He held it up to his face for a thorough examination and frowned. "This one has a worm."

"Oh."

"We'll leave that on the grass for the deer." Nathan rummaged for a minute and withdrew another specimen, one that apparently met with his approval. "Take this one—"

Eric took it. "Thanks, man."

"—and put it in a salad or a BLT—"

"Okay."

"Or you could make tomato sauce for spaghetti with it, but I'd have to give you about twenty more tomatoes, and I don't have that many."

"Right."

"Did you know tomatoes are *fruits?* Not veggies. *Fruits*."

Eric smiled at Nathan's particular emphasis on the word. "I did know, actually, but thanks for reminding me."

"You're welcome." Eric shot a furtive glance at the door.

"I'm going to go back to the house, but not if you're going to smash anything else—"

Eric held up a hand. "Don't worry."

"Okay."

Nathan backed up a step, hesitated, and then launched himself at Eric, hugging him around the waist and trapping Eric's arms at his sides. The warmth of the boy, the wiry feeling of his strong little body, his smell of grass and sunshine and shampoo, was almost too much for Eric. New emotions clogged his throat, but he choked them down, determined not to make any more scenes in front of this child.

He'd just started to extract his arms so he could at least return the hug when Nathan looked up at him, all wide-eyed innocence and exuberance. "You know why I'm hugging you?"

Eric shook his head.

"Because Mama Viv says my hugs are the best things for making her feel better when she's sad."

Eric swallowed, almost too moved to speak. "Mama Viv is right. I feel better already."

The embrace lasted two more seconds and then Nathan apparently decided that that was enough affection for the time being. Letting go of Eric and clutching the basket handle he raced down the path to the door, flung it open and nearly ran into Andrew, who was holding his own basket. After a beat or two of them trying to step around each other, Nathan darted around Andrew and disappeared down the path toward the house.

"*Hey.*" Andrew called after him and waved his basket. "I thought you needed this for tomatoes."

"That's okay," answered Nathan's now-faint voice. "Eric was smashing things, but he's calmed down now so don't be mad at him."

Andrew was just discovering this information for himself. His slow gaze traveled around the greenhouse, lingering on the one shattered pane of glass, the terra cotta debris and then, finally, settling on Eric's face.

They stared at each other for a minute. Eric's ears burned with embarrassment because he could just imagine how he looked right about now. Flushed, no doubt, a little sweaty and probably wild-eyed.

"Ah," Eric began. He was *not* in the mood for a round of Andrew's teasing.

Andrew cleared his throat and shifted back and forth on his heels, the picture of awkward discomfort. His gaze darted again to the pottery chards and then returned to Eric's face.

"So…you're good?" Andrew asked hopefully, backing toward the door.

Feeling an odd mixture of disappointment and relief, Eric nodded.

"Great." If Andrew had been strapped to the electric chair with the executioner's finger on the switch when the governor's call finally came through, he couldn't have looked more relieved. "That's what I thought."

Eric shoved his hands in his pockets and watched Andrew turn, walk to the door and put his hand on the knob. He was just looking around for a broom when Andrew heaved a harsh sigh and turned back. Looking deeply aggrieved, Andrew pointed to the wreckage on the floor.

"What the hell's going on?"

Eric couldn't answer right away. He dragged in a deep breath and hoped the burst of oxygen would give his brain some energy. "It's not good."

"I'd pieced that much together with my crack detective work."

Eric hadn't had any intention of discussing his personal life and, if he'd thought about it much, he'd've decided that he'd sooner appear on a TV shrink's show for advice rather than turn to Andrew.

But he was desperate, Andrew was here, and Andrew was happily married. Plus Andrew was shrewd and hard-headed, and maybe he'd have something worthwhile to say.

"Isabella…can't have children," Eric told him, nearly choking on the painful words. "And that's in confidence."

Shocked pity crept across Andrew's face in the second or two before he managed to hide it. He opened his mouth, faltered, closed his mouth, and tried again. "Damn, man." He paused, his Adam's apple bobbing as he swallowed hard. "I'm really sorry."

Nodding, Eric studied his shoes and tried to cap his emotions before they erupted again.

They lapsed into a painful silence during which Eric imagined Andrew was privately thanking God for blessing him with healthy children when Eric had none. Finally, just as Eric was beginning to wonder whether Andrew would deliver any advice, excellent or otherwise, Andrew cleared his throat.

"You could…adopt," he said.

This wasn't a revolutionary idea, of course. Objectively Eric knew that when people who wanted children couldn't have them, they adopted. It happened all the time. Big deal, right? Except he discovered that there was a huge difference between thinking about things in the abstract and applying them to your own life.

Andrew had adopted, though, and look how well it'd turned out. Nathan was a great kid, and Eric would take him or someone like him, no problem. But what if there weren't any more great kids out there like Nathan? What then? And Andrew had a biological child, too, and was soon to have another. Wasn't there a glaring difference between how parents felt about their biological kids and their adopted kids?

A flash of memory came from out of nowhere and intruded on his thoughts: Isabella's father in his recliner, looking at him with wizened eyes and infinite understanding. *It don't matter what kind of fam'ly you come from,* he'd said. *It's the kind of fam'ly you make that matters.*

At the time, Eric had interpreted this comment in terms of overcoming his troubled childhood and having a happy marriage even though his parents hadn't, but now the words had a whole new meaning.

Because if he and Isabella adopted, they'd be choosing the kind of family they wanted to make, wouldn't they? And any family with Isabella at the heart of it would be a blessed family.

Even so, the idea needed a little sinking in, a little thought. "Nathan's...great," Eric said.

Andrew grinned, overflowing with a father's pride. "I know."

"So...you love him, then?" Eric hesitated, realizing how stupid he sounded. "I mean, I know you *love* him, but...you have Andy, too, and I—"

His voice faded and died before Andrew's withering glare.

"You're a freaking idiot," Andrew said flatly, his heavy brows lowering into a shelf over his eyes, like Frankenstein. "Let's just get that out of the way right now."

"Yeah, let's," Eric said, feeling sheepish.

"What you're asking," Andrew snapped, "is whether, if a speeding bus was racing toward Nathan and Andy and I only had time to save one, whether I'd shove Nathan under the bus to save Andy. Right? Well, the answer is *no*."

"I didn't mean—" Eric began, although this was, in fact, pretty close to what he'd been wondering.

"I love both my boys," Andrew told him. "I'd kill for either of them, and I'd die for either of them. We clear?"

"Yeah, I'm thinking we're clear."

A stony silence followed. Andrew glowered, subliminally daring Eric to ask any more dumb questions, and then, when he seemed satisfied that he wouldn't, he softened.

"If you're worried about whether you can love an adopted kid as much as your own kid, you can." Andrew swung the basket and then looked down at it with surprise, as though he'd forgotten it was in his hand. Muttering, he put it on the nearest table and refocused on Eric. "And if you think it takes longer than a day of living with a kid—and knowing he's *yours* and he needs you—before you fall in love with him, then you don't know anything about kids."

That made sense, Eric thought. A lot of sense. There'd been plenty of times when he'd spent a few hours with Andy and Nathan and felt a hard pang of loss when it was time to hand them back over to Andrew and Viveca. Kids grew on you. It was hard not to love them.

"Thanks," Eric said. "I'm going to think about it."

"Good idea." Andrew, looking relieved, turned to go, but then he glanced back over his shoulder. "And I don't need to talk you into not letting Isabella get away, do I? 'Cause if I do, I'm gonna have to kick your ass for you."

Let Isabella go? When he'd only just realized her rightful place in his life and had a small taste of the joy they could have together? No way. Having Isabella and having kids with her were two separate and—as far as he was concerned—unrelated issues. "Oh, don't worry."

For the first time in hours, Eric felt light again, as though he had a plan and knew the path to choose. He grinned because one thing hadn't changed and would never change: he loved Isabella and meant to marry her. Come hell or high water.

"I have no intentions of letting Izzy go, kids or no kids."

Chapter 19

Isabella spent a good portion of the afternoon sitting on the cottage's front porch, swaying on the white wicker swing with Zeus in her lap and wallowing in her misery. There'd been no sign of Eric and she didn't really expect a sign anytime soon.

How she'd get back to Cincinnati, she had no idea. Originally they'd planned to drive home in Eric's SUV with the thought that he'd drop her off and continue on to Columbus, but Eric's SUV was still in Florida, waiting to be sent home, and so many things had changed since they left it wasn't even funny.

So now she was stranded two hours from home, not that she cared about the setting. Right now she'd be nursing her broken heart no matter where she was.

And speaking of locations, she didn't see how she could leave for South Africa. The bloom had begun to slip off that rose a couple of days ago when her father had said she'd just be packing her problems in the suitcase with her toothbrush if she moved to another country. He'd been right. Getting on a plane and flying thousands of miles away from Eric, whether he hated her now or not, wouldn't solve anything and, besides that, seemed impossible.

On the other hand, she'd always dreamt of visiting South Africa, if not teaching there. If Eric *did* hate her, a change of continent and new job would surely keep her busy and do her a world of good. Even if it would hurt to leave him.

She scratched Zeus's ears and wished she could sleep as peacefully as he could and block out the things that had happened this afternoon. If only a dog biscuit or two could cheer her up.

The wretched look on Eric's face when she'd told him about the secret parts of her life was something that would haunt her until her dying day and possibly follow her into heaven. If she'd ever doubted that he loved her, she didn't now, not after seeing his despair.

She'd hurt him. Truly, deeply hurt him, and it didn't matter one iota that she'd never meant to. The tight pain in her chest now was an expected but unwelcome side effect of injuring Eric. If he hurt, she hurt. Simple as that.

Would he forgive her for the lie? She thought he probably would. He was a fair man and he'd never been anything but understanding with her. The bigger question was whether he could get over the hurt of knowing she'd had a child with someone else. That she'd been young and foolish at the time was a mitigating factor, if a small one.

Had she destroyed his desire to marry her? That was the biggest question, and if so she could hardly blame him. Eric loved children and always had. And he came from a family to whom lineage and carrying on the family name was immensely important. Of course he would want his own blood children. She couldn't expect him to give up that dream just because she'd had years to adjust to the idea that she could never bear another child. It wouldn't be fair for her to ask it of him.

Her heart contracted and she stared up at the clear blue sky, blinking back her tears and letting the light breeze cool her face. She'd cried enough today.

If only she could get home, though.

Zeus groaned in his sleep and his little back paws scratched at the air. *Silly dog.* And she was a silly owner, wasn't she? Dressing him in his little kerchiefs and T-shirts, brushing his fur and taking him to the groomer's, making sure he had Fluffles. She knew what she was doing; any five-year-old could see that she was babying the dog because he was the only baby she'd have.

Another great wave of self-pity washed over her but a diversion arrived in the form of Viveca's singsong voice coming down the path from the main house. Zeus's ears pricked and he raised his head to look around with interest.

"Go to sleep, baby. It's past time for your nap. *Go to sleep... go to sleep.*"

Isabella saw Viveca emerge from the trees with Andy slung across her chest in a blue paisley sling. Andy, looking bleary-eyed and heavy lidded, rested his cheek against his mother's breasts, his thumb in his mouth. He did not look like he was about to go to sleep, although it was not for lack of trying on Viveca's part. She swayed as she walked, rubbing his curly little head and patting his bottom as she went. When her gaze connected with Isabella's, she rolled her eyes and gave her a tired smile.

"Andrew's little son here," she said in a soothing, high-pitched baby voice, "seems to think he doesn't need a nap today."

Isabella had to smile. "Isn't he your son, too?"

"Not when he's not behaving, no."

Zeus hopped down from Isabella's lap and trotted over to Viveca as soon as she climbed the steps to the porch. He stared adoringly up at her, tail wagging in anticipation of the belly rub he no doubt felt was his due.

"Hi, doggy," Viveca sang. *"Hi, doggy."*

Andy roused himself enough to take his thumb out of his mouth, lean down to better see Zeus, and point. "Doggy."

What a beautiful child, Isabella thought. What she wouldn't give to have her baby—Eric's baby—pressed to her breasts like that.

"Doggy," Viveca said again.

Isabella's throat constricted and some of her turmoil must have shown on her face because Viveca settled on the wicker chair nearest the swing, arranged Andy so that his legs dangled on either side of her hips, and studied her with concern.

"What's wrong? You and Eric have been acting funny all day."

Isabella thought hard. She and Viveca didn't know each other all that well although they'd always been very friendly, and she really wasn't one to pour her heart out. Even so, now that her relationship with Eric had imploded, the reason why would get around the family soon enough.

"I can't have children," she said, her voice hoarse. "I told Eric earlier."

"Oh." Viveca's face fell. "Oh. I'm really sorry."

Isabella managed a quick smile. "Thanks."

Andy pointed at Zeus again and the dog yapped a hello.

Andy grinned. "Doggy."

"You go to sleep," Viveca said, patting Andy's back, and Andy obligingly put his head back down. Viveca looked to Isabella, her expression now matter-of-fact. "Do you want to talk about it?"

Isabella tried to be polite, but it was pretty hard at the moment when Viveca had everything Isabella wanted—the husband, the kids, another baby on the way—and Isabella had only a dog that, more often than not, had muddy paws, fleas and gas.

"I would Viveca, but it's hard to have an in-depth discussion about my infertility with a pregnant woman who's got a baby strapped to her chest. No offense, though."

"Oh." Viveca's cheeks flamed, making Isabella feel bad for being abrupt. "Yeah. Right. Sorry. I'll just… I think I'll just go back to the house."

She got up and headed for the steps. After an initial moment of relief, Isabella regretted her hastiness because now was a time when she needed every friend around her that she could get.

"Wait," she said, and Viveca paused at the edge of the porch.

"I—sorry. It's just that…I'm really scared at the moment. I don't know what's going to happen. With Eric."

Viveca's expression clouded over with confusion. She absently patted Andy's butt, her brow furrowed. "What do you mean?"

Isabella's irritation swelled. Why did this need explaining? Wasn't it obvious? "I mean, my relationship with Eric is pretty much over. I don't even know if we can salvage the friendship at this point."

"Salvage the friendship?"

Viveca did something entirely unexpected. She laughed. Threw back her head and roared as if she was at an Eddie Murphy-Chris Rock concert. Poor Andy, looking perplexed, took his thumb out of his mouth and craned his neck to stare at his mother as though he wanted her to explain what the heck was so funny.

"What the heck is so funny?" Isabella demanded.

"Friends?" Viveca spluttered when she'd caught her breath. "Honey, Eric is in love with you. I knew it the first time I saw you together. If you think that man is going to want to be just *friends* with you, then you are obviously insane." She paused and then laughed again, muttering. *"Friends.* Right."

"Did you not hear me?" Isabella couldn't keep the annoyance out of her voice. "I can't have children, and Eric's going to want someone who can—"

"Honey, if Eric just wanted a uterus, he could go out and hire one. He's got the money."

This stopped Isabella cold. Eric had the money to do whatever he wanted. That was true enough. But he couldn't buy a woman who loved him the way Isabella did. He could search the world high and low but he'd never find another woman who'd love him better.

And yet…could she ask it of him? Ask a man to give up his chance to have a biological child? Wasn't that too much of a sacrifice, even for the woman you loved?

Helplessly stuck and confused, all Isabella could do was stare at Andy—precious boy—and wish he was hers. Suddenly the thing she needed more than she needed anything else was to hold a baby. Even if it wasn't hers.

"Can I borrow Andy?" she asked.

Viveca beamed at her. "Absolutely. See if you can get him to sleep for me."

Viveca freed Andy from the sling contraption and handed him over to Isabella, who moved to the wicker rocker and accepted his warm heavy baby weight gratefully onto her lap. She sat him facing her, his legs stretched along her hips, and he gave her a weary smile around his tiny thumb, which was now red and wrinkled from use.

Viveca fished a tissue out of the pocket of her dress and dabbled at her wet eyes. "Well. I'll just leave you two for a minute, okay?" She looked down at Zeus, who was patiently sitting at her feet, and tapped her thigh several times. "Zeus? You want some bacon? Let's go get some bacon. Come on. *Come on.*"

Zeus jumped up and yapped several times before turning and racing up the path toward the house, leading the way. Isabella watched them disappear through the trees and braced herself, ratcheting up her courage before she looked back at Andy's droopy blue eyes.

It had been a long time since she'd held a baby. Years, unless she was much mistaken. She'd avoided them like fire ants because the heartache that came from just a passing whiff of, say, baby powder, was enough to reduce her to tears of longing every time.

Older children were somehow different and that was how she'd managed to teach kindergarten all these years. They were little people with whom she could converse and negotiate. Babies were a separate species who brought misery with them whenever they crossed her path.

Andy, no doubt tired of being ignored, popped his thumb out of his mouth again and, with a murmur of what sounded like concern, patted her cheeks with his hands, leaving a wet streak on one side.

That did it. All the emotion that had been clogging Isabella's throat bubbled over into a weird sobbing-laugh noise.

Andy cocked his head, studying her.

"You're a precious boy," she said, laughing and crying, wiping her eyes and trying not to scare him. "You're a *precious boy*."

This seemed to reassure him. He grinned and cooed, showing dimples, miles of pink gums and those four white teeth. Undone, Isabella kissed his fat warm cheeks over and over, wanting to bite them, wanting to take this wonderful child home with her and keep him there.

His sweet skin smelled of milk and apricots and his sun-warmed curls were fragrant with baby shampoo. Someone had taken off his fancy white baptism shoes and his perfect little toes flexed and curled with delight.

Seeing this, she laughed again and loved him. Wanted him.

"You need a nap, baby boy." She settled him against her chest and he snuggled happily, at home with any available bosom. That weathered thumb went right back in his mouth and he sucked and snuffled, moving his head back and forth until he located just the right spot.

Once he settled down, she smoothed his curls, rubbed his temple and nape and rocked him, the melody of some long-forgotten lullaby on her lips. Soon his breathing evened out, telling her he'd finally stopped fighting the sleep he needed.

With the sun on her face, the breeze in her hair and the wonderful weight of a baby in her arms, even if it wasn't *her* baby, she leaned her head against the back of the rocker, cried, let go and forgave herself for the mistakes she'd made. She'd done the best she could at the time, and that was all she could ask of herself. She couldn't have a baby but she was still a good person, a real woman, and that was enough. With her sorrow, guilt and shame slowly drifting away like the clouds overhead, Isabella slept.

When she woke, the sunlight had shifted and her feeling of rejuvenation went far beyond anything that a short nap should be able to provide. She felt like a new person with no more than three minutes of life under her belt. She had no idea how much time had passed, whether it was an hour or two, but everything about her existence seemed to have shifted.

Andy was in the same position and nothing had changed as far as she knew, but Eric was with her. She felt his presence down to the marrow of her bones even if she couldn't see him. And then she turned her head to the right and there he was, almost to the porch steps, frozen and rapt, watching her and the baby with such a look of loss and longing on his face that she thought she might die from it.

Chapter 20

It was a long moment, one that was painful and poignant but mostly beautiful. Eric seemed not to blink the whole time and if he was still breathing she couldn't tell. She had no idea what to say; she had both the urge to say nothing, ever, and to apologize until her voice was hoarse. In the end all she did was give him a tiny smile.

Eric's lips curved at one edge, and then he dropped his head and stood there, just staring at his feet or the path—anything that wasn't her. His shoulders heaved, once, and then his hand went to his face and swiped past first one eye and then the other. Her chest tightened and she waited, wondering which direction her life was about to take.

When he raised his head, finally, he still looked sad, but also determined. A few of his long-legged strides brought him up to the porch with her, and he leaned against the rail, crossed his ankles and took a deep breath.

"This is hard," he said, low.

"I know."

"You look good with a baby."

"It feels pretty good." She paused. "I haven't held one in years. I haven't even been able to bring myself to hold the twins. My own brother's children."

"We all understand," Eric told her.

She nodded hastily, too choked up to say anything.

Eric looked away, his gaze tracking the drunken, swirling path of a monarch butterfly as it drifted past. In the smooth column of his throat she saw the rough bob of his Adam's apple as he swallowed hard. There was another swallow, and another, before he managed to continue.

"Here's the thing, Isabella," he said, his voice faint and hoarse. "I really want children. I always thought I'd have them one day."

She wouldn't have thought her heartbeat could stutter any more sickeningly in her chest, but she was wrong. So that was it, then. It was all over.

"I understand," she said, because she did. A man who wanted biological children was entitled to try to find a woman who could bear them. She wouldn't make him feel guilty for this choice. "You don't have to explain."

"Yeah, I do."

He shoved away from the porch rail, came to her rocker and knelt beside her, studying Andy. The baby was sleeping with his face turned toward Eric, and Eric stared, seeming to imprint him on his memory for all time. Then he raised a hand and ran it over Andy's head, caressing the way Isabella had done a little while ago. Finally he kissed the baby's cheek, a lingering kiss that was unbearably sweet and almost too much for Isabella to see.

And then Eric looked up, to Isabella, and there was a blazing intensity in his eyes that made her breath catch and her blood run hot and thick.

"I wanted us to make a baby," he told her. "But I can be happy without one."

Isabella blinked, rewound the words through her brain and digested them.

"Y-you can?" she stammered.

"Yeah. The thing I can't be happy without," he said, drifting closer, "is you."

Hope tried to gain a toehold in her heart but she ruthlessly knocked it back. "Me?" she said weakly, demanding confirmation. "You can't be happy without *me?*"

"Did you think I could?" he asked, holding her gaze as he picked up her hand, turned it over and pressed a kiss to her palm. "Did you think I would want to?"

She hadn't known what to think. Didn't know what to think now, although hope refused to die and seemed to be gaining more ground by the second.

"But," she began.

She was determined to take the high road and let him off the hook because he was obviously too nice to break her heart when she was infertile. *Yeah.* That was probably what was going on here. He felt sorry for her and would probably rather play the hero than dump her. *That was it.*

"But I can't let you sacrifice your chance to have biological children, and I don't want you to regret—"

Those dark eyes flashed, quieting her mid-sentence. "You're not *letting* me do anything. Let's get that straight. You don't make my choices for me. Okay?"

"Okay," she murmured, taken aback by his vehemence.

"I didn't *choose* to fall in love with you, but I'm glad I did. Okay?"

"Okay." She stared at him, feeling breathless and incredibly blessed.

"Even if I wanted to, I couldn't stop loving you now. Okay?"

"Okay."

"And the only thing I'd ever *regret* is losing you. Got it?"

Stunned dumb, she gaped at him with the fleeting thought that it would be a shame to catch a fly in her mouth just at the moment Eric asked her to marry him. *That* would be a Kodak moment, all right, but Eric wasn't slowing down to wait for any answer this time.

"So you're not going to South Africa." He paused for form's sake, but the look on his face was so determined, so ferocious, so utterly possessive, that arguing with him was the last thing on her mind. "Okay?"

She nodded frantically.

"We're going to get married. I'm sorry about you having to, you know—" he waved his hand, obviously trying to find the right words—"marry into my family, but there's nothing I can do about that. Okay?"

Happiness finally overwhelmed her to the point that she couldn't rein it in and didn't even want to. A burst of laughter erupted from her mouth, but she clapped her hand over her lips, afraid she'd wake Andy.

"Okay," she said, the word muffled by her palm.

"And we're going to adopt a few kids," he finished. "I'm assuming you've got no problems with that."

She dropped her hand and shook her head. "No. No problems."

They lapsed into a brief, awkward silence, during which Isabella tried to figure out what'd just happened. Frowning, she thought hard and finally decided she'd better just ask.

"Eric," she asked, "are we engaged now?"

Eric blinked. "Yeah." He paused, blinked again and nodded. "I think we are."

"Hallelujah."

There was one more stunned second of silence and then they both broke into joyous laughter. Eric grabbed her face and kissed her hard, almost tipping the rocking chair over backward in his enthusiasm. It didn't take long for the kiss to turn hot and deep but Andy slept on, oblivious to the passion surrounding him and Isabella's breathy whimpers.

"You two need to get a room," said a voice from somewhere nearby.

Startled and flushed, they broke apart to see Andrew emerge from the trees looking amused, his wide grin more wicked than usual.

Eric was already on his feet, gingerly picking Andy up from Isabella's lap and passing him over to Andrew, but only after pressing another kiss to his little drooping head.

"Take your boy, man," Eric said. His smile was so wide, so ecstatic, so amazingly bright, sexy and intent, that Isabella almost had to squint. Grabbing her hand, he pulled her to her feet and tugged her through the door to the cottage. "I need to spend a little quality time with my fiancée."

Isabella heard Andrew chuckle, but then Eric kicked the door shut and her mind emptied out of all things but one: she needed Eric inside her and she needed him *now*.

"Hurry," she told him.

Panting from the flaming heat of his intense gaze, she backed into the room and stopped when something hard—she had no idea *what*—hit her across the small of the back. With fumbling fingers she tried to untie the shoulder straps of her dress, but that was too difficult and she couldn't wait. Reaching up under her skirt instead, she wiggled out of her panties, dropped them to the floor, and opened her arms to Eric.

Luckily he was on the same page and had been working on his belt. But now, seeing her reach for him, he came straight to her.

With brutal strength he clamped his palms on either side of her face, tipped her head back and fused his mouth to hers in the kind of long, deep kiss that poured his body into hers, his soul into hers. Wild and frantic, she opened for him, sucking and biting and tasting this man who was *hers,* who would be her husband and partner for the rest of her life.

His big hands left her cheeks and slid down her back to her butt. Those long fingers dug in, kneading, pulling her tight against him until their bodies ground together with enough friction on her sweet spot to bring her right to the edge of what was going to be a convulsive orgasm.

Eric's sixth sense seemed to tell him she was close because he backed off and took those wonderful hands away. "Are you about to come?" he said into her mouth, licking and nipping as he did.

She nodded frantically.

"No, you're not. You're going to *wait*."

When she groaned, he flashed a crooked grin.

Putting his hands on her shoulders, he turned her roughly around and pushed her so that she bent over something. With quicker reflexes than she'd thought she could muster at the moment, she threw her hands wide and braced herself on a hard, cool surface.

The counter. It was the kitchen counter.

Oh, man, she thought, shaking now with anticipation. This was going to be wild and hot and *good*.

At the welcome sound of his zipper, she moaned with encouragement and rubbed her butt against his bulging groin lest he have any confusion about what he was supposed to do next. He didn't. He thrust one hard leg between hers to widen her stance—she felt the soft scratch of the fine wool between her thighs—and raised her skirt.

Yes, she thought, weak with relief as he took the bulbous head of his penis and rubbed it against her, spreading her juices and making her wetter and slicker. Yes…yes…*now*.

But he didn't enter her. Distraction seemed to hit him in the form of her butt, the globes of which he was now caressing, over and over. He crooned with enthusiastic appreciation.

Desperate and irritated, Isabella looked over her shoulder and tried to focus her dim gaze. "Hello-ooo?" she said with the little bit of sarcasm she could muster. "Do you think you could do that later—"

With of laugh of pure male satisfaction, he surged his hips, sinking inside her, all the way to the hilt. Isabella cried out, ecstatic with pleasure. One of his frantic hands grasped her throat and turned her face around until he could kiss her as deeply as he was thrusting. The other hand pulled down the bodice of her dress and her strapless bra and rubbed over her swinging breasts, back and forth, back and forth.

Their rhythm was quick, hard and absolutely perfect because each time he plunged inside her he hit the exact right spot, the one that made her hotter and louder. Isabella's knees weakened and the room grew dark.

He freed her mouth only long enough to say one thing: "*Now* you can come for me, Sunshine."

Isabella didn't need telling. The spasms had already begun radiating out from her sex and contracting through her belly, generating a pleasure so bright, so fierce, that she would have yelled from it if he hadn't caught the sounds in his mouth.

Determined to give him as much pleasure as he gave her, she tightened her inner muscles around him and closed her thighs as much as she could. That did it. Shouting her name, he pumped into her, shuddering and convulsive.

Spent at last, he stilled and sprawled across her back. She rested her cheek on the cool counter and tried to catch her breath.

"And to think," she said tiredly, "that we could've been doing this for *years*. If only you'd noticed me before this."

"To think you made me promise we'd only make love for one night."

"I never proposed an idea that stupid, did I?"

She felt the curve of his cheek against her as he smiled. "You did, but don't worry." His hot tongue ran up her spine and stopped right between her shoulder blades, where he planted a long, wet, kiss that had her groaning again. "We're going to make up for all that lost time."

Epilogue

Isabella saw the girl first, on the sixth day of their honeymoon.

They were touring the Leadership Academy while they were there—Isabella was hoping to convince Eric to make a significant donation so the girls could have new computers when classes started in the fall—and were walking across the courtyard with the matron when Isabella looked around and saw the girl crouched under a baobab tree twenty feet away, teasing a sleeping dog.

At first glance, she wasn't much to look at—just a tiny little girl of about five, mostly short braids and skin and bones in an ugly sack of a yellow dress. But there was...something about her, and Isabella couldn't look away.

"And here is the library." The matron, a stern woman named Mrs. Hobbs, gestured to an enormous building, all windows and light.

Eric murmured appreciatively.

Isabella watched the girl.

On all fours with a thin stick in her hands, the child crept forward, silent but vibrating with a mischievous excitement that Isabella could feel despite the distance. The dog, which looked like he had some yellow Lab somewhere in his family tree, along with a whole lot of mutt, remained on his back, belly exposed and ears pricked as the girl came closer.

Clamping one hand over her mouth to stifle her giggles, the girl used the stick to worry the dog's ear, which twitched. The dog groaned, wriggled and batted at the stick with a paw.

The girl laughed harder and tickled again, and the dog apparently decided he'd had enough. Flipping over, his tail wagging hard enough to shake his whole skinny body, he licked the girl's face.

Isabella, feeling unaccountably touched, had the distinct impression that girl and dog had played this game before with each other, many times. Drawn to the girl by forces she couldn't understand, she walked off, leaving the matron mid-sentence and Eric glancing after her.

"Izzy?" he said.

Isabella barely heard him. "Hello," she called to the girl, approaching slowly so as not to startle her. "What's your name?"

The girl gave her a stormy look, her brows drawn together over flashing, wary eyes. "I didn't bother him," she said in a wonderfully exotic and cultured voice that didn't quite sound British and didn't quite sound Dutch. "I was just playing."

"I know." Ignoring the dust and the dirt, Isabella sat crosslegged under the tree and arranged her purple-flowered skirts around her legs. The dog, seeing a potential new friend, sniffed her hand and, upon deciding Isabella was okay, licked her cheek. "The dog likes you."

The girl pursed her lips.

"My name's Isabella." Isabella held out her hand and the girl shook it with a grip that was strong but reluctant. "What's your name?"

"Thandiwe," said the girl.

"Thandy?"

"Than-di-we," said the girl again with the kind of deep exasperation with an adult's failings that only a child can manage. "Don't you speak English?"

"Not very well," Isabella said.

Eric and the matron wandered closer and Isabella had the irrational urge to shoo them away and tell them to leave her alone with Thandiwe. There were things she needed to say to the girl and things she needed to know, and nothing and no one could interfere. A need was growing inside Isabella, centering in her chest and causing an ache that was too strong to ignore. This child compelled her, made her need to reach out and find common ground that they could walk together.

Rummaging in her purse, Isabella pulled out her wallet and flipped it open to a picture of Zeus. The long-suffering dog was dressed in the black Darth Vader costume and helmet Eric had bought him last Halloween. Isabella had snapped the picture in the thirty seconds before Zeus had shaken off the cape and hidden under the coffee table, refusing to come out.

"Here's my dog." Isabella gave her the wallet. "His name is Zeus."

Thandiwe peered at the picture and grinned. "Darth Vader!"

That delighted little smile, all white teeth, dimples and sparkling brown eyes, stopped Isabella's heart. "You—you know Darth Vader?"

Exasperated again, Thandiwe rolled her eyes and clicked her tongue. "*Everyone* knows Darth Vader."

That was when Isabella *knew* and, judging from Eric's surprised gasp from somewhere above her, he knew it, too. Raising her chin and blinking back her sudden tears, she looked up at him and he met her gaze with his mouth slightly open in astonishment and his heart in his eyes.

Afraid to reveal too much emotion to this poor little girl and, more than that, afraid to hope, Isabella swiped her eyes and struggled with her composure.

"Where's your mommy, Thandy?" she asked.

"Than-di-we," said the girl matter-of-factly, now studying the rest of Isabella's Zeus pictures with rapt interest. "Dead. She had the AIDS."

This information was too much. Pressing a hand to her heart, which now threatened to burst, Isabella bent at the waist, sobbing and laughing but trying to do it discreetly lest Thandiwe think she was insane.

Eric reached down, grabbed Isabella by the shoulders, and pulled her into his arms, absorbing her shudders and kissing her cheek, over and over again.

The matron gaped at them.

Thandiwe paused in her picture review long enough to glance up at them with concern. "Barking mad," she muttered.

Isabella and Eric stared at each other in perfect understanding, words unnecessary.

This was not what they had planned. In fact, they hadn't planned anything at all beyond this honeymoon and enjoying each other's company for a year or two. Isabella would travel with him, they'd decided, and they'd spend a lot of time in Hong Kong for business.

And then they'd think about children. Maybe surrogacy, maybe adoption. They'd talked about adopting an American child because charity begins at home, and they'd talked about a baby, an infant.

Now, seeing this sarcastic little girl who loved dogs and Darth Vader, all of that went out the window.

Holding on to Isabella for dear life, Eric backed her up a step and gestured to Mrs. Hobbs, who followed, looking wary. "Is she available for adoption?" he whispered.

Mrs. Hobbs's jaw dropped in open horror. "Yes, but you don't want *this* child. She's nothing but mischief and trouble."

Isabella and Eric exchanged another glance and laughed. They'd expected nothing less from any child of theirs.

"She's perfect," they said together and laughed again.

Turning, as one, they watched Thandiwe show the pictures

of Zeus to the yellow dog, who yawned with obvious boredom. And Isabella knew that, no matter what bureaucratic hoops the State Department and the South African government made them jump through, she and Eric had just met their first child, their daughter.

"Thandiwe," she told Eric. "Our daughter's name is Thandiwe."

"Thandiwe," he echoed, and pulled her into his arms as they watched the girl, their eyes filled with tears of joy.

Essence **bestselling author**

DONNA HILL

TEMPTATION AND LIES

Book #3 of T.L.C.

Nia Turner's double life as business executive
and undercover operative for covert crime-fighting
organization Tender Loving Care is getting even
more complicated. Steven Long, the man she's seeing,
suspects she's stepping out on him, and Nia's caught
in a web of lies that threatens her relationship. Will
any explanation make up for not telling the truth?

*Available the first week of February 2009
wherever books are sold.*

KIMANI™
ROMANCE

www.kimanipress.com
www.myspace.com/kimanipress

Can he overcome the past to fight for the future…?

Favorite author

YAHRAH ST. JOHN

THIS TIME *for* REAL

For years, widow Peyton Sawyer has avoided romance…
until, volunteering at the community center, she
experiences an immediate smoldering connection
with director Malik Williams. But Malik is haunted
by the past and doesn't think he can give Peyton the
relationship he knows she deserves.

"St. John has done a fantastic job with her debut
release."—*Romantic Times BOOKreviews*
on *ONE MAGIC MOMENT*

*Available the first week of February 2009
wherever books are sold.*

KIMANI™
ROMANCE